"Yeah." I slapped snow fr⟨...⟩ ⟨...⟩ppened to the missing people no⟨...⟩

"Uh huh." Logan sho⟨...⟩. I don't like the looks of that."

"Of..." Then I saw the tall, white figure loping toward us, something flapping from its shoulder. "Oh, that. What is it?"

"Golem."

"A what?" I asked, but he was moving, charging toward the golem. "Dude!"

"It's ice," he called back. "I've got it."

"Okay, I'll just stand here looking stupid," I muttered, watching as the distance between them narrowed. "I mean, it's not like I could melt it or anything."

Discord Jones

Frost & Bothered

Gayla Drummond

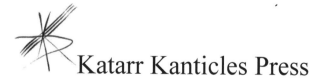

Katarr Kanticles Press

Katarr Kanticles Press
Texas, USA
Edited by Tonya Cannariato
Copyright © 2014 Gayla Drummond
Cover by Gayla Drummond

ISBN-13: 978-0692355619 (Katarr Kanticles Press)
ISBN-10: 0692355618

Acknowledgments

Super big thanks to you, the reader!
Without you, this series wouldn't have happened.

Frost & Bothered

One

"My son wouldn't take off," the woman sitting across from me insisted. She was gripping her black clutch purse tightly enough to whiten her knuckles. "He's a good boy. He wouldn't do this to me."

I ignored the flicker of movement at the periphery of my vision. Nothing was there, especially not what, or rather who, my mind insisted was. There was work to do. I didn't need my recently reoccurring nightmare distracting me during my waking hours. I nodded and said exactly what she needed to hear. "I believe you, Mrs. Guerra. But if we're going to find out what's happened, we have to ask certain questions."

My new partner, Dane Soames, offered her a sympathetic smile and the cup of coffee he'd poured. Mrs. Guerra was a short, plump Hispanic woman in her late thirties or early forties. She released her purse, her hands trembling as she took the cup, and I winced, expecting hot coffee to slosh all over her.

Fortunately, Soames hadn't filled it to the brim. The dark liquid did make an escape attempt, but it was unsuccessful. "Gracias."

"You're welcome."

She turned her bloodshot brown eyes back to me. "I'm sorry. I'm..."

"Terrified," I said. "It's all right. I completely understand."

Boy, did I. After my mom's kidnapping. I had a whole new level of sympathy for clients with missing loved ones. "Did you bring something of his with you?"

"Sí." She placed the cup on my desk and fumbled with her purse. Its clasp stuck, causing her to mutter a couple of choice words in Spanish before forcing it open. I hoped the boss was giving her a big discount on our services. She had on a light brown dress with a white apron and nametag under a worn workman's jacket. Above the bold "Helena" was the name of a small diner I'd had breakfast at a few times, with my dad. Jobs like that didn't pay much.

She retrieved a little, tissue-wrapped bundle, handing it to Soames when he held out his hand. Unwrapping it first, he put it on my desk next to the open folder in front of me. A class ring from W. H. Preston High School, the only high school for the Palisades, sat in silver glory in the center of the tissue.

"Frederico is proud of that ring. He wears it often." A single tear escaped from Mrs. Guerra's left eye. "He's the first of our family born here, the first to graduate high school and go to college."

"That's awesome." College required math, and math had broken things in my brain once I'd gotten past the simple stuff. Who needed trigonometry to be a private investigator? Not me. "Which college?"

"'The community one," she said, lifting her chin as though daring me to think less of her son. I didn't, because college was college as far as I was concerned. You just had to pay a hell of a lot more for the ones with fancy names.

"Cool." I looked down at the folder Tabitha had given me when seeing Mrs. Guerra into my office. There was a short list of names included under the scanty details of Frederico's disappearance, as well as a small photo of him. None of the names was female. I studied his photo. Frederico was a good-looking guy. "He doesn't have a girlfriend?"

"He dates, but no special girl yet. My boy has plans for his future, so he's not interested in anything serious."

"Okay." I glanced at the ring, debating whether or not to handle it in front of her. If my psychometry felt like working, I could find out whether her son was alive.

"They say you are a bruja."

I looked up, wondering exactly who "they" were. "No, Kate's the witch. I'm a psychic. Basically, I have more than the usual five senses." Among other things, but since I didn't understand exactly how my abilities worked, just that they did and how to control some of them, I left it at that. "Not any magic."

If people wanted to believe what I could do was magic, nothing I said would convince them otherwise, but I always tried. Truth in advertising wasn't a bad thing. I smiled, and she returned it. She hadn't touched her coffee. I wondered if she'd slept last night while glancing at the ring again.

"Can you tell me that he's still alive?" Her voice was small and soft.

Crap. I closed the folder and pushed it aside before pinching the corner of the tissue and pulling it closer. "Maybe. This doesn't always work immediately."

She nodded, her gaze on my hand as I reached for the ring. I hated trying this in front of clients, because when it came to being clubbed over the head with death, my poker face needed loads of practice. Picking up the ring and closing my eyes, I waited. For several seconds, nothing happened, and I felt a guilty rush of relief. "I'm not get..."

The loud brrrrring of a school bell. A flash of satisfaction over a test with a perfect score. Annoyance as someone yelled, "Hey, polla!" A girl's giggle. Boxes stacked next to store shelves. Music with a heavy beat. Mrs. Guerra's smiling face and a thick, warm rush of love.

And thank you, God, a golden shimmer. I opened my eyes. "He's alive."

Mrs. Guerra burst into tears.

Once we'd calmed her down and seen her out, Soames looked at me as we stood in the waiting room. "What do you think?"

"You first." This was only our fourth case together, but he'd proven to have good instincts and not to jump to conclusions.

Tabitha, our still-new receptionist, folded her arms and propped them on the edge of her desk, her gaze avid. I had the feeling she found the private investigation stuff fascinating, but she hadn't quite reached the point of feeling comfy enough with us to offer her opinions—yet. She'd only been with us for about a month, and I felt certain she'd realize no one would mind if she started participating in our case discussions soon.

"She's a nice lady, loves her son and thinks the world of him, but she could be overreacting. Just because he didn't go home last night, that doesn't mean anything's happened to him. He's an adult." Soames paused. "Then again, parents don't always know what's going on with their kids, and he might not be as great as she thinks he is. They do live in the Palisades. He could be in a gang and maybe ran into some trouble last night."

I nodded. "But..."

"I know. Living there doesn't mean he's a bad kid. He did graduate, and is going to college. Maybe it's something really simple, like the stress got to him, so he's taking a break. Maybe with a girl."

"All good possibilities. What I picked up is that he's proud of his accomplishments, and loves his mom. Felt like he's a hard worker, but I heard music too, so I think he takes time out for fun." I shrugged. "I'm going to grab my stuff. We'll have lunch and hit the campus to look around."

"Okay."

"Do you want to go eat with us?" I asked Tabitha, who smiled.

"I'd love to, but Kate has an appointment coming in at one, and I've already ordered Chinese for us."

"Maybe tomorrow then." I'd yet to time a lunch invite right where she was concerned. Tabitha aligned with Kate's unique fashion sense, and self-preservation had pushed me away from wearing so many tees to work.

Jeans were a requirement, but I'd traded my running shoes for a pair of black, combat-inspired boots with good tread. My royal blue, scoop-necked sweater looked more professional than a T-shirt. I went to my office and grabbed the dark blue peacoat I'd found at a thrift store, as well as my new black purse, which was a lot smaller than my old zebra print one.

Soames was pulling his leather jacket off the coat rack in the waiting room. Mr. Whitehaven's gray trench hung from it. Funny how only the men in the office used the coat rack. "We'll see you later."

Tabitha waved us out, and we crossed the small parking lot to my car. A light dusting of snow made my beloved chariot sparkle in the weak sunlight. "I love my car so much."

My partner chuckled. "You should've seen Logan working on it. Biggest job we had at the time, and he wouldn't let anyone else touch it. Did everything himself."

"Wow." My car had been reduced to a nearly complete junk pile by a couple of angry vampires some months prior. "That was a lot of work for one guy." I brushed snow away from the driver's door lock, chilling my finger, and tried to ignore the faint flutter in my stomach at the mention of Logan's name.

"Yeah it was. He's really proud of it. Has before and after photos hanging in the garage office." Soames grinned at me over the roof of my car. "There's a rumor going around that you two are supposed to have dinner sometime."

I felt my cheeks warming and ducked my head to unlock the door. "We talked about it."

Actually, I'd babbled like an idiot and embarrassed the hell out of myself, because Logan had been shirtless and washing my car.

Soames waited until we were seated before saying, "And?"

"Nosy."

"Yes, I am. And?"

I started my car. "We're probably going to have dinner sometime. After I've moved and stuff."

That changed the subject. "How much longer is that going to be?"

"Final meeting tomorrow." My shiver wasn't from the cold, but excitement. "I get my keys then. Dad's promised to get a lawn crew out as soon as possible. It's his housewarming gift to me."

Warm air from the vents began to fill the car as I backed it out of the parking space. Soames changed the angle of the vent on his side. "Housewarming gift?"

"Presents for family or friends who are moving into a new place. It's a traditional thing, but I think it's going out of style." I was driving slower than normal. It had been decades since Santo Trueno had seen heavy snows, or for that matter, even regular snowfalls. There hadn't been any of the white stuff the previous two winters, just occasional bouts of freezing rain.

Long enough for everyone to forget how to drive when it did snow. There'd been accidents galore the past two days, mostly minor fender benders. The alternating icy and slushy road conditions freaking everyone out meant hair-trigger overreactions, and I'd narrowly missed being sideswiped on my way to work that morning.

"What's acceptable aside from lawn crews?"

"I don't know. Bottle of wine? House plants? I don't want any house plants though. Always forget to water them. Not that you have to get me anything. Housewarming gifts are optional." I slowed down to a complete crawl a few seconds before the car in front of us hit an icy patch. Its back end slewed sideways as the driver tapped the brakes and over-corrected. I concentrated, using my telekinesis to stop the slide before he hit a station wagon with a "Baby on Board" bumper sticker. Regaining control, the driver managed to straighten out his car without sliding again. "I'm seriously considering teleportation as my main means of transport this winter."

"I can see why. What's for lunch?"

"There's plenty of places to choose from around the campus."

"Pizza?"

I groaned. "Dude, we ate pizza four times last week."

Soames shrugged. "What can I say? I like pizza."

"So do I, but not in excess." I barely swallowed a gasp of surprise as a figure stepped in front of my car. The car ahead showed through her as Ginger smiled and lifted her hand in a wave.

Guess she was tired of being ignored. I drove right through her, checking the rearview as she disappeared from sight.

"You seem kind of jumpy lately," Soames said.

"I haven't been sleeping well. One of the perks of being psychic is really vivid dreams."

"Dreams, or nightmares?"

"Both. I'm used to it." I was, to a degree. The constant dreaming about Ginger was new, and I'd begun seeing her while conscious roughly two weeks ago.

Soames gave me a healthy side-eye. "Uh huh. Any chance you're regretting breaking off things with Nick?"

"No. I mean, I feel bad about hurting his feelings, and I miss some of the stuff we used to do together, but I know it was the right decision." Completely true. It'd taken me a couple of weeks to figure out why I'd jumped into dating Nick, but I had finally admitted it was mainly because I'd been lonely. Almost all my friends had significant others, so I'd also felt left out.

Terrible, awful reasons to get involved with someone.

Throw in the fact Nick had been a bossy butt and overprotective, it's a wonder we'd lasted even a few months. Besides... "There are some things," I saw Ginger standing on the sidewalk to the right, a stake jutting from her chest and her blood-coated nightgown glued to her figure. "You just can't come back from. He went through my phone to see who I'd been talking to. People who trust each other don't do stuff like that."

When I'd broken up with him, Nick had also gotten angry enough to nearly lose control and shift. Why? Jealousy of Logan.

And what had I turned around and done? Agreed to a future dinner date with Logan.

Gah, why did everything about life and adulthood have to be so damn complicated? I downshifted and used my TK to nudge another car when its front tires lost traction. Ginger waved at me from its backseat as we passed, baring her bloody fangs in a smile. The teen sitting beside her, furiously texting on his phone, obviously had no clue he was sharing the backseat with my delusion.

She was a delusion. A visual hallucination brought on by guilt and lack of sleep. Had to be that. No one else ever reacted to her presence, not even the dogs.

I seriously needed to find a new therapist.

A clump of snow fell from a traffic light, hitting the hood of my car with a thump. Soames sighed. "I love this weather."

"It makes a huge mess and results in tons of accidents."

"Wow, aren't you the little downer? Think of the fun. Snowball fights and building snowmen."

I wrinkled my nose. "That requires being outside and freezing off body parts."

"Fine. How about the fact it'll melt and help fill up the lakes?"

"Okay, that's a plus." Texas had been suffering from drought conditions for nearly a year.

"See? Bright side to everything." He smiled at the street ahead. "Plus, it's beautiful."

I scanned the slushy street, dirty cars, and hunched, scurrying people on the sidewalks. No sign of Ginger now. The sky was a dreary mass of gray clouds. "You need your eyes checked, dude."

He laughed. "Winter used to mean the clan spent a lot of time together, after working hard the other seasons to make certain we'd live through the cold months."

Ah, the simple life of days gone by, before the Melding. Back when the supes were merely scary stories to humans. They'd been stuck in their own realm, circa the Dark Ages or similar, and apparently had spent a lot of time trying to kill each other, from everything I'd learned.

Yeah, I could see why he'd find the depressing view beautiful. No one was after him, and all he had to do to fill his belly was stop at a restaurant or a grocery store.

For some, times were easier in the modern world.

Two

Santo Trueno Community College's campus spread out over six city blocks, and to my eyes, looked way more inviting than either of the other two colleges the city boasted.

For one, the buildings were more modern, none taller than four stories, and the landscaping had been handled with an eye to student safety. Trees were spaced well apart, with their lower branches trimmed to provide a clear line of sight up to about five feet. All the shrubbery was less than two feet tall. There were benches, every one of them placed under a light. The sheltered benches had clear plexiglass on their sides and backs, with only their little roofs opaque.

It wasn't a place someone could easily sneak up on you, even at night. I'd driven past hundreds of times, and the campus was always lit up like an over-achieving Christmas tree at the first hint of dusk.

If we'd had books or backpacks, Soames and I would've fit right in with the students walking around. Most seemed to be heading toward classes, but a few groups stood around, smoking, or hanging out and talking.

"Where are we going?" Rock salt crunched under Soames' hiking boots.

"I think the Admissions Office first. Someone there can either give us a list of his classes, or tell us who can." I shoved my hands deeper into my coat pockets, my purse dangling from my wrist. "I need to invest in some long johns."

"Some what?"

"Thermal underwear."

"Wuss."

I bumped him with my arm. "It's thirty-two degrees. That's cold to us mere mortals."

He chuckled. "You're a psychic. Make yourself a nice pair of warm air mittens."

"I'd probably set my coat on fire, and I like this coat."

"Then I guess you'll just have to suffer."

We reached the first building and I checked the sign. "Bingo."

The interior felt like a blast furnace after being outside. I unbuttoned my coat as we walked down the hallway, our soles occasionally squeaking on the blue and white tile flooring.

The Admissions Office was at the other end of the building. Soames pushed open the door, letting me enter first. I'd noticed that most of the male shifters I knew tended to open doors for women. Personally, I liked it, because I'd had plenty of practice opening doors for myself. The guys got bonus points if the door handles were icy.

"Hi, how can I help you?" The girl behind the waist-high counter smiled. She was blonde, her hair held back with barrettes on both sides, and she wore a pair of red-framed glasses. Very studious looking.

"Hi. My name's Discord Jones. We're private investigators, and I need to see about getting a list of classes for one of your students. He seems to have gone missing, and his mother's hired us to find him."

"Oh. Um, I don't know if I can give that information out." She bit her bottom lip, her shoulders dropping.

I smiled. "We don't need any personal information. Just a list of the classes he's taking, so we can talk to his instructors and classmates."

"Well," she looked at Soames, who leaned against the counter with a smile.

"You could write that down for us," he suggested, and gave her a wink. "Maybe your phone number too?"

Gah. I felt like kicking him in the ankle, and almost hoped she'd be offended. But no, she nodded and went to a computer, returning a few minutes later with a sheet of paper. Soames glanced at it while taking it from her. "Thank you, Sheila."

I waited until we were in the hallway before saying anything. "That was crappy."

"What was?"

"Pretending you wanted her number."

He stopped. "I wasn't pretending. She's cute."

She had been rocking those red glasses of hers. "So you're really going to call her?"

"Yes. I'll ask her out for coffee. That's the no pressure kind of thing, right?"

I had to realign my thought processes. "Uh, yeah. Pretty much."

"I mean, unless you tell me not to call her."

"Come again?"

Soames shrugged. "You're clan now, and a queen."

"I'm what?"

He hesitated, studying my face. "No one mentioned that to you?"

"Uh, no, or I wouldn't be asking 'what the hell'?"

"Right. You're clan, and an adult female. That makes you one of our queens. So you get to boss us around. The men, I mean." He snorted. "Come on, you know we're the only shifter species ruled by women."

"Oh." I did know that, but hadn't really thought what it meant. Especially not in context of me joining the clan.

His eyes twinkled. "I'd bet money Logan wouldn't mind you bossing him around."

Instant face fire. "Dude, shut up, or I won't let you call Cutie Pie back there."

"Sorry." The grin on Soames' face said otherwise, but we'd reached the outer door. I buttoned my coat.

"You really wouldn't call her if I told you not to?"

"I really wouldn't."

"Oh, the power rush." My own grin made an appearance as his faded. "Kidding. Just one thing."

"Yes?"

"You do know that 'no' actually means no, right?"

He pushed the door open for me. "Doesn't everyone?"

"Actually, no, everyone doesn't."

Soames grunted. "Well, we do."

"Mega Douche didn't," I said while walking through the door.

"Mega...oh, you mean Harrison. He's not a typical tiger. Guy has some serious issues."

I snorted. "You think?"

"But our Queen made her point, loud and clear."

We both smiled, and I said, "Yeah, she did."

Terra had stomped the guy into the ground even though he was three times her size. "And it was a glorious thing to behold. Where to first?"

He checked the list. "History class."

We didn't have much luck throughout the afternoon, not until a girl stopped us on our way out of the building where Frederico's last class met. "Hey, wait up."

She was shorter than me, with dark brown hair, blue eyes, and a round face. "Lacey Carter. I heard you say you were looking for Rico."

Well, if she'd heard us, why hadn't she said something then? "Yes. Do you know him?"

"We're working on a project together. Well, we're supposed to be, but he postponed last night to hang out with his friends." Her lips tightened, the only sign of miffiness about being blown off.

"I see. Are those friends students here too?"

"Two are. They hang out at O'Banion's after class most days. I can point them out to you if they're there."

"That'd be great. Thanks."

Lacey cocked her head, scanning us. "You two are really private detectives?"

"Yes."

"Huh. I thought only old people were. Rico's really missing?" She began walking, surging ahead to lead the way. We fell in behind her. Soames wasn't able to reach the door first, and Lacey shoved it wide as she went through.

"He didn't make it home last night. His mother is worried." I followed her out as Soames stretched to keep the door open for us.

"The first thing she does is hire a couple of PIs?" Lacey shook her head. "Helicopter mom much?"

I nearly snapped at her, Mrs. Guerra's relief that her son was alive still fresh. "Like I said, she's worried."

Dusk was on the way, so all the lights had come on. We crunched our way down the sidewalk. The college's rock salt expense must've been astronomical.

The girl snorted. "Maybe he got drunk and crashed at a friend's."

"Possibly." The negative vibe coming from her was grating at my nerves. However, she was helping. "We'll find out."

"Does being a PI pay much?"

Rude much? I tried for neutral. "Pays enough."

"I'm wondering because they're always poor in books and movies. I'm going to be a film maker," she said, her tone turning lofty. "I'm going to do all the important stuff on my movies. Writing, direction," she waved her hand. "I'll be famous someday."

"Fame's overrated." I was still worrying about my name being leaked to the press. The bodies we'd found during the case we'd worked for the vampire lord, Derrick, were still popular news fodder.

Lacey frowned as she glanced at me. "Don't be silly. Everyone dreams of being rich and famous."

Yeah, and eventually, they grew out of it. I didn't want any part of it, having enough headaches to deal with. Not in the mood to argue with her, I looked across the street as we paused at the curb. "O'Banion's awaits."

The three of us sloshed across the street road and into the place, which proved to be a sports bar. The tables were tall, and so were the chairs. Everything was made of metal and looked spindly. People perched on the chairs like overgrown bugs. A huge, flat-screen TV dominated one end of the rectangular space.

"Over there." Lacey pointed to a table halfway between the entrance and TV. "That's Jake and Marty."

"Okay. Thanks for your help." I headed toward the two guys, hoping my polite dismissal was enough. Once there, I introduced myself. "Hi, I'm Cordi Jones."

"She's a private detective," Lacey chimed in, slipping around to stand beside me.

"Yeah, and I'm looking..."

"For Rico. His mom's freaking out because he didn't make it home last night.

I looked at her. "Thank you. I'll take it from here, if you don't mind."

"I don't. Go ahead."

"She doesn't know how to take a hint," one of the guys said. "That's why we call her 'Lacey the Leech'."

Wow, rude. I had an instant where I didn't know how to respond, because they might have useful information, but pissing them off wouldn't result in getting it from them.

Fortunately, Soames decided to step in. "That was pretty damn rude."

"So?"

My partner smiled, his eyes turning a clear gold, and spoke in a silky growl that reminded me of the one time I'd badly aggravated Logan. "So, I think maybe you should apologize to Lacey."

Both guys went stiff, and the one who'd called her "the Leech" swallowed hard enough for us to hear. "Sorry, Lacey."

She smirked, but I really couldn't blame her. My partner was still smiling. "Thank you. Now, I believe my friend has a couple of questions for you."

Just like that, I had their undivided attention. "When's the last time you saw Rico?"

"Last night, at the club."

"That's Jake," Lacy said. "Marty's the rude one."

I nodded. "Which club?"

"Dreamland. It's new, and pretty cool. Lots of hot waitresses." Jake's gaze flicked toward Soames. "And, uh, it's kind of the in place right now."

"Was he with someone?"

"Rico danced with a couple of girls, but I don't think he was hooking up with anyone. I'm not sure when he left. He didn't tell anyone he was leaving, but that happens."

"Okay, where is this club?" Jake gave me the address. "Great. You've all been really helpful. Thank you."

We managed to beat Lacey out the door, and once on the sidewalk, discovered snow falling again. "Crap. Rush hour's gonna be a bitch."

"And your car's on the other side of the campus."

"That's not a problem." I held out my hand, and Soames took hold with a laugh.

"You are such a wuss about the cold."

"Quit picking on me." I teleported us to my car. He released my hand and walked around to the passenger side. I dug out my keys, but turned my head just as a dark figure leaped out from behind the two-feet-tall bushes on the other side of the sidewalk that lined the parking lot.

A quick grab of TK, and the guy hung in mid-air. With more leisure, I realized it was Nick's older brother, Patrick. "No fair, Psychic Girl."

"Dude, you have about three seconds to explain what the hell you thought you were doing before I stick you on top of the flag pole."

"I was leaving class, and saw your car. Thought it was a golden opportunity to put an end to Nick's moping."

Soames leaned on the roof of my car and snorted. "By mugging

Discord?"

Patrick rolled his eyes. "No, I was going to kidnap her."

"Okay, yeah. Flag pole topper is so a part of your immediate future. Because seriously, kidnapping me?"

"Well, yeah. The plan was, I kidnap you, take you home, and then Nick and you have a nice talk. You get back together, and no more mopey little brother." Patrick grinned. "Good plan, right?"

"You're an idiot," Soames said. "I'm voting flag pole too."

"Oh, come on." Patrick kicked his legs. "Can I get down now?"

"Why should I let you down? You're planning to kidnap me."

"Not for nefarious purposes. For a good cause. Big difference."

I sighed and lowered him to the ground. "Nick and I aren't getting back together. Your good cause is a lost one."

Patrick shoved his hands into his pockets. "He loves you."

Not sure how to respond to that, I simply nodded.

"Won't you please give him another chance?"

Soames groaned. "This is the problem with wolves: The men don't know how to deal with rejection."

"Oh, and you pussy," Patrick paused to smile. "Cats do?"

My partner smiled back, showing plenty of teeth. "Most of us do, because we're taught that women are people too."

"I know women are people."

"Too bad your dad doesn't," I muttered.

"Dad's old-fashioned." Patrick flapped his hand. "Come on, Psychic Girl. Nick's heart is broken. He's suffering."

As though I didn't have enough guilt weighing me down lately. I had to work to keep my voice pleasant. "Look, it's great to find out you really care about your brother, but you'd help him more by convincing him to find someone who wants the same kind of life he does. I'm really sorry he's having a hard time right now, but dude, I'm not responsible for anyone's happiness but my own."

Patrick's face crumpled into a frown. "You don't love him."

"No."

"Then why were you looking at houses together?"

I managed to keep from sighing. "I was looking for a house for me. It would've been rude not to include Nick because we were dating then."

"Oh. So you're definitely not going to go with me to talk to him?"

"Definitely not." What good would it do to see Nick and possibly explain exactly why I'd gotten together with him in the first place? None. The only results would be more hurt.

"What if I got on my knees and begged?"

Amusing as the idea was, I shook my head. "Not even then."

Patrick sighed. "I tried."

"Yes, you did." I had to fight a smile, because funny as it was, his "try" had included attempted kidnapping, and then laying a big, old guilt trip on me. Heart in the right place or not, both were jerk moves.

"All right." Patrick pulled his hands free of his pockets and squared his shoulders. "Please accept my apologies for bothering you."

I studied his face for a second before saying, "Apology accepted."

"Thank you." He inclined his head to first me then Soames. "You two have a good evening."

"Thanks. You too." We watched him turn and walk away. I looked over at Soames, who shrugged. "Might be just me, but he seemed less douche baggy than usual right then."

"If you say so."

I unlocked the door. "I did. Must be running a fever."

Opening the passenger door, Soames laughed before dropping out of sight to take a seat. I followed suit after a final glance in the direction Patrick had taken, and started my car.

THREE

A layer of ice had formed on the windshield, and I switched to defrost. In doing so, I glanced in the rearview mirror to find Ginger had returned. She crouched in the cargo area, her face lurking between the front seats. Her eyes were red.

Determined to ignore her, I cast about for a conversation starter. "Why do you still call me Discord, instead of Cordi?"

"Habit, I guess. That's how Logan introduced you to us."

"Well, we're partners, friends, and clan now. You can call me Cordi."

"Okay. Should I mention you prefer that to the others?"

"Sure. Would it be weird if I called you Dane?"

He chuckled. "A little, since only my parents call me that anymore, but it's cool."

"Awesome." I turned the windshield wipers on, clearing away bits of melting ice. They skated over a good portion of it, but I left them on. "I've been wondering. Do you think of yourself as a tiger, a human, or...?"

Soames, I mean, Dane, shrugged. "A person. We're just people who happen to have two shapes we can switch between."

Had that been rude to ask? He didn't look offended. "Sorry. I'm being too nosy."

"Nah, you're just trying to figure us out, and that's fine." He scratched his chin. "What's our next stop?"

"It's Friday night and we have a club to check out. Next stop is Mom's. I'll change and then we'll go to your place so you can do the same." The wipers and defroster had done their job, clearing the last of the ice.

"Sounds like a plan."

I glanced in the rearview to discover Ginger was gone once more.

Even though the trip was business-related, I decided to dress up for the occasion because I hadn't been to a club in ages. Thanks to some advice from Sal, my fairy godfather—heavy emphasis on the "god" part—I'd learned to build a better mental shield. It cut way down on the energy drain of keeping other people's thoughts muted.

Telepathy wasn't all it was cracked up to be.

When I returned to the living room where Dane waited, he whistled. I sucked in my cheeks, put my hands on my hips, and did a catwalk turn with my head high, to show off the clingy black and green dress. Long-sleeved and low-backed, its hemline ended just above my knees. It was made to go clubbing in. I'd chosen a pair of black pumps with two-inch heels.

"You're really going to freeze in that."

"I'm going to wear a coat." Actually, I kind of needed his opinion on the one I had in mind. "Be right back."

Back in my room, I pulled out the second of my thrift store finds. Mom's eyes had bulged when I'd first shown it to her, until she'd realized it was fake fur. Slipping it on, I hurried back to the living room, watching Dane's face when he saw me.

"Terra's going to want one," was the first thing he said. I relaxed. "Where'd you get it?"

I stroked the soft lapel. "Thrift store. Isn't it cool?"

The coat was white tiger skin. The interior was lined with black Sherpa, adding weight to the outer, acrylic shell. I'd locked and targeted on it the second I'd spotted it, and held my breath while trying it on. The coat was fitted to the waist, with a full skirt, and it had buttons up top, but tied at the waist.

"Very cool," Dane assured me. "But be prepared for Danielle to hate it."

I hesitated, my fingers on the buttons. She already didn't like me very much. According to Alanna, Danielle had her eye on Logan, and our few interactions definitely supported that theory. Danielle didn't like that he and I were friends, and she was probably going to completely flip her lid when we did go on that future dinner date. "Maybe I should I wear a different coat."

He grunted. "I wouldn't change."

I stroked the coat's skirt, trying to decide. There hadn't been a chance to wear it before now, and I really wanted to. "Are you sure Terra won't be offended or something?"

"I'm sure she'll love it, and it looks great on you. Come on, I have to have time to clean up, too."

That was persuasion enough. "Okay."

Rush hour traffic had died down, allowing the falling snow to collect on top of the refreezing slush. End result: We barely made it to the tiger clan's building. Small sports cars weren't made for winter traveling.

Someone had salted the walk and wide drive that led to the garage section's bay doors. Teague responded to Dane's knock on the metal front door of the apartment side. "It's laundry night. Hi, Discord. Nice coat."

The tall, lean man with rusty black hair was a lion shifter, on loan to our clan as a bodyguard for Terra. "Hi, and thanks."

"There's room if you want me to pull your car in."

"We should take one of the trucks," Dane said, and I nodded.

"Yes, please." After handing my keys over to Teague, I added, "Thanks."

"Is Alanna up or downstairs?"

"Your sister's in the laundry room."

Dane looked at me. "I need to talk to her before I get ready."

I hadn't known the two were related. Teague chuckled. "What he really means is that he's going to beg her to do his laundry."

That made me laugh. "Can't blame him. I hate doing it. Go ahead. I'll visit with Terra until you're ready."

"Okay." Dane loped down the first floor hallway, dodging basket-laden people.

Teague asked, "What are you dressed up for?"

"We have to check out a club for a missing person case."

He twirled my key ring. "Which club?"

"Dreamland. Have you heard of it?"

"Nope. Terra and Logan are upstairs. I'll get your car inside."

"Okay, thanks." I headed for the stairs, trading smiles and greetings with the clan members I passed on their way down. Fortunately, I didn't see Danielle or her two cousins on my way up.

Terra answered my knock, her pale green eyes widening when she saw my coat. "Oh, wow, it's gorgeous. Where did you find it?"

"A thrift store. I'm at loose ends until Dane's ready to go. Is it okay if I hang out here?"

"Sure." She hugged me before stepping back to allow me inside. "Hey, Logan, Discord's here."

We heard the muffled slam of a drawer before his bedroom door opened. He wore gray sweatpants, a red tee, and a welcoming smile. The smile faded as he had a good look at what I wore. Terra giggled. "She looks awesome, huh?"

Logan blinked. "Yes, she does."

"She's waiting for Soames, so came to visit."

It may have been my imagination, but it looked as though Logan clenched his jaws. "Oh. Where are you two going?"

"May I try your coat on?" Terra asked at the same time.

"Sure." I untied the belt and slipped it off. "We're on a missing person case and need to check out a club."

The teen squealed, shoving her arm into a sleeve.

He waved his hand at the kitchen while checking out my clingy dress. "Do you want something to drink?"

"Thanks, but no. We're going to stop for dinner first." I moved out of Terra's way as she tied the belt, knowing what she'd do next. Something about full skirts caused an urge to twirl.

She did twirl, the coat belling out. "Oh, I love it." she stopped and struck a pose. "How do I look?"

"Beautiful," Logan said with a smile, finally leaving the doorway of his room. She purred, stroking a coat sleeve, and spun around again.

I decided to sit down. So did Logan. We both went for the recliner, halted, and he chuckled. "I promise the couch is more comfortable."

"Okay." I moved to the couch's end and sat, crossing my ankles. Feeling flustered was an unwelcome bonus. The only other time I'd been in a dress around him had been when demons had wanted to sacrifice me to meld their realm to the regular world.

"Would you mind if I go show Alanna?" Terra proved she had a wicked "puppy eyes" expression.

"Sure, go ahead."

"Thanks, I'll be right back." She flung open the apartment door and hauled buns. Logan sighed before walking over to shut it.

"Soames is working out okay?" he asked while walking back to sit down.

"Great. We get along way better than Nick and I did."

"Good, glad to hear it." His tone didn't match the words.

"Yeah. Um," I groped for something else to say. "Hey, I get the keys to my house tomorrow."

"Congratulations. When do you plan to move?"

"Maybe next weekend? I guess it'll depend on the weather."

"Right." The silence that followed did not feel comfy.

Crap, we'd never had trouble talking to each other before. My stomach fluttered again, and not pleasantly. My issue was simple: I'd made an ass out of myself before and after he'd admitted to being attracted to me. It also wasn't fair he looked better every time I saw him. Logan even made sweatpants look sexy.

I sighed before I could stop it.

"Is something wrong?"

"No. I mean, not really. Kind of?" The hem of my dress became really interesting. I began fiddling with it. "Maybe it's just me, but it feels like we've entered Awkwardville city limits since we, uh, talked about going out."

"Oh. Well, we haven't talked much since. We've both been pretty busy."

"Yeah."

"It's okay if you've changed your mind."

I quit picking at my dress to look at him. "No, I haven't. Have you?"

"No, but... You and Soames seem to be getting along really well. I know he thinks highly of you." Logan glanced at the door.

I laughed. "Nice to know, but I'm pretty sure he doesn't 'like' like me. He hit on someone today and has her number. I like him, but not in a dating way."

"So..."

"So we're still on. I mean, unless you change your mind."

His shoulders relaxed. I hadn't noticed he was tense. "I won't."

"Great." And there we were, out of conversation again. Damn it. "Um, I was kind of thinking."

"About what?" Logan asked when a few seconds passed.

I took a deep breath. "About us dating. It's not that I don't ever want a serious relationship, but..."

He raised his hands to stop me. "I know. We're going to, what's the phrase? Play it by ear?"

Instant relief, because we were on the same page. "Yes, that."

"Sounds good to me. I haven't dated a human before. Actually, I haven't had time to date at all since the Melding. I'm going to be rusty."

"That's okay." Better than okay, because it meant no recent ex-girlfriends to worry about. Just Danielle and her crush or whatever. An idea struck. "Hey, can Terra spare you?"

Logan grinned. "She'd be happy to get rid of me for a little bit. According to her, I've been looming too much."

"Then how about a practice run?"

"Practice run," he repeated, and I nodded.

"Yeah. Come with us tonight. It won't be a date because we're on a case and Dane will be there, but we'll be hanging out. You know, together."

He rose from the recliner before I finished talking. "Love to."

The smile on my face felt goofy as all get out. Terra burst in as his bedroom door shut. "I'm back. Alanna loves it, and I let her try it on. That was okay, right?" Before I could respond, she rushed along. "It's too big on her. I wish I could find one like it."

"I'll keep an eye out for another one," I promised. "If it's okay, I'm going to borrow Logan tonight."

The teen grinned. "All night?"

"Terra!" Logan shouted from his bedroom, and she snickered.

Club wear for men who bought clothing for work instead of play consisted of jeans and non-tees. Both men wore black jeans and boots—ropers. Dane wore a dark red, short-sleeved shirt, while Logan's was a long-sleeved button up in forest green.

On our way downstairs, I wondered if he'd chosen his shirt to match my dress, or because he knew how great he looked in green. I didn't ask. It's sometimes nice to have things like that to ponder.

Just my luck that Danielle appeared at the foot of the stairs as we reached the last flight. She was around Logan's age, with the sharp-boned face of a super model, and dark hair and eyes. Her long legs were bared, thanks to an itty bitty pair of black shorts, and so was most of the rest of her, since her only other item of clothing was a bright purple sports bra. Danielle was lean and toned, and I felt out of shape looking at her.

She noted my hand around Logan's forearm, our clothing, and a frown appeared on her face. "Where are you going?"

"Out," Dane said, already halfway down the last flight. He paused to look up at us. "Are we taking your truck?"

"No, we'll go in my car," Logan replied, and I felt the attention of everyone in earshot coming to bear on us at the sound of his voice. Behind Danielle, Teague crossed his arms and leaned back against the outer door. I wasn't sure who he was watching, her or us, as Logan led me down the steps.

"Can I drive?" Dane bounced down to the ground floor.

"Have I ever let you drive my car?"

My partner smiled. "Nope, but I intend to keep asking."

Apparently tired of being ignored, Danielle spoke. "Your place is with our Queen."

By then, we'd gone far enough that I could see at least three other people in the hallway, trying to pretend they weren't loitering.

"I'm off duty tonight." Logan smiled at her. "Our Queen is sick of me hovering around now that she's come into her own."

Danielle, her frown deeper, moved back to let us off the final step. I was her next target. "Your coat is a mockery of what we are."

"Terra loves it." Point for me, but I knew she'd score one of her own, sooner or later. It looked like it'd be later, as she sniffed and began climbing the stairs. Relieved she was leaving, I said, "I thought you drove a truck."

Dane opened the door to the garage. "You're not the only one who has a massive love affair with a car."

"Oh?"

"Took him three years to hunt down all the parts and restore it."

"What is it?"

Logan pointed a finger at Dane when he began to answer. "She'll see it in a minute."

I nodded at Teague, who smiled, before we entered the garage. Dane trotted to the far corner, and as we followed, I realized there was a door back there.

"He named it."

"I couldn't think of a cool enough name, or my car would have one too."

"Logan called yours 'Baby' while he was working on it. He talks to the cars he likes."

"That's enough, Soames." Logan's cheeks had acquired a touch of pink.

I giggled. "I think that's cute."

Dane opened the door, reaching in to flick on the lights. "This is our personal garage."

Having wondered where they kept all their vehicles, I went through to find a line of about half a dozen trucks. We walked down to the far end, where a car sat under a gray cover. I let go of Logan's arm. "Mystery car is mysterious."

The two men took up positions on either side of the car's hood, preparing to remove the cover. Logan smiled. "Do you want to take a guess?"

"Hello, psychic here. Unveil and surprise before one of you thinks too loud."

"Sure." They bent and flipped the cover over the hood, which was painted a deep, super glossy dark green. Away from direct lighting, the car would look black.

"I think lime green was a stock color for a '69 Challenger , not this green."

"This green is my favorite color." Logan and Dane finished pulling the cover off. "I didn't go straight stock on everything."

"Wanna race for pink slips?"

He laughed. "Your car's too new for me."

"Yeah, I see that. Bet I get better gas mileage."

Logan came around to open the passenger door for me, while Dane put the cover away on some shelves built into the side wall. "You do, but I have more horsepower."

"Them's fighting words, dude. Now we have to race."

My partner snorted. "You'll lose."

Probably, but I was having fun teasing Logan, and pretended outrage. "I'm sorry, have you not been riding with me the past few weeks?"

"He has nitrous."

"That's cheating."

They both laughed, and we climbed in.

FOUR

We rolled into Dreamland's parking lot about eight-thirty, after having stopped to enjoy a steak dinner. The outside of the club wasn't much to look at, just a square shape painted tan, with a covered entrance. There was a short line of people waiting to get in, and to my surprise, a couple of large bouncers guarding the door.

"Someone has an over-inflated ego," I said when we cruised by the entrance in search of a parking spot. "Wonder if we're cool enough to get in?"

"Guess we'll find out."

Dane leaned forward. "I am, but I don't know about you two."

I tried to shoo him back. "Ha, ha. You're so funny."

Logan chose a spot in the corner of the lot farthest from the entrance. "Sorry, we're going to have to walk."

"I'll live, but it may be too much for Dane. He's such a fragile flower."

My partner rolled his eyes. "You're being sillier than usual."

"Jitters. I haven't been to a club in over a year, and not to many before then anyway. Here I am, dressed to the nines, with two handsome men, and we're sitting in a gorgeous set of wheels." I pulled my licenses and a twenty from my purse. "Did you install an alarm on it?"

"Oh, yeah." Logan cut the engine.

"Good. Will you hold this for me?" I handed over my stuff, before shoving my purse under my seat. It took him a few seconds to realize I didn't mean just for the moment, but when he did, Logan tucked my licenses and money into his wallet. "Dane, you have Rico's photo, right?"

"In my wallet," he assured me.

Logan exited, leaving Dane to crawl out of the back seat on his own. A moment later, he appeared out of the evening gloom to open my door. The snow had stopped again, so I left the hood of my coat down.

Doors shut and locked and the alarm set, we walked across the lot.

We had to pass the door to go to the end of the line, but as we neared the door, one of the bouncers stepped forward. "Tiger lady. Come on in."

"I knew this coat was a wise purchase," I whispered to Logan. "My friends too?"

The bouncer, about seven feet tall and some type of supe I'd never seen before, surveyed them for a second before nodding. "Your friends, too, Tiger Lady."

"Thank you." We passed between the bouncers, the second one turning to open the door for us. The room we entered was silent, and painted white. Everything was white: Walls, floor, ceiling, the back of the door we'd come through, the counter, and even the cash register sitting on it.

An elf sat behind the counter. She was a white blonde with the palest skin I'd ever seen, dressed as a sexy angel. White feathered wings stuck up above her head. Her eyes were pale pink. Albino elf. Neat.

Once at the counter, I saw the discreet sign that informed us the cover charge was five dollars. That was amusing, after the whole "You shall not pass unless you're cool enough" charade outside. Logan and Dane began pulling out their wallets, but the elf spoke. "There's no charge for you or your companions, Miss Jones. Be welcome, and enjoy your evening."

"How do you know who I am?"

She inclined her head. "Prince Thorandryll owns this establishment."

"Seriously?" She nodded, and I wondered if he'd passed my photo around the old sidhe so all his people would know what I looked like.

"Yes, Miss Jones. Your refreshments are complimentary as well."

Huh. Partying on Thorandryll's dime did have a certain allure, but we were there for a reason. I glanced at Dane, who stepped forward and held up the photo of Rico. "Have you seen this man recently?"

She looked at the photo. "Yes. He's been in several times since we opened. I believe he was here last night."

Woohoo, we were getting somewhere. "Did you see him leave alone, or with someone?"

The elf shook her head. "I'm afraid not. This is the entrance."

I hadn't seen another door outside. "Where's the exit?"

"You'll find it when you're ready to leave. My apologies, but there are new arrivals incoming." She gestured to a door at the right of her post. "Please enjoy your evening."

"Sure. Thanks." Had the door been there before? I couldn't remember as we moved toward it. At least we'd confirmed Rico was a regular.

"Welcome, Miss Jones," an elf said the second I walked through the door. This one was a guy, dressed in clinging black pants, highly polished riding boots, and a white poet's shirt. His hair didn't match the romance cover outfit, being dark blue. The room we were in was little more than a rectangular box, with doors at each end. It was also painted white, but the overhead lighting picked out glints of green, blue, pink, and gold on the walls, floor, and counter the new elf stood behind. It was like standing inside a giant opal.

"May I take your coats?"

Fancy. I untied the belt of mine as the guys shrugged off their jackets. The elf took them, not offering a number or anything. "Um, don't we need a ticket or something?"

"We never forget which article belongs to which guest," he assured me, and gestured to the far door with a fluid gesture. "Please, enjoy your evening."

"Thank you." I sincerely hoped the next door actually opened into the club. The gauntlet thing was growing old.

Onward we went, and a blast of warm air, music, and loud conversations smacked me in the face as Dane opened the door. He went through first, I followed, only to back up and bump into Logan after looking down. The floor was water, fish flashing neon colors darting around under the surface. "Whoa."

"It's solid," Logan said, and I looked up to see people dancing on the water in the middle of an underground grotto. The place was huge, with thick coral columns spaced around the dance floor.

I took a step forward, my gaze moving up the nearest column. A greenish fog concealed the ceiling. "Pocket realm, glamour, or super interior decorating?"

"My vote is pocket realm." Logan moved to my right side. "The air smells salty."

It did. "Okay, this is actually kind of awesome."

"There's a bar." Dane pointed off to our left. "And tables. Unless we find some clues on Rico, I vote we make Thorandryll really, really sorry about that complimentary drink thing."

"I'll be under the table in three drinks."

He laughed. "You're a wuss. We can drink gallons."

"Seriously?" I looked at Logan, who nodded. "How?"

"Our metabolism is higher than humans'. That's why we heal far faster. We break down alcohol and drugs extremely fast too."

"That is so unfair. Wait, does that mean you can't get a buzz?"

"We can, but we have to drink a lot to keep it going." Dane grinned, looking around. "I hope he has a big stock room."

"Uh huh. How much is a lot?"

"I'll show you if we're here for a while." His grin widened. "I really like this place."

I followed his line of sight to a waitress in a skin-tight cat suit of glittering blue scales and matching go-go boots. Her eye makeup and lipstick matched the suit. Way too much glitter for me. She looked human though, under it all.

"I think I'll start questioning the waitresses." Dane made a beeline for her.

"You do that," I called after him, noticing a small school of fish trailing his footsteps. "I can't tell if there's non-watery floor over there."

"There is." Logan took my hand and led me after Dane. "Do you want a drink?"

"Yes, please." The neon flashing fish were darting around us too, and I couldn't stop watching them, expecting to plunge through whatever was holding us above the water. "Have you seen *Jaws* yet?"

"No, what's it about?"

"A man-eating shark." An eel slid by, trailing red lightning, and I squeaked.

He laughed. "I doubt there's sharks."

"Thorandryll might be here." We stepped from "water" to what looked like stone, but felt like thin carpeting under my shoes. The music went from loud to muted, but the buzz of a lot of people laughing and talking continued. I checked my new mental maze shield for weakness, but all its walls were firm. One area was humming, but not loud enough to be irritating.

Straight to the bar we went. I fought laughter at the sight of the bar stools: Coral columns, loads shorter and more slender than those holding up the roof, topped with upturned clam half shells for seats. "Dare you to sit on one."

"Ah, think I'll stand, but you go right ahead." Logan patted the stool closest. "Nice and cushy."

"And kind of tall." I didn't see an easy way to climb aboard the stool. Logan turned, put his hands around my waist, and hello! I was on the stool. Even managed to find a slight protrusion to plant the heels of my shoes on. "Thanks for the lift."

"My pleasure." He rested his forearm on the bar's edge. "What would you like to drink?"

"Pina colada."

"All right." It wasn't necessary to wave for a bartender's attention, because one arrived then. "A pina colada for the lady, and a Weirding Pale for me, please."

The bartender, yet another elf dressed like Coat Check Guy, inclined his head and walked down the bar a short distance.

"What's a Weirding Pale?"

"Dwarf-brewed ale. It has a stouter taste than any of the human ales I've tried."

"Oh." Dwarves were real. Of course. It struck me again how little I'd learned about supes. They had different cultures, just like humans did. "In fairytales, dwarves mine and make stuff like weapons."

Logan nodded. "They are master miners and weapon smiths, but they're also famous brewers. At least with us."

The bartender returned with our drinks. Mine was in a fishbowl glass I'd have to use both hands to carry, and lowered my "under the table in three" estimate to one. Logan's was in a stone tankard, sans lid. He tipped the elf a five while I tried a sip through the green straw stuck in my drink. "Mm. I may need help with this."

Logan lifted his tankard, shaking his head. "You're on your own with fruity drinks. They make my ale taste funny."

"I won't be having a second, that's for sure." I moved, and the seat twisted. Sliding my over-sized drink closer to him, I turned until I could see the dance floor. Dane was talking to a waitress in red. "He seems to have things under control."

"Does that mean you're off the clock unless he finds something?" Logan watched me over the lip of his tankard as he took a drink.

I checked my mental Rico file, and the gold shimmer was present. "Delegation is such a useful tool."

"Good. Want to move to a table?"

"Sure." He helped me off the stool before I hefted my drink. "Lead on."

He chose a table about ten feet from the edge of the dance floor. We both eyed the chairs—they had stubby tentacles and were orange—but the tentacles stayed on the backs. We sat down, and I realized the table's top was glass, showing a scene of gently waving seaweed. A soft green glow emanated from the table. "Weird. The air and lighting all looks green, but people don't."

"Magic lighting." Logan scooted his chair a bit closer to mine. "I like your dress."

"Thank you." Suddenly nervous, I took another drink, only to wonder if I looked like a fish sucking on the straw.

He settled back in his chair. "Are you excited about your house?"

Ooh, conversation I could handle. "You have no idea. It's been crazy at Mom's."

"I bet. How's Leglin and the Pit Crew?"

"They're doing good. They don't mention Red much, though." My eyes grew hot. I blinked before taking another drink. "How's the search for a new place going for you guys?"

"A couple of possibilities. It's kind of hard to find something that'll work for as many people as we have."

"Yeah."

Dane walked up and squatted between our chairs. "A couple of the ladies remember Rico being here last night, but no one remembers seeing him leave. Hey, is that Weirding?"

"Yes."

"I'm getting one, and then I'll do some more asking around." Dane rose and strode off to the bar.

"He likes the job," Logan said.

"He's good at it, and fun to work with." The music slowed down, and I glanced at the dance floor as people began pairing off for 'Lady in Red'.

"Found your sea legs yet?"

"What?"

Logan smiled. "Would you like to dance?"

"Oh. Um, sure." I needed his help to escape my chair. Once on the dance floor, Logan pulled me close and right into a slow Two Step. A warm tingling sensation spread through me, one I'd felt before when we'd touched. It only lasted a few breaths, so I didn't think it was sexual. Those kinds of tingles tended to congregate a bit lower and stick around until something was done about them. "Where'd you learn to dance?"

"Television."

I laughed. "You learned well."

"Thanks." His hand settled more firmly on my back. "You should see me do the Lambada. It probably works better with a partner though."

Imagining him dancing alone in his living room drew another laugh from me. "You'll have to teach me. I can waltz, Two Step, shake and shimmy to rock, but that's it."

"What, no tango?"

"No tango," I confirmed. "But I do a mean Cotton-Eyed Joe, and a not bad Electric Slide."

"I should make a request." Logan spun me while looking around. "But I have no idea where the DJ booth is."

"Darn. Or not darn, since I'm not wearing my boots."

"What if," he spun me again. "For our first date, we have dinner and go dancing somewhere Cotton-Eyed Joe is welcome?"

"Mm," I said. "That depends. Are you going to wear a Stetson?"

"That's a cowboy hat, right?"

"Yes."

"I'll see what I can do," he promised. I squinted at him. "What?"

"Trying to imagine you in a Stetson, doing the Cotton-Eyed Joe. Or maybe the Schottische."

His teeth flashed in a grin. "I know that one too."

"You're kidding."

"When in Texas," Logan said as the song ended. He stepped back, holding my hand, and doffed an imaginary hat. "Ma'am."

It's entirely possible I fell a tiny bit in love at that moment, looking into his eyes and watching a cute grin spread across his face. The same grin I'd seen the night we met, when he'd shoved his hands in his pockets to try to look harmless.

Then I saw Ginger behind him and to his left, her mottled, gray skin flaking as her mouth stretched into a mocking grin.

"What?" Logan asked, glancing that way. Fortunately, Dane was at the edge of the dance floor, waving at us. "Oh."

Just as well she'd decided to turn up, or I may have embarrassed the holy crap out of myself again. You know, by blurting out something stupid like "can I keep you?" to Logan. "We better go see what he's found."

FIVE

Dane hadn't found anything, or rather, he had found more of the same. Club employees who remembered seeing Rico around, some of them recalling that he'd been there the night before, but none had noticed when he'd left.

I sighed. "So this is a dead end."

"Guess so." Dane chugged the rest of his ale. "We don't have to leave, do we? You want another one, Logan?"

He didn't bother asking if I wanted a refill, since I'd barely made a dent in mine. Logan accepted, and leaned close once Dane headed for the bar. "There's still whoever watches the exit to talk to."

"True. I'll go look." I managed to lever myself out of my chair.

"Do you want some company?"

"Um, no. I need to powder my nose first."

"Okay. I'll be here."

I left in search of the restroom, and after asking a waitress in glittery purple, found it. No magic present in there. It was just a restroom, clean and, amazingly for a club, nothing broken. While waiting for a turn at a stall, I wondered if asking Logan along had been a mistake. Maybe I hadn't been in love with Nick, but we'd spent a lot of time together. People grow accustomed to being part of a couple, and when they aren't, they miss it.

At least, I did. Witness my realization about why I'd been with Nick in the first place.

The truth was, I did miss the cuddling while watching movies, or watching Nick try new foods, and yes, the sex. I also missed seeing Nick wake up in the morning, stretching with a drowsy smile.

Missing those sorts of things, and the person they were attached to, was what caused rebounds. When you were rebounding, you never chose a person for themselves. You chose them to fill the empty space.

"Have you guys seen Becky?"

More than eager to quit my current line of thought, I looked at the woman who'd walked in. She was a pretty brunette in jeans, pirate boots, and a black leather corset.

"She probably hooked up with Tommy," another woman said. She had neon red hair.

"He's dancing with Michelle."

The line shuffled forward, the two before me hurrying into vacated stalls.

"She got mad and left then. After all, draaaaaama queen!" Neon Red sang.

The brunette wrinkled her nose, considering her friend's response. "Yeah, I guess. Hurry up. We're ordering jello shots."

My turn arrived. I took care of business, made certain of my dress, washed my hands, and left. I avoided the bar and looked for an exit sign, but didn't find one. The restrooms, a door with an "Employees Only" sign, but nothing else.

Not even the door we'd entered the club through. Weird. I flagged down one of the waitresses. "Hi, I was wondering if you could help me. Where's the door that was here?"

She smiled. "This is like, the weirdest place. It's there, but only when people are coming in."

"But it leads to the coat room, right?"

She nodded, orange glitter flashing. "Yeah, it does. I mean, it kind of does? Like I said, this is the weirdest place. When you're ready to leave, it'll be the exit, and you'll be on the other side of the coat room. That's where you'll pick up your coat, and then, you'll go out the Night Room, instead of the White one."

I sighed. "Friggin' elves and their magic."

The waitress laughed. "Right? But they pay well, and we don't have to wear heels."

"Big perks," I agreed. "Thanks."

"You're welcome."

Skirting the dance floor, I walked back to the table and sat down. "Can't find the exit, because it's a magic exit and doesn't appear until you're ready to leave."

Dane put his tankard down. There were a total of seven on the table, but he didn't look drunk. "Kind of not ready to leave yet."

I wasn't either. Personal worries aside, it was nice spending time with Logan without Danielle scowling at me. I checked my mental Rico file to make certain the gold shimmer was there. It was.

We didn't know anything bad was going on in regard to him. He wouldn't be the first twenty-one-year-old to check out for a day or two. As had been suggested, Rico could be shacked up with a girl, having a little vacation before returning to his daily grind. Mrs. Guerra would probably yell at him for an hour or two for scaring her, and he'd promise never to do it again.

It wasn't like we had anything else to go on anyway. I looked at my drink. It appeared to be mocking me. "Challenge accepted. We are off the clock."

About halfway through my pina colada, I stopped flinching each time Ginger popped up, and the practice run I'd talked Logan into appeared to be turning into a real date.

Dane checked in from time to time, often with a girl or two attached, but for the most part, Logan and I were left to ourselves.

We danced, talked about my new place and his hopes for a new place for the clan. He wanted to know all about the period of my life when I'd woken up from the coma to beginning to work at Arcane Solutions.

"I'm in the tub for the first time in a year, and kind of dozing because hey, bubble bath and no worries about freezing myself into a giant block of ice again." I had to pause as we both laughed. I'd already told him about that misadventure. "And I thought I heard Mom call me."

Logan was beginning to chuckle. "And?"

"I opened my eyes, and there I was, standing in the kitchen wearing nothing but bubbles, with Mom and five of her friends staring at me. That's how I learned I could teleport."

He began laughing.

"It wasn't funny, dude." My statement had no force, because I was laughing too. "I nearly died from embarrassment."

"Sorry." Logan, his face flushed, reached for my hand. "Really."

"No, you're not." My attempt to pout failed for two reasons. One, that event was funny now, with a few years' perspective. Two, he was holding my hand, his thumb stroking the back of it.

"Okay, you're correct. I'm not sorry, but I'll tell you some of my most embarrassing moments sometime. Then you can laugh at me. Deal?"

"Deal." Tingles were attacking me again, and they weren't the warm, fuzzy kind. I squeezed his hand before pulling mine away. "Nose powdering time again."

"Okay." He looked at my drink. "Your ice has melted. Do you want a fresh drink?"

"Mm," I checked my balance as we both stood. There was a faint buzz in my ears. "No, but maybe more ice?"

"I'll take care of it."

We went our separate ways. There wasn't a line at the restroom this time, and I noticed a clock on the wall when I went in. It gave the time as a few minutes before midnight.

It felt as though we'd been there longer than a few hours. Maybe Thorandryll had a stretchy time spell on the place, to sell more drinks or something. I could totally see maximizing profits being a thing for him.

Once at the sink, I checked my makeup as I washed my hands, ignoring Ginger darting from side to side behind me. Two women walked in while I was leaving, so I exchanged smiles with them.

Logan was at the table, and there was fresh ice in my drink, bringing the level up to about three-quarters to the top.

Out on the dance floor, Dane was rocking with a blonde to Def Leppard's "Pour Some Sugar on Me". I sat down. "He's having a blast."

"Looks like it." Logan watched Dane spin his partner out and back. The blonde planted a laughing kiss on my partner's cheek. "He's always been one of our more outgoing people."

"And you're not?"

"Let's just say I'll be glad to retire from the clan's limelight when the time comes."

"When will that be?"

He shrugged. "When Terra choses her mate."

Puzzled, I asked, "But isn't she the leader now?"

"She's our Queen, yes, but turning the reins over takes time. She has to learn how to handle everything herself. What's okay to delegate and not worry about, what she needs regular reports on, and what she'll need to stay on top of herself instead of depending on someone else to take care of it."

I propped my elbow on the table and rested my chin in my hand. "You're kind of peeling the shiny off the whole royalty thing."

"Sorry. It's more complicated here than it was back home. We didn't have to depend on things like money, working for other people, or if the grocery store is out of something."

"My mom says life always seems simpler when you're looking back."

"Sunny's a wise woman."

"Yeah. Think I'll keep her." I took a drink, wondering if I'd ever reach the bottom of the damn glass. "Do you guys celebrate Christmas?"

"Winter Solstice, which I hope you'll be able to join us for. It's December twenty-second this year."

I'd dropped my arm to rest on the table, and he slid his hand closer, our fingers barely touching. "I'd love to. Is there a ceremony or something?"

Leaning forward, Logan put his hand completely over mine. "There will be food, drink, and a huge bonfire. The high point of the evening is dancing naked around it."

I stared at him. His lips twitched after a few seconds. "Dude, that's so not funny."

"The look on your face was."

"Meanie." I hesitated. "You are joking, right?"

He laughed and sat back. "Yes. What we really do is write down our wishes for the new year, tie them to a twig or pine cone—something that will burn to ash—and toss them into the bonfire."

"Neat idea. Does the smoke carry the wishes to the gods or something?"

"You'd have to ask Moira about that. We collect the ashes. Before the Melding, we used them to fertilize our fields."

Interesting. "What do you do with them now?"

"Save them. When we have land of our own again, we'll use them in flowerbeds or whatever we have available."

"So the ashes are," I thought about it for a second. "Positive energy?"

Logan nodded.

"That's pretty cool, and you'll have eight years of it to spread around. Have any of your wishes come true?" None of my birthday wishes had, unless I counted my last one: Live to see my next birthday. I'd made the same wish a couple of weeks before, on my twenty-third birthday, and felt certain I'd be repeating that wish for years to come.

"A few have. We made some useful connections, found a place to live, and we haven't lost anyone."

We both moved to take drinks. Once I'd swallowed, I asked, "You haven't made any wishes for yourself?"

One corner of his mouth quirked. "I did last year."

"And?" I prompted, my curiosity quick to rise.

"It may come true. Looks promising."

"Hm. Not going to tell what it is, are you?"

"That jinxes them." Logan hid a smile in his tankard. I could tell because the corners of his eyes crinkled.

"Well, I hope it does come true for you." Didn't matter what his wish had been. I had ample evidence that Logan was a great guy, one who cared about and for his people. Other people too. He deserved having a personal wish or three come true.

"Thank you." The music had slowed down again. He placed his tankard on the table. "How about another dance?"

"Absolutely."

We danced more than once, because I dared Logan to try Two Stepping to rock songs. It was a dare he accepted, picking up the pace and adding enough spins that I was slightly dizzy and breathless when the fourth song ended.

"You were right," he said.

"Told you so," I replied while fanning my face and trying not to pant. "Need my drink."

"Okay." He put his arm around my shoulders, graciously ignoring the fact my dress was slightly damp from my dancing exertions.

Logan hadn't broken a sweat, nor was he breathing any harder than normal. I needed to think about putting together an actual exercise regimen, or I was going to have trouble keeping up with him.

Assuming keeping up with him was in my future. I liked the idea it might be, but not the potential drama with Danielle.

"Ladies and gentlemen, last call. We do hope you've enjoyed your evening at Dreamland."

"If you want another, better go get it," I said while taking my seat.

"Do you want anything else?"

I pointed at my drink. The fresh ice had melted, and it was basically full again, though watered down. "I'm good."

"Okay, be right back." Logan turned and hesitated at the sight of the purple-suited waitress. She held up a tankard.

"Weirding Pale, right?"

"Yes, thank you." He took the tankard and tipped her. With a smile, she whirled away, and Logan sat down. "That was strange."

"Why? Serving drinks is her job."

"I know." He sniffed his ale. "She's the first one to come to the table, at least when we were sitting here. We've had to go the bar all night."

"Maybe Dane said something to them." I looked around. "Speaking of, where is he?"

Logan scanned the club. "Probably the restroom."

My partner had been putting away the ale. "Yeah, I guess. Hey, this has been a lot of fun tonight."

"I agree. We should definitely do it again. When you're ready," he added.

"About that, um," I hesitated. "Do you know that Danielle has a thing for you?"

He blinked and put his tankard down. "I'm aware she's been paying close attention to my activities."

Oh, boy. "Because she likes you."

"Huh." Logan's forehead furrowed slightly, his gaze moving from my face to a point over my shoulder. "Her birth clan was more traditional. She's been critical of how we do things."

Maybe I should've minded my own business. Then again, Danielle's dislike of me did make her disapproval my business, in a limited fashion. I tried a different approach. "Dane said I count as a clan queen."

The furrows on Logan's forehead deepened as he looked at me. "You're clan and an adult female. Yes, that makes you a clan queen."

"All right. He also said that means you guys have to mind me."

Logan blinked twice before his expression cleared, and he directed a smile at me. "Oh. You think if Danielle is interested in me, she'll order me not to see you beyond clan matters and events."

Close enough, so I nodded. "Can she do that?"

"She could," he said. "And I could appeal her order with Terra."

Who loved him, and liked me. Right, time to drop the subject. "Okay."

Logan wasn't done with it, probably seeing it as a teachable moment. "Any member can go to Terra to appeal an order they don't like. It doesn't happen often, because the queens seldom interfere with anyone's personal life."

I nodded again, watching his smile widen, and Logan leaned toward me. "But there is one queen I wouldn't mind taking an interest in my personal life."

Ooh. He meant me, and I felt a blush warm my face, along with a huge, more than likely goofy, smile. "Anything you say may be used to unfair advantage in the future."

"Then I have something to look forward to."

Oh, my God. I had to look away, my face completely on fire. "And there I go, embarrassing myself again. My favorite hobby."

Logan's soft chuckle reached my ear a second before he kissed my cheek. "I'm sure I'll embarrass myself too."

"Right. You have it way more together than I do." And he didn't have Ginger lurking around behind people, baring her fangs as though she were about to bite them.

"Not when it comes to some things." The dance floor went dark, causing us both to look toward it. "I think they're trying to tell us something."

"Yeah, 'go home'." I looked over my shoulder. "Hey, the magic door has graced us with its presence. Guess it appears at closing time whether we're ready to leave or not."

Logan stood. "We'd better go then."

"What about Dane?"

"He knows where we're parked."

"But he has Rico's photo." I stood and looked around, hoping to spot my partner. Logan touched my hand, and I let him take hold.

"He'll remember to ask."

"Okay." We headed for the exit, only to end up in a line of people waiting to leave. It wasn't a long wait. Logan took charge of my coat and his jacket when a different Coat Keeper elf handed them over.

"The Prince hopes you enjoyed your evening, Miss Jones."

Was Thorandryll here, spying on us? Surely not. "We did, thanks."

Logan held my coat at the ready, and I slipped into it before we stepped into the Night room the waitress had warned me about. It was painted black, with tiny pinpoints of white light blinking overhead. One more elf, another woman, stood by the exit. She wore all black, and a delicate net of twinkly stones over her pale blue hair. "Please join us again soon, Miss Jones."

"Sure, thanks." With that, we made good our escape.

SIX

Outside, the cold felt like a slap in the face. I shivered. "Wow, I do kind of feel like I'm waking up from a dream."

Logan crooked his arm, and I slid my hand around it to rest on his forearm. "That coat looks really good on you, Tiger Lady."

"Thanks. Rrawr." We began walking.

"Have you been practicing your roar with your little brothers?"

"Oh, you know it. Sean's convinced he'll be able to turn into a tiger when he's older." Ice crunched under my heels. "Brr."

He fished out his keys, and when we neared his car, hit the button to disarm the alarm. After settling me in the front seat, he went around to the driver's side, and offered my cards and twenty back once he'd settled in. "Here you go."

"Keep the twenty. You tipped the bartender and waitress."

"Yes, but thanks to being Miss Jones's escort, I didn't have to pay for my drinks, or the cover charge."

"Hm. Okay." I accepted all three items and retrieved my purse from under my seat. While putting them away, I checked my phone. No texts, voicemails, or missed calls.

Logan had started the engine and set the heater on a higher setting. "This is going to sound dumb, but how'd I do?"

"Huh?"

"I told you I'm rusty on the dating thing." He wasn't looking at me, too busy fiddling with the stereo. It was the same one he'd put in my car. "Was I too pushy or anything?"

"You know, I normally do date dissections over lunch with Jo. It's a girl thing. But no, you weren't too pushy. I had a great time, and feel less awkward about things now."

"Good." Logan turned up the stereo enough for us to hear the music, but too low for me to easily hear the words. "Trying to keep in mind the not-pushy thing, but I'm curious if you have any idea when you might be open for a repeat?"

I was looking forward to another date with him, and was glad he'd asked. "How about weekend after next, if neither of us are busy?"

"Saturday?"

"Sounds good." I wondered if he'd try for a kiss once we were back at the garage. Probably not, unless Dane left us alone before I left. Darn it.

Several cars had left the lot. Turning in my seat, I looked out the rear window. "No Dane yet."

"He may be collecting phone numbers."

"That wouldn't surprise me." A few more cars left. I turned around, watching the tail lights of one as it drove down the street in front of us, and a sense of disconnection struck right before my vision went dark.

I groped for Logan's arm, and he caught hold of my hand. "What is it?"

"Vision." My shoulders thumped into the seat's back, my neck popping as my head jerked backward. "Ow."

"You all right?"

"I can't see anything." Warmth enveloped me, and I felt pressure across my eyes and wrists. "I think I'm tied up and blindfolded. It's warm."

There was a sound. I turned my head from side-to-side, trying to pinpoint where the quiet sound was coming from. "I hear...whispering."

The driver's door opened, a rush of cold air displacing the heat. Darkness turned lighter, and I blinked at the front windshield as Dane said, "Sorry. No luck with the last elf about Rico. Oh. Am I interrupting something?"

"Nothing really useful," Dane said, and I shook my head, listening to the rumble of the engine as Logan braked for a stop light. "Any guarantee it had anything to do with Rico?"

"No, but generally if I only have one case, anything my abilities throw at me have something to do with it. It's when I'm working more than one case that things get confusing."

The light changed. Logan checked both directions before letting off the brake and easing down on the gas pedal. The snow had returned, and was coming down heavily. "It's confirmation the kid's still alive and hasn't been hurt, right?"

"I didn't feel any pain or panic, but I don't know if was a retrocog or a precog. At least not yet. But Rico is alive," I added after checking my mental folder. "Whoever it was, they felt sleepy and not particularly afraid."

"Drugged?" Dane asked.

"Possibly. I'd be pretty damn worried if I were blindfolded and tied up."

My partner sat back with a gusty sigh. "Day One, no bueno."

I didn't completely agree with his assessment while glancing at our driver. Our case may not have brought good news, but my impulse to invite Logan certainly had.

"You're welcome to stay here tonight," Logan said as we pulled into the garage. "It's late, and that was a big drink."

"Ooh," Dane murmured from the back seat, and I blushed.

"Soames." Logan shot him a frown via the rearview mirror.

My partner grinned back, not cowed in the least. "What?"

"I didn't mean it that way."

"Too bad, huh, Cordi?"

My blush grew about fifty degrees warmer. "You can stop any time."

"Where's the fun in that?" Dane asked.

Logan turned off the engine, glaring at him in the review mirror. Dane huffed. "You two have no appreciation for the fine art of teasing."

I had to laugh. "The teased seldom do."

"Sucks for you then."

Logan rolled his eyes and exited the car.

"He's going to smack you."

It was Dane's turn to laugh. "No, he won't. Logan's fine about being teased. He's only protesting because it embarrasses you."

"Yeah, and thanks for that."

He leaned forward to press his cheek against mine. "I only tease people I respect."

Logan opened my door, and my partner took the opportunity to exit out the driver's side. I swung my legs out, intending to stand, but Logan squatted down instead of offering his hand. "I know you'd probably be fine, or that you can teleport home, but the offer's open to stay here. You can bunk with Terra, or take my bed, and I'll sleep on the couch."

After a few seconds of thought, I nodded. Teleportation was fine, but then I'd be without my car. As heavy as the snowfall was, driving it home didn't seem like a great idea. "Okay. I'll need to call my mom and let her know."

Which I did while we walked upstairs. My first choice was to sleep in Terra's room, but I hastily shut her door after opening it and peeking in. "Okay, not sleeping in there. No room. Does she sleep in tiger shape often?"

"No, that's a...what is it humans say? A security blanket?"

"Oh. Yeah. I can sleep on the couch. I don't want to put you out."

"It's okay. I don't mind." Logan waved away my half-hearted attempt at protest. "I'll loan you a T-shirt."

That put a stop to the idea of protesting. I closed my mouth, having never slept in something that belonged to a guy before. None of my exes had left clothing over at my place—not even Nick, though he'd spent a few nights nearly every week with me. "Okay."

"Give me a couple of minutes to change." Logan disappeared into his room, closing the door behind him. Taking off my coat, I laid it over the back of the recliner and slipped off my shoes. My feet hurt because I seldom wore anything with more than an inch-high heel.

My job required running a little too often.

Logan returned, carrying a pillow and blanket. He wore the sweats and tee he'd had on when I'd arrived earlier. "All yours."

"Thanks." I picked up my shoes and crossed to his door, stopping to look up at him. "Guess I'll see you in the morning."

"Yeah." He bent, turning his head, and pressed his cheek to mine. It was a tiger thing, not nearly as good as a kiss would've been, but it put a smile on my face. "Sweet dreams."

"You too." I went into the room, noting the turned-down bed, with a dark gold tee folded and waiting at the foot of it. He'd also set out a clean washcloth and towel on the bathroom counter. Thoughtful.

I washed my face, used some of his mouthwash, and changed before climbing into bed. Rico's gold shimmer was in his file.

And Ginger was lurking in the corner.

I sighed and closed my eyes, shutting her out. There wasn't anything I could do about her. You can't change the past. No one can.

The best I could do was curse Merriven. It was his fault I'd murdered her, according to the revelations he'd made. He'd used her as bait, wanting to turn a psychic into his little vampire princess. I shuddered, remembering the sound of his voice as he'd mockingly repeated the things Ginger had said to me.

I cracked one eye open and flinched, swallowing a scream of surprise. Ginger was bent over, her face mere inches from mine. Her blue eyes were scummy with the white of death. She'd never gotten so close to me before, not when I was awake.

Rolling over, I closed my eyes again and did my best to pretend she wasn't there.

It's not like she actually was there. Nope, I was beginning to lose it. That's what was happening. I'd made a terrible mistake, and losing my mind appeared to be the consequence.

Which meant I shouldn't be trying to start something with anyone.

Or maybe it meant I should, before I went too crazy and ended up as a resident of Happyville Manor. Who knew? Not me.

I didn't particularly want to end up crazy and babbling to anyone who'd listen about the vampire haunting me. I just didn't know how to handle the knowledge I'd murdered her, and not because she'd wanted to die. I mean, die again. I hadn't killed her the first time she'd died. He had.

Freakin' bastard. I didn't even know if he'd been telling me the truth, because Merriven had been in my head. He'd combed through my memories. There were still traces of his slimy mental touch in my mind. I'd hoped his death would erase them, but no luck.

I'd felt guilty before, back when I'd believed I'd done what Ginger wanted. When I thought I'd saved her from eternity with a sadistic monster. That guilt was nothing compared to what I felt now.

Calling Leglin was an option. Sometimes snuggling the giant hound helped drive Ginger away. But he was probably sprawled out on my bed and asleep. I trashed that idea.

Eventually, I fell asleep, and Ginger found me in my dreams. She chased after me as I ran, ignoring my tearful apologies. Strangers pointed at me as I ran by with her on my heels. They whispered "Murderer", one after the other.

It wasn't a restful night's sleep.

"Discord."

I opened my eyes and focused on a line of light. Someone had opened the door, but not wide enough to poke their head inside.

"Discord, Sunny called," Logan said. "She said you're supposed to be at Rita's office at ten-thirty. It's eight-forty-five, and it's still snowing."

"Shoot!" I threw back the covers and lunged out of the bed. "I'm gonna be late."

There wasn't time to drive home, shower, and change, before driving to the real estate office. I stood there, trying to decide whether to teleport and leave my car, or not.

"Are you decent?"

Looking down, I shrugged. His tee reached about mid-thigh on me. "Yeah."

He pushed the door open. "There's a lot of...you look really cute."

My hair was probably waving hello, and I could feel sleep crusted in the corners of my eyes. "You have an odd idea of cute, but thanks."

"You're welcome. The radio's reporting a lot of minor accidents, and there's over a foot of snow already, with ice under it. You might not want to try driving your car in it."

"I guess I'll teleport home."

Logan nodded in agreement. "I can pick you up from Rita's office, if you want to come get your car later. The road crews are out, so you might be able to drive it home then."

"I guess. I kind of wanted to go to my new house. You know, to sit in it and soak up the fact it's finally mine."

"Oh."

"You haven't seen it. Any chance you'd feel like driving me out there and watching me act completely goofy?"

Logan chuckled. "Love to."

We settled a few details before I grabbed all my things and teleported home. "Mom, I'm home!"

She came to my room as I tossed everything onto my bed. Leaning against the doorframe, she asked, "Is that Logan's shirt?"

"Yep, he loaned it to me." I stripped. Being naked in front of Mom wasn't a hang up of mine. After all, she'd given birth to me, and used to change my diapers and give me baths. "I'm going to hop in the shower."

"All right. Do you want something for breakfast?"

"That would be great. I'm going to teleport to the meeting."

"No, you're not. Your father's on the way over. He should be here in twenty minutes."

"Oh. Okay. I'll be out in a few." After I'd taken the quickest shower ever, dressed, and hung up my tiger coat, Mom called me to breakfast.

Purse and less-dressy pea coat in hand, I hurried to the kitchen. Dad was drinking coffee and sitting at the table with Tonya. I kissed the top of his head in passing, and ruffled Tonya's auburn curls. "Good morning. Where are the dogs?"

Tonya pointed at the window. "Bigs are outside, littles are hiding under a blanket on the couch."

"Here." Mom handed me a plate of scrambled eggs and bacon. "Eat."

"Thank you." I kissed her cheek and plopped down in a chair. "Were you guys excited when you bought this house? Because I'm on Cloud Nine."

"We were," Dad said. "First houses are special." He smiled at Mom, and she returned it. Something, or someone, thumped into the back door then Leglin galloped past the large window, Kyra in hot pursuit.

"Well, they're having fun." I began eating.

"You're not the one who has to dry them when they come in." Tonya sighed.

"Sorry, but thank you. I promise I'll do something nice for you." Mr. Whitehaven gave us generous bonuses at Christmas, and I'd missed Terra's birthday. Taking both teens on a shopping trip after Christmas might work.

Tonya shrugged. "You don't have to."

"I know, but I want to. It'll have to be after I move though. Ooh, maybe we can have a slumber party at my house."

"That would be fun. Will Terra be able to go?"

"Yes."

Dad cleared his throat. "We need to leave in five to have enough time to get there."

"Right." I gobbled down my breakfast, and left with Dad.

In his car, he glanced at me. "Your mother said you stayed over at Logan's last night. Are you two seeing each other now?"

Dad increased the wiper speed to combat the snowflakes trying to collect on the windshield.

"Kind of easing into it. He slept on the couch," I added, because my first response sounded weird by itself.

"He seems like a nice guy. Definitely an incredible mechanic."

"You should see his car. It's a '69 Challenger he restored. Slow down, someone's going to..."

Dad was already applying the brake, and the truck that slid through the intersection missed us by a foot. "Good job, co-pilot."

"Thank you, Captain. You may proceed."

"I thought Nick was nice too. The boys really liked him."

Insta-guilt. "Yeah, he was, but we argued too much."

"Ah." Dad left it at that.

"Oh, I forgot to tell you. Logan's picking me up."

"Lunch date?"

"No, I want to go bask in being a homeowner, and he hasn't seen my house yet. Plus, my car's at his garage and I need to pick it up."

"All right. Looks like it'll be a while before I can have a lawn crew go out there."

I frowned at the falling snow. "Well, at least I won't have to worry about snakes until spring."

SEVEN

When we finally left Rita's office, Logan was sitting in the waiting area. I held up my new keys in my left hand, flexing my right—holy crap, there'd been about a billion things to sign!—and jingled them with a grin. "All done. I'm a home owner."

"Congratulations." He stood and held out his hand to my dad. "Hello, Mr. Jones."

"Hello, Logan." They shook. "You did a superb job with Cordi's car."

"Thank you, sir."

"Call me Ben." Dad turned to me and held out his arms. "Give me a hug, and go have fun."

"Thank you for helping me with everything." I threw my arms around him. "I couldn't have done it without you."

"You're welcome, honey."

"Be careful driving home, and tell Betty and the rug rats hi for me."

"I will. You two be careful. Bye." Dad left, and we followed him a moment later, once I had my coat on.

"The turn's coming up on the left." I was bouncing in my seat. "Look, they added the 'Sold' part on the sign."

"I see that." He began slowing his truck.

"I'm being annoying, aren't I? I'm sorry." I'd yapped non-stop about my new house the whole drive.

"No, you're not. I don't blame you for being excited. It's a big deal." He made the turn, the tail of his truck slipping a bit, and brought it to a halt after entering the drive. We could see the house and garage down the unbroken lane of snow. "That's a pretty picture."

"It is." All of my worries about home ownership had melted away. "That's my house. Gosh. I'm like, officially an adult now."

Logan chuckled. "Do you need a minute?"

"Nope. I need to get inside and see if it's as awesome as I remember."

"All right." He began to drive forward.

"It does need paint, and there's an unfinished efficiency apartment at the back of the garage."

"How much land?"

"Twenty-four acres."

"Nice." He slowed the truck and pulled up in front of the garage. "It's a good-sized place."

"I know, right? The dogs are going to love it." Unbuckling my seat belt, I was out the door before he'd shut off the engine. "Come on."

"Right behind you."

I giggled the whole way to the front door, unlocked it, and stepped inside. Most of the first floor was an open plan, and I scanned it, hardly able to believe it was really mine. "That's my fireplace, and my kitchen. Ooh!"

"Wow." Logan had come inside. "This is really nice. I like it."

I spun around with a smile, and my jaw dropped because he was carrying a picnic basket and a blanket. "What's that for?"

He tilted his head toward the fireplace. "Soames mentioned you'd have a fireplace. I brought wood, thought we could have a celebratory lunch."

How thoughtful, and kind of...no, it was pretty much romantic, unless he'd packed cheese sandwiches. "You're awesome. But first, the grand tour, okay?"

"Sure." He put down the basket and blanket, and I immediately began leading him around.

It took half an hour, because I wanted to coo over various things. Logan went outside after we'd returned downstairs, and brought in the wood. He began building a small fire after checking out the fireplace.

"You can make it bigger."

"It'll burn for hours."

"I can put it out when we're ready to leave."

"Right," he said. "Tiger Lady is also Psychic Lady, with Amazing Fire Powers."

I laughed and opened the basket. "Holy cow, dude."

The basket was packed, with two wine glasses and a nice bottle of pinot noir front and center. I pulled it out. "How did you manage this in just a couple of hours on a Saturday?"

No brightly colored plastic plates or paper napkins to be found. The plates were bone china, the silverware heavy, and the napkins were linen. Even the food was packaged in nice, glass serving dishes. My mouth began watering as I unloaded them. Coq au vin, green beans almandine, and parsleyed potatoes. There was cheesecake drizzled with chocolate for dessert, two mugs and a black thermos full of coffee, too.

"I pulled a few strings." He'd turned around. "One of the clan works at a French restaurant. I hope the food's good."

"Are you kidding? This is fantastic." I couldn't believe he'd gone to that much trouble. Well, okay, he hadn't had to cook any of it, but still...I felt my eyes narrow and cocked my head. "You wouldn't happen to be trying to seduce me, would you?"

He blinked, a strong feeling of genuine surprise emanating from him. "No, why?"

"Because there's candles." I pulled them out. "There's wine, and a fabulous French meal. Plus the cozy fire. It's all quite the romantic setup, dude."

Logan surveyed everything. "When you put it that way, I guess it is, but I swear my intentions are pure. I just wanted a nice lunch, since this is a special day for you."

"This is an extremely nice lunch." My God, how sweet was he, doing something like this without an ulterior motive? "Thank you."

He smiled. "You're welcome."

"Come eat before everything gets cold."

An hour later, I savored the last bite of cheesecake and sighed. "Yum. Absolutely delicious."

"The French have gained a new fan. That was fantastic." Logan held up the thermos. "More coffee?"

"I'm good, thank you." I checked my phone. "It's almost two."

"And you have a case to work on." Logan began repacking the basket. "What's your next step on it?"

"I don't know. Someone would've called if Rico had turned up." I checked. "He's alive. The last place he was seen was Dreamland, and you know how much luck we had there."

"Yeah."

"About the only thing I can do is try to find more of his friends to talk to, unless something pops up on the psychic radar." I looked out the front window. "And it's still freakin' snowing."

"You can use my truck. Or my services as a chauffeur, because Soames has zero winter driving experience." Logan scowled down at the basket. "This isn't working. How the hell did they fit it all in here?"

"I'll help." I moved to my knees to assess the situation, and began rearranging dishes. "You don't have stuff you need to do?"

"Garage is closed due to inclement weather. Alanna is chaperoning Terra and our other teens." He handed me the wine glasses. "I'm not allowed to supervise the play dates because I intimidate the boys."

"Imagine that. I bet you stand where you can see everyone, with your arms crossed and that super serious look on your face."

He rubbed the back of his neck. "Ah, yeah. I guess I do."

Laughing, I closed the basket. "There, all done. I'm going to guess it doesn't help that you call them hanging out together 'play dates' either."

"They're children."

"They're teenagers, Logan. Entirely different. Also, Terra is Queen."

"True. I just," he sighed. "I don't want her to get hurt. She's mooning over Devon and he's not remotely Consort material."

I sat and pulled my knees to my chest, hugging my legs. "Is there a rule that the Queen can't play the field until she figures out what she wants in a guy?"

Logan opened his mouth, closed it, and swallowed before answering. His expression wavered between surprise and a little sick. "No, but she's just a kid."

"See, there's where you're going wrong. Sure, she's a teenager, and unless shifters develop way different than humans, there's hormones and stuff running wild, but she's also a young woman." I held up my hand when he started to speak. "A young woman who is aware of what's expected of her, and who desperately wants to make good decisions."

Logan thought about that for a minute. "You're saying I'm worrying too much."

"You're worrying too much. She might get her heart a little bruised, but that's part of growing up, and life in general. You can't protect her from it. When she's ready, I have no doubt she'll make a good decision." I frowned. "I don't know if she'll make it for herself and the clan, or just the clan though."

He had to think about that too. "We want her to be happy."

"Might want to make sure and tell her that. A lot."

Logan studied me for a few seconds. "It sounds like you may have been worrying about her too."

I shrugged. "I like her, and we kind of have stuff in common. I mean, neither of us signed up for the gigs we have. Both of us kind of wish we were normal girls. The big difference is that I was a normal girl for fifteen years. Terra's never been a normal girl."

Very quietly, he said, "I know."

"Not that being a normal girl is all fun and games. But she doesn't know that." Heck, I realized I didn't even know any "normal" girls anymore. My friends were witches and shifters. Oh, and one elf: Alleryn, Thorandryll's healer.

"What can I do about it?"

Perfect time to make good on that promise I'd made to Tonya. "You can't do anything, except okay her going out with Tonya and me. We'll do fun, normal stuff. Hit the mall and shop. Stuff like that."

He began to shake his head, stopped, and looked me straight in the eyes. "You'll keep her safe?"

"Duh."

A half-smile appeared on his face. "Would you be insulted if I wanted Alanna to go along?"

"Nope. I like her too. She'd probably have fun."

"Okay, but I'll warn you that I'll probably be a nervous wreck until she's home."

I released my legs and moved to my knees again. Leaning over the picnic basket, I crooked my finger at him. "Come here."

Logan leaned forward. "What?"

I kissed him. Just a quick smackeroo on the lips. "Thank you."

"For what?"

"Trusting me. My first meal in my new home. Being a total sweetheart. Take your pick, dude."

He turned slightly pink while I spoke. "Oh. Uh, we'd probably better get going."

"Right." I climbed to my feet and looked at the fire. A little concentration, and no more flames. I added a touch of cryokinesis to cool the remains. "Let's go."

A clan member I didn't know by name yet was on guard duty at the door. He greeted us before saying, "Soames wants to talk to you. Something about your case."

"Okay, thanks." I wondered if I'd missed a call and pulled out my phone to check while following Logan to the stairs.

"You're neglecting your duties." We both stopped and looked up. Danielle stood at the top of the flight. She looked pissed, her eyes narrowed and her lips a thin slash across her face. She glared down with her arms crossed. "Your place is with the Queen."

"I know my place, and my duties to our Queen." Logan's voice was the same silky growl he'd used to stop us from sniping at each other while we were searching for my mom. I shivered, and he added, "Apparently better than you do."

"Ooh, burn," I murmured.

"Discord."

"Sorry."

Danielle growled. "You fail to show proper respect."

I didn't know if she meant me or him, but Logan responded as though she meant him. "I've shown you nothing but proper respect since you joined the clan."

"That's the problem," I said, and they both looked at me. Oops. "Sorry. My mouth isn't always under my control."

The guy on guard duty chuckled. Danielle's face reddened. "And you. You don't belong here among us. You're an insult to our status, parading around in your sad excuse of tiger skin, pretending yourself an equal to our Queen."

"That's enough," Logan said.

"No, it is not," she yelled, and I flinched. Danielle had a serious set of lungs on her. "She's an affront to us. Makes us a mockery to others. She weakens us, and she weakens you."

Her shout had opened doors on the first floor. People began gathering in the hallway. Down at the far end, I saw Terra come out of a room, with Alanna and other teenagers on her heels.

My mouth ran away with me again. "Wow, you really are a queen. A drama queen."

Logan sighed. "Discord, please."

"Yeah, I know, I'm not helping, but holy freaking crap." I dropped my phone into my purse. "I hate drama. You," I pointed up at Danielle. "Don't like me. Fine. That's something I can deal with. But back off of Logan."

"I am a queen of this clan."

"Newsflash: I am too."

Danielle laughed, and it was a nasty, sharp sound. "You're human."

"Eh, there's been some debate about that." I waved my hand. "Point being, whether you like it or not, we're equals here."

"You're not my equal." She dropped her arms, her fingers flexing.

I sort of lost my mind as Ginger appeared behind her. My delusion pulled a theatrical vampire pose, baring her teeth and lifting her clawed hands in the air as though she were about to attack Danielle. "Yeah? How about you come say that to my face?"

Totally the wrong thing to say to her. Logan grabbed my arm when Danielle snarled and leaped, shifting as she came toward us. I threw up my hand, stopping her in mid-flight with my telekinesis. She thrashed, her tail thumping off the wall and railing, her claws shredding air.

Logan released my arm and stepped back. I took a deep breath, trying to figure out what the hell I should do now. Letting her go before she calmed down wasn't an option. She'd rip me to shreds. Apologizing was, but it's not like I'd ever done anything to her to start the whole mess.

Terra was halfway down the hall, and she did not look happy. I decided to wait until she reached us before doing anything else.

Danielle stopped snarling and clawing the second Terra stepped into view. The teen looked up at her before looking at me. "Put her down."

I obeyed, relatively certain Danielle wouldn't charge down the stairs now that our Queen was present. She didn't, but she did crouch down, glaring at me with slitted, orange eyes.

Terra looked at Danielle again, and I felt a curious sense of pressure. The older woman shifted from tiger to human again, and stood naked as the day she was born in front of us. The teen asked, "What's the problem here?"

"Danielle doesn't like me, and she used that as an excuse to jump all over Logan when we got here." I heard Logan mutter something, but couldn't make what he said out. Not that it mattered, because my explanation was the truth.

"I call for a queens' council to discuss the Protector's neglect of his duties."

That set off some serious whispering among those watching our little drama unfold. Terra's shoulders twitched, and her pale green eyes shot to Logan before settling on Danielle again. "Go put some clothes on. We'll meet in the conference room."

Danielle shot me a smug look before turning and stalking upstairs. I blew out a breath, wondering what the hell a queens' council was, and turned around to look at Logan. He shook his head when I started to speak, and I closed my mouth. He looked pretty grim. Great, I'd gotten him into big trouble.

Terra gave the order to have the other queens informed, and marched away, back down the hall. I stood there until Alanna gestured for me to follow her.

Right, I was a queen here too. With a last glance at Logan, I followed the petite brunette down the hallway.

The conference room was down at the end, through the same door I'd seen Terra leave a few minutes before. Chairs were the only furniture present. I sat next to Alanna, and looked at Terra. She offered a tight smile in return.

No one was talking, and I received the distinct impression we weren't supposed to until the other queens had arrived. It was hard to stay quiet, the lovely luncheon Logan and I had shared beginning to congeal in my stomach.

EIGHT

Ten minutes passed before all the other queens joined us. Danielle glared at me as she entered the room behind Moira, the red-haired shamaness. Moira chose to sit on my other side, which was strangely comforting.

Once all the women had arrived and sat down—there were about twenty of us in total—Terra stood up. "This council has been called by Danielle. Stand and state your reason."

The dark-haired woman inclined her head while rising from her seat. "I believe the Protector has neglected his duties to Queen and clan several times since I joined. His duty lies first with our Queen, and second to the clan, yet over the past few months he has forsaken his duties and placed our Queen in danger." Danielle's glare made it super clear who she blamed for it.

"Part of Logan's duties as Protector have been to lead the clan until our Queen was ready to take her place," Alanna said. She didn't bother standing up. "In pursuit of those duties, he's made certain alliances. He'd be a poor leader and Protector if he failed to uphold our end of those alliances."

"He shouldn't place the Queen in danger to do so," Danielle countered.

"You're assuming I was in danger." Terra smiled. "I was protected by Teague, two powerful witches and their familiars during the search for Discord's mother."

The older woman inclined her head. "Perhaps you weren't in danger then, but last night and today? What if we'd been attacked?"

I raised my hand. "Do I get a turn?"

Terra nodded. "Go ahead."

"Thanks. Okay, Logan's spent what? Eighteen years leading the clan and protecting Terra? Everything I've heard points to him doing a damn good job of it." When I paused for air, most of the queens made quiet noises of agreement.

"Unless I've missed something, Terra is officially Queen now. She's eighteen, and came into her own over a month ago, whooping the holy hell out of that overgrown douchebag in the process. I think that means she's pretty capable of taking care of herself. Especially here, at home, with everyone around."

That earned some more murmurs of agreement, and gave me the nerve to keep talking. "I don't think you realize it, Danielle, but insisting Logan's the only one who can keep Terra safe isn't a good thing. It kind of undermines her, and the clan. I mean, if people start hearing our Queen can't take care of herself, they'll begin believing it. They hear that they're not capable of protecting her, they'll start doubting themselves." I had to stop for air. "And if they start believing that they're weak, that Terra's weak, then others will begin to believe that too. Words have power, and the feelings words convey have power."

Moira nodded, a smile playing about her lips. "Our newest queen has raised valid points."

"That is not my intention." Danielle's glare was gone, her face slightly slack with surprise. "My intention was to assure that the Protector is reminded of his foremost duties."

"Sure it was." I winced, not having meant to say that out loud. But there it was, dangling in the air. "You made it perfectly clear not twenty minutes ago that you don't like me, and you don't like the fact that Logan and I are friends."

"Until he is no longer our Queen's Protector, he has no right to pursue any personal interests."

Alanna suddenly snorted. "If he hadn't done that, the clan would be in bad shape. It's his personal interest in vehicles that gave us our start after the Melding. His personal interest led to us finding a home, and to our financial stability."

"That's important, but what's more important is that I want my cousin to be happy." Terra wasn't smiling. "It's not fair that he spends years and years taking care of everybody, and never has time for things that will make him happy. It's not fair to make him wait to build a life for himself that isn't centered solely on the clan."

"It is his duty," Danielle insisted, and she may have said more, but the teenager cut her off.

"Screw duty. He's done it for years, and I know he'll continue doing it, but he's earned time off to do his own thing too."

"But..."

"I have spoken," Terra snapped, her lips drawing back to expose her teeth. "Does this council agree with my decision that the Protector can begin reaping the rewards of his years of selfless devotion to Queen and clan?"

"Yes," Alanna said, and others repeated her answer, including me. Danielle was the only hold-out, remaining silent.

"Then this meeting is ended."

I felt like jumping up with my fists in the air, but refrained after checking Danielle's thunderous expression. That would probably set her off, and this time, she might not check herself because of Terra.

Instead, I stayed quiet and followed everyone out of the room, grateful that Alanna and Moira continued to flank me as we walked.

While we'd had our meeting, the rest of the clan had assembled in the hallway or on the stairs. Logan was leaning against the wall next to the front door, but he pushed away to stand straight, his face impassive.

Terra took the opportunity to do him a little dirty. "The queens' council has made a decision on the claim of dereliction of duty leveled at the Protector. We have taken into account your many years of service, and the results of those years." She paused. "Our decision is as follows: You will continue to fulfill your duties to Queen and clan."

Logan bowed his head. "Yes, my..."

"Don't interrupt, I'm not finished."

"My apologies."

"However, we have decided to lessen those duties."

Logan raised his head, a look of hurt flashing across his face before his expression settled back into neutral lines. I felt sorry for him, and I guess Terra decided not to jerk him around anymore, because she said, "This is not a punishment, but a reward. We've made the decision to allow you leisure time to pursue personal interests. You have more than earned it."

He blinked, and a slow smile found its way onto his face. "Thank you, my Queen."

"You're welcome. I think you should start by taking a two-week vacation."

Logan's jaw dropped.

"But we need to discuss..."

"Geeze, Logan, can't you take a hint?" Terra spun around, her hands flying to her hips. I quietly shut their apartment door and leaned against it. "I don't need a babysitter anymore. What I need is a chance to really be Queen."

"Okay, I get that, but..."

"No buts. I need an advisor more than a bodyguard now. Advisors don't have to hang around constantly. They get to lead their own lives too."

He nodded, and I had the feeling he hadn't really been listening to her. "All right. I just..."

"Need to go pack. I don't want to see you for two weeks, unless something comes up and I call you. So don't forget your phone."

"Wait. You're kicking me out of the apartment?"

"Well, yeah, dummy. I know you. You won't do the vacation thing if you stay here. So you need to go somewhere else." She dropped her hands. "And the rest of us need some practice at not running to you for every little thing."

Logan ran his hand over his hair before slowly nodding. "Okay."

"Good. Go pack, ask Alanna for some cash, and then go have some fun."

"I could just stay in another..."

"Dude." When he turned to me, I grinned. "When the boss offers you an all-expenses paid vacation, you do not argue. You say 'thank you', and you hurry to pack before she changes her mind."

"I, uh," he threw his hands in the air. "Okay, fine. I'll go pack."

He crossed to his room. Terra waited until he'd closed the door before pointing at the front one. Out in the hallway, she pursed her lips. "Why did Danielle try to jump on you?"

Uh-oh. I winced. "It was my fault. I got smart with her."

She nodded, but said, "We can't have two queens fighting. It's bad for morale."

"I'm sorry. It won't happen again."

"You mean, you'll try not to let it happen again."

Well, yeah. It wasn't as though I could control Danielle or make her stop disliking me. "Yes."

Terra tugged at the ends of her pale blonde hair. "I'm not saying don't defend yourself or anything like that."

"I know, I get it. Don't be a jerk. I'll try not to be," I promised. "It just made me mad that she jumped all over Logan like that. I know it was because of me."

"I can understand that, but I think you need to hear something. Logan likes you. Danielle doesn't have a chance with him. She'll want to be the boss in any relationship she has, and he won't go for that. He's been a leader too long." She wrinkled her nose. "That didn't come out right. What I mean is, he'll be equal, or he'll lead, but he won't choose someone who'll try to boss him around all the time."

"I have gotten that impression."

Terra flashed a smile. "Just saying it because I want you to know that Danielle's not a threat to anything you and Logan decide to do. She doesn't realize that yet, but it won't hurt you to ignore her comments and stuff. Okay?"

Look at me, being schooled by an eighteen-year-old about showing some maturity. "Okay. Thanks, and I'm sorry I caused trouble."

"It's okay." She nibbled on her lower lip for a second. "You know, it would help if you could find a way to spend more time with us. Not like every single day, because I know you're busy most of the time. But maybe Sunday evenings? We all eat together and watch movies or play games then."

Bonding time. Definitely something I should take part in, since I still didn't know every clan member on sight or by name. "That sounds fun. I'll come as often as I can."

"Great. But not tomorrow or next Sunday, okay? I need you to keep Logan as busy as possible while he's on vacation, or he'll turn up and there goes that idea."

I saluted her. "Ma'am, yes, ma'am."

Terra giggled, and we heard muffled footsteps inside the apartment. "Here he comes."

Opening the door, Logan gave us a suspicious look. "What are you two conspiring about?"

"Nothing. I have to go see what Dane wants to tell me. Come with?"

"Well, since I'm at loose ends." He lifted the dark blue duffle bag he held. "I guess I will."

"Cool."

Logan grinned and kissed Terra on top of her head. "Don't burn the building down while I'm gone."

"I'll try not to."

"And call me if..."

"Shoo!" She flapped her hands at him.

Dane opened his front door at my knock, and stepped back. "Come in."

His apartment didn't have much by way of furniture. A small, round table with two chairs sat between the living and kitchen areas. A beige sofa was sandwiched by two square end tables, and fronted by a matching coffee table. Mismatched bookshelves lined the other walls, filled with paperback books.

One of the work laptops sat on the coffee table, next to a small printer and a box of manila folders. My partner took a seat on the sofa in front of the laptop. "I try to think of stuff that will help me be a better PI, since I don't have your psychic leg up on it."

Logan dropped his duffle by the door, and we crossed to sit on either side of Dane.

"I've been learning about social media sites and stuff. You know, bookmarking forums and sites that people from Santo Trueno hang out at." Dane clicked on the favorites icon in the browser, and a list of folders appeared in a dropdown box. The folders were labeled with titles like "City" or "Colleges", and "Clubs", etcetera.

"Wait, you're cataloging Santo Trueno?"

He smiled. "Well, I'm trying to. At least, everything I can find online. You know, the Internet is available to just about everyone, as long as they have a smart phone, or a library card, or use one of the Internet cafes."

"No, I didn't know that. I use the Internet at work, and I guess my phone isn't smart." I felt compelled to add, "I do know what social media is though."

"You should upgrade your phone. Anyway, I've spent the day poking around, looking through social media sites and forums. I found those friends of Rico's that his mother gave us the names of."

"Awesome. Did you get their addresses?"

"Yeah, but none of them know anything." Dane grinned at my raised eyebrows. "Email, Cordi. It's the wave of the future."

"Oh."

"Well, email and social media. But that's not what I wanted to talk about. Rico's not the only person who's recently gone missing. Or," he tapped around on the keyboard. "Is suspected of missing. Here it is."

I looked at the screen, and the text document he'd opened. It was a list of seven names, with dates beside each that went back two weeks. Five of the names had red Xs beside them. "What's the X for?"

"To mark the ones who were all last seen, or talked about going to, the same place. I don't know about the other two yet."

"The same place. Dreamland?"

He nodded.

I stared at the list. The final name, below Frederico Guerra's, was Rebecca Spears. For some reason, I couldn't look away from that name. It took me several seconds to make the connection. "Have you guys seen Becky?"

Both of them looked at me. I felt like punching a wall. "One of my trips to the restroom last night. A girl came in, looking for one of her friends."

"Becky, Rebecca." Logan touched the screen, pointing out the date beside her name. "Last night."

"Son of a...we were right there." I took a breath, and held my hand up to Dane. "High five, partner. You done good."

Dane high-fived me. "We're going to make a house call, aren't we?"

"Oh, you bet. I'm sure Thorandryll will be thrilled to see us."

NINE

When I'd been released from Alleryn's clinic after the Merriven ordeal, I had learned where Thorandryll's sidhe was located. Actually, it seemed all of the elves' sidhes were located in the same area: an older section with well-established estates in the north/northeastern-most end of the city.

Logan volunteered his chauffeuring services. Upon our arrival, the two elves standing on the other side of the beautifully carved wooden gates opened them, allowing us entry, truck and all.

"This is freaky as hell," I complained as we left the truck. It wasn't snowing in Thorandryll's pocket realm, or his sidhe. I wasn't sure if there were a distinction between the two or not. The sky overhead was blue, with a few fluffy clouds slowly travelling across it. We left our coats in the truck, but that didn't help me much, since I'd worn a sweater.

"You're not allowed to go home for two whole weeks?" Dane asked. We'd had to fill him in since more than one person had told Logan to "have a nice vacation" when we'd left the clan's building.

"That's what she said."

"Wow." My partner shook his head and ambled ahead of us.

I tapped Logan's arm. "Why did you back off after I TKed her?"

"You can take care of yourself. I shouldn't have tried to interfere between two queens."

"But you've helped me out before."

He nodded. "Against people who weren't clan. That's different. We're supposed to protect the queens against outside threats. It's our job."

"But not inside threats?"

Logan made a face. "It's a respect thing. A queen isn't much of one if she can't handle her own problems with other clan members."

"Oh."

"Usually, those problems don't result in one queen trying to physically attack another," he said. "I had a moment of dumb, grabbing you like that. If I'd messed up what you doing, it would've undermined your place in the clan."

"I see. Okay." Internal clan politics, something else I obviously needed lessons in. Personally, I liked the idea he'd been so ready to protect me from several hundred pounds of pissed-off tiger queen. Yet, I also liked that he knew I could take care of myself in such a situation.

"I apologize for interfering. I could've gotten you hurt."

"Apology accepted, but thanks for being ready to step in. My telekinesis doesn't always work, you know." Though it usually did, since it was my most practiced ability, being such a useful one. In fact, thinking about, I realized I couldn't remember the last time my TK hadn't worked. At least not without help, like Merriven's interference.

Logan nodded. We were nearing the steps to the graceful, white stone edifice that was Thorandryll's home. "You're welcome. Mind doing me a favor?"

"What?"

"Don't goad Danielle anymore. Her birth clan follows the old traditions to a T, and one of them is that queens who can't settle things peacefully do so by physical combat."

Yikes. "I've already promised Terra I wouldn't be a jerk to Danielle again."

"Okay." Logan glanced at me. "Sorry."

"You're supposed to keep the peace in the clan, right? You're just doing your job." I shrugged. "I'll try not to make your job harder than it is."

"Thank you."

"You're welcome." We climbed the steps to join Dane and a dark-haired elf dressed in light gray.

"Welcome, Miss Jones. If you'll follow me, I'll lead you to the Prince."

"Sure. Thank you." It peeved me that the elves ignored Dane and Logan, but throwing a fit about it wouldn't change anything.

The elf led us through a grand hallway, a room with a lot of seating that looked like it was meant to be used for socializing, and out a set of French doors onto a side patio.

"Miss Jones, please join me." Thorandryll gestured to a few lounging chairs near the one he was using. His golden blonde hair was loose around his broad shoulders, and dark-lensed shades hid his icy blue eyes. He wore a pair of clingy green riding britches and tall, highly polished brown riding boots. No shirt, because it was hanging over the back of his chair.

I wondered if all elves were smooth-chested while noting that his muscles were as well-defined as Logan's. Including his abs.

"To what do I owe the pleasure of this visit?"

Crap. I was staring. Embarrassment warmed my face, and I grabbed Logan's hand to pull him over to one of the lounge chairs. "We're investigating a series of disappearances."

Logan waited until I sat before sitting next to me. Dane picked another chair. I tugged at the neck of my salmon pink sweater and squinted at the blue sky. Thirty degrees cooler would be nice. "Nice weather."

"I prefer summer." Thorandryll snapped his fingers, and the gray-suited elf who'd brought us to him stepped forward. "Shade and drinks for my guests."

"At once, your Highness."

Nice that he'd included the guys. While we waited, I looked around, and recognized the balcony I'd jumped off of during an earlier visit. It was a good twenty yards down the side of the house. Mansion? Palace? Architecture wasn't a specialty of mine.

The servant brought out a crimson umbrella to shade us from the sun. A second servant—light gray clothing seemed to be the uniform for them—carried out a tray of drinks. The drinks were some sort of juice mixture over ice. I caught hints of orange and raspberry in it. "Thank you."

"Quite welcome." Thorandryll smiled as cool air began to flow down from the umbrella. I refused to look up. There wouldn't be anything to see, because magic.

The elf prince took a second to call attention to his shirtless state with a lazy gesture. "Forgive my disarray. I was riding earlier, and didn't expect visitors."

My eyes were not behaving themselves. Silently scolding them, I took a sip of juice and moved my foot, putting my leg in contact with Logan's. A faint smile appeared on his face, which he immediately hid by taking a drink.

"Yeah, sorry to barge in like this, but we kind of have seven missing people to find, and discovered the weirdest coincidence. There's one thing they all have in common."

Thorandryll laced his fingers together and rested his hands on the waist of his riding britches. The move called his abs to my attention again. Damn it. "Which is?"

"The last place they were seen, or told others they planned to visit." I smiled. "Your club, Dreamland."

"Interesting."

"We thought so. Me especially, since I learned a while back that elves have a history of abducting humans. I mean, pretty ones, and wouldn't you know it? All seven missing people are damned good-looking."

Thorandryll chuckled. "Times have changed, Miss Jones. Since the Melding, hardly a day goes by that I don't receive an invitation to intimacy from a few people."

He'd said "people" and I blinked, giving that word choice some serious thought. "Men hit on you?"

"Some men do prefer their own sex."

Before I could stop, I asked, "Do you?"

Dane choked on his drink, and I felt Logan quiver. I'd probably just broken a huge supe rule about being nosy, and really, the question wasn't one I'd have asked a human. But it didn't faze the elf prince. "No, but the offers are flattering."

"Not that I care." Boy, that was just as rude as asking in the first place. "I have a hard time keeping my curiosity to myself these days. Sorry."

"I'm certain your curiosity is a boon to your chosen profession."

"Yeah. Anyway, missing people, your club, and history. My curiosity is on fire."

He smiled. "I'm afraid I know nothing about the disappearances."

Okay, if he wasn't lying, I needed to try a different angle since Dreamland was the only connection we'd discovered between the missing. "Then I guess we'll go to the cops and dump it on them. Mayor Wells has been keeping a close eye on cases involving supes ever since the vamps went public about those bodies. I imagine he'll be all over the fact they went missing at a club owned by an elf prince."

His laughter was an unexpected response. "I do enjoy the way you think, but threatening media exposure of crimes I have no part in isn't the best leverage."

"No? I wonder how many people will continue going to a club others have a history of disappearing from? I'm going with 'not many'. Logan?"

"Not many is my guess too."

I tsked a few times. "It's a really nice club. Shame it won't last, but I'm sure you can eat the loss, right?"

Thorandryll was still smiling. "My businesses don't fail, Miss Jones."

"There's a first time for everything." I watched him while having a sip of juice. "How expensive is it to build a new pocket realm? Can they be moved?"

His smile dimmed. "You're more than welcome to search the club, if that is what's behind your questions."

"Great, but I doubt we'll find anything on our own."

"What is it you wish for me to do?"

"Give us a tour. Stand around looking all princely while we question your employees. Maybe one's playing games." I tapped my nails against my glass. "Or, if you're lying, just confess."

"The last time I failed to divulge all I knew to you, it proved costly." Thorandryll removed his shades. "I swear by Danu I have no part in the disappearances of any humans in this time."

Huh, worded like that, it sounded like he was admitting to past kidnappings. I looked at Logan, who said, "He's telling the truth. Elves don't swear by Danu lightly."

"Okay."

"However," the elf continued. "It's possible you may have uncovered someone using my club as a hunting ground."

"Hunting implies killing, and the man we've been hired to find is alive."

"For now."

Sometimes, I kind of hating dealing with supes. Then again, humans could be just a blood-thirsty. "And the motive for that would be?"

"Failure of my newest business pursuit."

His ego was amazing. "Let me get this straight: Someone's kidnapping people to make you look bad?"

Thorandryll raised his eyebrow. "You find that unlikely?"

He had a point. After all, he was the reason Dalsarin, the last of the dark elves, had chosen Santo Trueno as Ground Zero for his world domination plan. "Honestly? Nope. I bet you've pissed off scads of people since you learned to talk."

Logan's turn to choke on a drink, and I patted him on the back, which in turn reminded me of something else in regard to the Dalsarin business. "You know, I spilled blood for you again, thanks to your buddy, Dalsarin, and Logan nearly died from one of his poisoned arrows."

"I loaned you the use of my hunting pack when you were searching for your mother." The elf's gaze flicked to Logan. "And there are some we aren't beholden to in matters of spilled blood."

Right, because elves considered shifters nothing more than animals. "You didn't exactly divulge everything you knew then either. You didn't give me any heads up about the whole Cernunnos and Hunt thing."

"Be that as it may..."

"Blood," I said, an idea striking.

"I beg your pardon?"

"I spilled blood for you again. We're even on that, but Logan spilled blood for you too, and I guess maybe you haven't gotten the memo: I'm a member of his clan. A queen, which makes him one of my people because we've shared blood. So one of my people nearly died because of you. Doesn't that mean that mean I technically spilled blood twice on that little jaunt?"

The tips of Thorandryll's ears began turning red as he stared at me. His face had become an expressionless mask. I could see a wide-eyed Dane watching us from the corner of my eye. Logan, recovered from his juice misadventure, was sitting perfectly still.

Judging by their reactions, I either had a compelling argument, or had just stepped in it big time. "Well?"

"What would you have of me, Miss Jones?"

Yay! I had a debt from an elf prince in my pocket, but not an answer to his question since I hadn't planned on bringing up the matter. "I'll get back to you on that. Right now, I'm thinking you might want to speak to Mr. Whitehaven."

"For what reason?" Thorandryll's tone was frosty.

"To hire us to investigate whether or not someone's trying to smear your name." I smiled, more pleased with myself than I probably should've been.

It's not like I managed to put an elf over a barrel every day.

"You didn't have to do that." Logan started the truck while Dane climbed in. Being sandwiched between them meant I didn't instantly grow cold as we drove out of the elven summer into the Texas winter.

"No, but if you'll remember, he has me on the hook. I have to go to dinner with him sometime, to repay him for turning me back from a dog. Turnabout's fair play."

Dane pulled the center seatbelt out from under his leg and handed it to me. "What are you going to ask him for?"

"Whatever Logan wants me to. He's the one who almost died."

Logan shook his head. "A blood debt's a big deal, and he owes it to you."

"Dude, don't even argue with me over this. Instead, start thinking. When you know what you want, tell me."

"Discord..."

I lifted my chin and stared at him. "That was an order."

Dane snickered. Logan's lips parted as though he were going to protest again. I silently dared him to. It was only right that he reap whatever reward I could wrangle out of Thorandryll.

"All right. Thank you," Logan finally said.

"You're welcome."

Dane let a few seconds pass before asking, "Where to now?"

"Good question." I sighed, unable to think of what to do next, other than hang out at Dreamland that night. It was too early for that, and it'd be a little bit before we learned whether Thorandryll had called the boss. "Mom's house. I need to take a turn with the dogs, and maybe cook dinner too. We can get ready to hit the club after that."

TEN

"Argh." I rolled over, spitting and swiping snow off my face. "Diablo, you are in so much trouble."

The black pit whirled around with a yip. *More where that came from!*

I laughed as snowballs rained down on him, and he raced away. "Hah! Thanks, guys."

Logan grinned, tossing a snowball at Leglin. My hound ducked and ran, his tail held high as it waved. Dane scored a hit on Bone's shoulder, and the white pit charged him, barking happily. They went down in a shower of snow.

I rose to my feet, only to fall again when Leglin bumped into me. "You too?"

Kyra, Tonya's husky, leaped into the air and hit Leglin in the side with all four of her paws. He went over, thrashing snow everywhere. "Way to go, girl!"

The park had been deserted when we drove by on the way to Mom's. Snow had left a two-feet-deep blanket on it, with drifts up to four feet. No one objected to my suggestion we take the big dogs there for some exercise.

Bone bounded up as I climbed onto all fours and swiped his tongue across my face. *Chase me!*

I did for about twenty minutes, slipping and sliding all over the place thanks to the snow building up in the tread of my boots. The exertion quickly wore me down, and the white pit stopped to look back at me when I halted. His tongue lolled out in a laugh, right before a pair of arms closed around my waist.

My shrieks filled the air as Logan lifted me and spun around several times. When he stopped to put me down, he stepped back. I turned and swayed toward him like a drunk. "No fair, now I'm all dizzy."

"Yeah." He shook his head. "Little dizzy myself."

"And I'm cold."

"Aw, poor baby."

"You're mocking me. That's not nice." Equilibrium restored, I bent and scooped up some snow to pack.

Logan followed suit. We began circling each other, and he said, "My arms are longer."

"Yeah? I can teleport." I did, rising on my tiptoes to smash my snowball on top of his head. He whirled, throwing one arm around me, and shoved his handful of snow down the back of my coat.

"Holy crap, that's cold." I did my best to knock him over, trying to escape the freezing clumps sliding down my back.

Laughing, he leaned back to shake snow from his hair. His other arm settled around me. "Bet you're really cold now."

"You jerk. Some of that made it all the way down." I wiggled, unable to hold still as icy water made a line down my panties and jeans. "Oh, my God. That is way too cold."

"You did try to freeze my brain." The tip of his nose brushed mine. I could see the gold flecks scattered in the dark pine green of his irises. "I say we're even."

He didn't seem interested in letting go, and I'd stopped wiggling. "Not yet."

"Oh?"

I grinned, and shoved snow I'd gathered with telekinesis down the back of his jacket. Logan's eyes went wide before he closed them, grimacing. "Okay, it's on, woman."

"Aw, poor baby. Are you cold?"

He opened his eyes, looked at me, and proceeded to wipe my grin away with his lips. His weren't cold, and suddenly, I wasn't cold anymore either.

"Ooh, Cordi and Logan, sitting in a tree, K-I-S-S-I-N-G."

Logan pulled back. "I think I'll go kill Dane now."

"Uh, okay." I had hold of his jacket.

"Or it could wait a few minutes," he decided before his lips met mine again. I slid my hand up his chest and around the back of his neck. He purred, and I nearly melted.

"Guys. Oh, come on," Dane said. "Break it up or get a room."

I giggled, and Logan smiled, both breaking our lip lock. He rested his forehead against mine. "That was pushy of me."

"I was pushy back. We're even."

"I like even."

"Me too." I was also enjoying gazing into his eyes, but shivered. "Brr, for reals."

"I can kill Dane later. Let's go." He released me, but held out his hand after stepping back. I grabbed it as he asked, "Do you think Sunny has anything hot to drink?"

"You crazy kids." Mom shoved mugs of hot, spiced cider into our hands. "Drink and warm your insides."

"I was going to help with dinner."

She tousled my chilly, damp hair. "There's a pot roast in the slow cooker, and it's almost ready. Plenty for everyone."

We cheered her, and Mom retreated to the kitchen with a laugh.

Not long after that, we were seated in the kitchen and busy stuffing our faces. Playing in the cold and snow had definitely worked up my appetite. Mr. Whitehaven called as I neared the bottom of my second bowl.

"Would I be correct in thinking you have no objection to accepting another case for Prince Thorandryll?"

"You would. He's sort of involved in the Aguerra case, and two paying clients is better than one, right?" I knew the boss wouldn't give Prince Snooty Pants a discount. The elf hadn't been truthful with him either, during the first case we'd worked for him.

Mr. Whitehaven vented one of his deep chuckles. "Yes, indeed. However, there's one detail I need to clarify with you. The prince's impression that Logan is your bodyguard persists, and I didn't disabuse him of it. Will Logan be assisting you two on the prince's case?"

"Is it a problem if he does?"

"No, I simply need to know to properly bill the prince, and assure adequate remuneration for Logan."

"Okay, hang on." I pulled the phone from my ear and tapped mute. "Mr. Whitehaven wants to know if you feel like temping again."

Logan swallowed the roast he was chewing. "I have two weeks of vacation time and no idea how to spend it. Temping works for me."

"Cool." I unmuted the phone to tell my boss, "He's on board."

"Excellent. Someone will meet you at Dreamland this evening. Make certain to keep me updated on your progress."

"Yes, sir. Bye." I ended the call and checked the time. "We need to get a move on, guys. We have a meet at Dreamland to make."

In spite of our best efforts, it was after nine before we arrived at the club. The same tall bouncers passed us through the door, and Angel Elf greeted us with a smile. "Welcome back, Miss Jones. A moment, please."

"Sure, thanks." I untied my coat belt. No dress and heels for me this time. I'd chosen jeans, a teal, short-sleeved top, and my favorite pair of brown, aviator-style boots. Clothing I could run or fight in, if either became necessary.

The guys had both gone with short-sleeved polo shirts. Logan's was the dark gold that looked positively scrumptious on him. Dane's was baby blue. The color complemented his coloring, too, brightening his rather dark blue eyes. My partner was an attractive guy, but the reasons I liked him had nothing to do with his looks. Dane was smart, dedicated, and fun. It didn't hurt that he was easy-going and loyal too.

"Miss Jones?" An elf with unusually short hair had opened the interior door. "Welcome. If you'd come this way, please?"

"This way" wasn't into the opalized Coat Room, but led directly into a short, bland, beige hallway.

"I'm Merlandon, and have the honor of managing Dreamland for my Prince. My office is," he hurried past me to open a door. "Here. Please, come in and have a seat."

His office was little more than an over-sized closet. Also done in all beige, it held a desk and five chairs. They were molded plastic, four of them lined up against the wall to face his small, student-style desk, the fifth behind it. Not exactly the most comfortable seats in the world, but we wouldn't be there long enough for that to matter. I hoped.

"We'll cooperate to the fullest extent," he said after sitting down. He leaned forward, giving me full eye contact. His were a muddy brown. "Anything you need, Miss Jones, anything at all, please just tell me."

"Thank you." Something was way off about him. I noticed a tic start twitching in his left cheek, and watched his Adam's apple bob as he swallowed. He was extremely nervous. "We'd like a tour of the employee areas."

"Of course." Merlandon jumped to his feet, his thighs bumping the desk edge. That unbalanced a glass of water sitting near the side edge. It tipped over, spilling water, and rolled off the desk top. The office was so small, Dane simply leaned forward to catch the glass before it hit the tile floor.

"Goodness." Merlandon's ears reddened, and he came close to dropping the glass when Dane offered it to him. "Terribly clumsy of me."

I'd never seen a clumsy, or nervous, elf before. "Merlandon."

"Yes, Miss Jones." His hands fluttered away from the glass he'd placed on the desk.

"Do you have something to hide?"

He paled, and for a second, I seriously thought he was going to faint. "No, Miss Jones. Nothing to hide. It's...this is my first true opportunity to prove myself to my Prince, and it was going so well. Now this terrible thing is happening to our guests, who are my responsibility, and I wasn't even aware of it until his Highness called me earlier."

His pupils were enlarged. The poor dude was in full-on panic mode. What the hell kind of boss was Thorandryll, to instill such terror with a phone call? "Okay, do me a favor?"

"Anything, Miss Jones."

"Take a deep breath, and let it out slowly." I'd never thought I'd feel sympathy for an elf. Merlandon obeyed, but his hands were trembling.

"And another one, same thing."

"Terribly sorry."

"It's okay, just calm down. We're not the Spanish Inquisition." My attempt at humor failed as he gave me a blank look. "We'll figure out what's going on and handle it. I'll personally make certain Thorandryll is told how very helpful you were."

"You will?"

"Yes." That calmed him down. He even managed something resembling a smile. "Now, that tour?"

"Of course. Please come with me."

The tour was a bust, aside from being a peek into a world I'd never been a part of. I didn't know if it was a good or bad thing I hadn't had any other jobs prior to working at Arcane Solutions.

I had to drag Dane away from the casks of Weirding Pale in the stockroom. "But there's so much of it. Can we take a break now? I'm thirsty."

"No, now we need to question the employees." I aimed a smile at Merlandon. "One at a time, please. We'll set up in the break room."

"Of course. Bartenders or servers first?"

It didn't matter, but an elf being so eager to please was a novelty, so I pretended to give it a moment's thought. "I think the waitresses first."

"Very well, but we do prefer 'servers' here at Dreamland, Miss Jones. It's the PC term."

"Sorry." Ah, political correctness from an elf, when his people referred to shifters as animals. "I'll try to remember that."

"Thank you." Merlandon half-bowed before striding away, leaving us to make our way to the break room alone.

"Either of you notice anything weird?"

"Yeah, casks of ale with my name on them," Dane said, casting a longing glance over his shoulder before walking out of the stockroom.

I rolled my eyes. "It was a serious question."

"Nothing, aside from Mr. Nervous," Logan said, and Dane agreed. "There's magic everywhere, but as far as I know, it's because of the location. Pocket realms are magic."

Not helpful, but since we hadn't come across any signs with arrows and "This way to the bad guys" painted on them, I hadn't expected a different answer.

Ginger was in the break room. I hadn't seen her since the mini-drama with Danielle. She crawled around on the walls and ceiling the entire time we questioned the employees.

It was really distracting.

"Thank you for your help. We're going to walk around the club and look things over. I'll let you know if we discover anything."

"You're quite welcome. Remember that your, and the gentlemen's, refreshments are complimentary."

Nice to learn I hadn't ticked off Thorandryll enough to have the free-drink offer rescinded. The mention put a smile on Dane's face while he gathered the missing people's photos into a neat pile.

"And if you'd like, you may leave your coats and whatnot in a locker. That exit," Merlandon gestured to the door at the end of the break room. "Is the door that opens into the club, next to the bar. Just return through it to reclaim your belongings."

"Thanks." The lockers had stubby little keys, making it simple to determine which weren't already in use. We dumped our coats, the folder of photos, and my purse before hitting the bar.

Dane drank his first ale before the bartender finished mixing my mojito. Thankfully, the mojitos were served in more normal-sized glasses.

Irritated by our lack of progress, I didn't notice the change in décor until I turned away from the bar. The underwater grotto was gone, replaced with a jungle. The coral columns had become huge trees, their uppermost branches forming a canopy over the dance floor. White mist wafted along at ground level, swirling with the movements of dancers. The tables, chairs, and bar stools had changed to bamboo creations.

Instead of flashing, neon fish, there were glowing birds roosting and flitting about. "Wow, now I'm getting the name."

"Hate to say it, but I like the place." Logan sipped his ale. "Do you want to circle around?"

"That's as good a plan as any," I agreed. It was also a plan that netted nothing before last call. We collected our belongings, and one of the bartenders helped us shortcut from the back rooms to avoid the exit line.

Out in the parking lot, Logan stopped short halfway to his truck. "Damn."

"What?"

"I completely forgot to figure out a place to stay."

"Oh." I covered a yawn. It'd been a busy day. "It's late. You can both stay at Mom's tonight. She won't mind. I have a trundle, and there's an airbed we can pull out too."

"You're already crowded enough."

"Dude, it'd be like five AM before you dropped us both off and found a motel. They kick you out at noon."

Logan glanced at Dane, who shrugged. "I'm good with whatever you decide."

"Well, if you're certain Sunny won't mind."

"She won't. Come on." I was tired and cold. "Forward march, then home, Jeeves."

"Yes, madam." Logan jingled his keys the rest of the walk to his truck.

ELEVEN

My first peaceful night's sleep in weeks was destroyed by the sound of my bedroom door rebounding off the airbed with a deep boing, followed by a high-pitched shriek. That second sound sent me rolling over, off the edge of my bed, and directly on top of Logan, who'd won the coin toss for the trundle bed.

He grunted when I landed on him, a wince following as I tried to scramble off and managed to hit a sensitive spot.

Dane snickered.

"Ooh, sorry. Let me..."

"Yeah, just don't," Logan sucked in a breath, and I stopped moving. Well, everything but my head, which I turned so I could see who was at the door.

Grandma Jones stood there, her brown eyes wide and her jaw slack. Her short, white hair trembled as she closed her mouth.

"Hi, Grandma."

Mom appeared, looking over her shoulder. "Good morning. I'll set two more places for breakfast."

"Morning, Sunny," Logan said after spitting some of my hair out of his mouth. I settled for giving the best deer-in-the-headlights impression of my life.

My mom winked at me. "Let's allow the children to rise, Estelle. You did want coffee?"

"I...yes." Grandma about-faced and followed her to the kitchen.

Tonya stuck her head around the edge of my door to survey us, a grin immediately blooming. "Did you see her face?"

I groaned. "I hate mornings like this."

Twenty minutes later, everyone was dressed and in the kitchen.

Grandpa Jones, a burly man of over six feet with hazel eyes and a shiny pink, bald head, bear hugged me. "There's my little doll."

"Hi, Grandpa."

He released me. "Now, who are these two, and do I need to have a talk with them?"

"Logan Sayer and Dane Soames, and no. They're working with me."

"In your bedroom?"

"Grandpa," I whined. How did grandparents do that? Make you feel about ten years old, and act like it too? "It was snowing last night and they live all the way across town."

"Ah." He ruffled my hair before shaking hands with them. "Theodore Jones. Call me Ted."

"Nice to meet you, sir." Logan smiled and glanced at my mom. "Did you need any help, Sunny?"

"No, have a seat."

Hah, no escape for him. We all sat down under Grandma's thin-lipped, narrow-eyed gaze. The morning didn't improve as Leglin, Bone, and Diablo burst into the kitchen. My grandmother uttered another loud shriek when Diablo planted his front paws on the table's edge, right next to her.

"Dude, down."

"*Bacon.*"

"No bacon. Get down." Grandma was leaning away from him and about to fall into Dane's lap.

"*Bacon,*" he repeated with a snap of his teeth, and she cringed.

"*I'm sitting,*" Bone said. "*Can I have bacon for being a good boy?*"

"Argh." I tossed him a slice from the plate already on the table. "Diablo, down if you want bacon."

The black pit dropped to the floor. I tossed him a piece, and one to Leglin too.

"My Lord, what are these beasts? Oh my, they're those killer dogs that..."

"No," I snapped at her, only to wince when Grandma glared at me. "Sorry. No, they're rescues."

"Pitties," Grandpa said. "Come here, boys. You like bacon?" Bone and Diablo took up station next to his chair. He began feeding them and Leglin softly whined. "What kind is that one? You come here too. He's a handsome fella."

"Elf hound, Grandpa. Guys, come on. Go to the living room."

"I don't mind," my grandfather said, collecting more pieces of bacon. "Who's a good boy?"

"*Me, me.*" Bone's tail swished across the floor. "*I'm a good boy. Give me all the bacon.*"

"*I'm sitting. I'm a good boy too.*" Diablo wagged his tail. "*Don't be a pig, Bone.*"

"Well, I do mind sharing the table with beasts," Grandma declared.

Jeeze. I closed my eyes for a second.

"Now, Estelle, let's not toss that word around at the breakfast table." Mom deposited a platter of pancakes in the middle of the table. "Logan and Dane are shifters, and 'beast' is a derogatory term some use for shifters."

My grandma eyed Dane as he transferred a few pancakes to his plate. He'd eaten with us several times, and felt totally at home. "You're a shifter?"

"Yes, ma'am. Tiger."

"Oh." She looked at Logan. "And you?"

"I'm tiger, too."

My turn for scrutiny and a question. "You're sleeping with two shifters?"

"Oh, my God." Instant face furnace, because her tone made it clear what she meant by "sleeping".

"Estelle," Grandpa snapped. "That's enough. Cordi's sex life..."

"Oh, God. Kill me now," I begged the ceiling, which failed to respond by falling on me.

"...isn't any of our business."

Dane poured syrup over his pancakes. Logan's gaze was glued to his empty plate, but I saw his lips twitching.

"No, I'm not sleeping with both of them. Holy crap, Grandma."

"Not that there'd be anything wrong with it, if you were." Mom patted Logan's shoulder as she put the coffee pot on the table. In that instant, I knew exactly why some people spontaneously combusted.

"Mom."

"What?" She went to the swinging door to call Tonya to the kitchen.

"Stop. Please. My embarrassment quota has been exceeded for the day."

"Cats have spines." Grandma was studying Dane. "Do you have spines in your...?"

I couldn't believe my ears. "Holy frickin' crap, don't finish that question."

She didn't, but Dane answered anyway. "No, ma'am. We don't resemble normal felines that closely."

"Oh. Well, good, because spines would be," Grandma shuddered.

Tonya entered the kitchen. "What spines?"

"Penis spines. They," Grandma waggled her forefinger between Dane and Logan. "Don't have them."

I groaned and planted my elbows on the table, in order to hide my face in both hands. "Could everyone please shut up?"

Instead, everyone ignored me. Tonya dropped into a chair. "I'd wondered about that."

I peeked through my fingers to watch Mom pile pancakes on everyone's plates.

"Well, we don't in human shape," Dane said between bites. "We do in tiger shape."

"Does it make taking a leak as a tiger difficult?" Grandpa wanted to know, and I lifted my head.

"Okay, people. Enough. Seriously." I didn't yell, but spoke loudly enough no one could ignore me. "No more talk about spines, penises, or sex at the table. Ever. I'm beyond serious about this."

My grandma sniffed after a few seconds of silence. "I was merely curious."

I shushed her and we glared at each other. Make no mistake, I loved her to death, but holy cow she could be a total pain in the...

"Spines," Tonya muttered before stuffing a chunk of pancake into her mouth. All three men snickered. Mom was smiling.

God, what a way to start a Sunday.

"They're staying here?" I tried to keep my voice down. "Why?"

"Betty's parents and her sister's family are staying there for Christmas. I'm not going to have family staying in a hotel during the holidays." Mom glanced over her shoulder. I was helping her wash dishes. "They can have my room. I'll sleep on the couch."

"Aw, Mom. I'll be waking you up all the time, coming in late. This case might take a while."

"That's all right."

At the table, Grandma asked one of the guys, "Do your people have sex in both shapes?"

"Holy frickin' hell, Mom, make her stop."

"She's curious, and neither of them seem to mind her questions."

I scowled and put a little extra elbow grease into drying the plate I held. Once the guys were gone, my grandmother would bombard me with questions. Oh, but wait...I had a new house. "Mom."

"What?"

"It's too crowded here and Grandma doesn't like my Pit Crew. I'm going to stay at my place."

"The weather's too bad for moving."

"I'll camp out there then. There's a fireplace."

Mom sighed. "All right, if you're set on it."

She had no idea how set I was on it. "Yes."

My attempts to apologize were waved aside by Dane and Logan. Apparently, they'd found the entire situation hilarious, including my horrified interjections.

On the other hand, my request for a lift out to my new place became something much more. By Monday evening, a combination of them, Logan's truck, Tonya's help packing my stuff at Mom's, and my teleportation ability saw me moved into the new house, though not fully unpacked.

Weather be damned. The guys had handled the stuff in storage, and once everything was present, I realized I didn't have enough furniture for a house.

Since Dreamland wasn't open on Sundays and Mondays, we'd been at loose ends anyway. I'd considered trying to collect items belonging to the other missing people, but finally decided against it. When we found Rico Guerra, we'd find them. I didn't believe in coincidences enough to think otherwise, not with the Dreamland connection.

I'd been alone in my new house a few times during the moving process. Enough to realize how far from town it was, and how quiet. Ginger's habit of jumping out of closets, rooms, or from around corners hadn't helped. She'd earned a few screams from me, mainly because she'd grown less translucent and looked far more real.

I'd invited Logan and Dane to stay, and after a little discussion, they'd agreed to until Logan's vacation time was up.

Dane was upstairs in the guest room, inflating the two airbeds I'd bought. Logan built a fire while I made hot chocolate.

Glancing out the kitchen window, I said, "It looks like Narnia out there. All I need is a lamp post."

"I don't remember them seeing a house when they came out of the wardrobe."

"Well, no, but snow and trees? Those I have in spades."

He finished his fire building and moved to the couch. "Right."

"It occurs to me that Narnia could be real."

"How's that?"

"Think about it: A different world behind a magic entrance. That sounds like a pocket realm to me."

"You have a point," Logan agreed, propping his feet up on the coffee table and stretching his besocked toes toward the fire. He turned his head. "Do you need any help?"

"Nope."

I picked up the mugs and went to join him, stepping over sleeping dogs to hand him one before sitting down. "Aslan could be a god or maybe an elf transformed into a lion."

"Maybe. And the Snow Queen?"

"Ooh, I have it. She's his wife, and cursed him into a lion because he consorted with one too many nymphs."

Logan sipped his hot chocolate. "Is this a remix? Because that sounds like a Zeus and Hera sort of relationship."

"Remixes are fun." I leaned back, and propped up my feet, too. "Of course, no one noticed the kids were missing because time ran differently in Narnia from the real world."

"True." He petted Speck, who lay tucked between us.

Dane thumped downstairs. "Don't you two look cozy. Is that hot chocolate?"

"Yes." I left the couch to fix him a mug, and we spent the rest of the evening speculating on the potential of a real Narnia.

TWELVE

I yawned my way downstairs, following the big dogs, with Squishy cautioning Speck as the Chihuahuas navigated the steps in my wake. Downstairs, Logan was on his phone. I let the dogs out the front door, promising the Chihuahuas I'd buy them coats soon.

"Discord," Logan said, holding his phone out where I could see it had been muted, as Dane thumped down the stairs.

"Cordi. I was supposed to let everyone know she'd prefer for us to call her Cordi."

"Oh. Cordi, we have another missing person. The Rex's youngest son."

Great. "He's our ally, right? Tell him," I paused. The only lion shifter I knew was Teague. Being part of the clan made me the lions' ally too, and them, mine. It would probably be a good idea to meet more of them. "Scratch that. See if he wants to meet, and invite him here."

From the quick smile Logan tossed me, I'd made the correct call on the matter. I let the Chihuahuas in and dried their tiny paws and legs.

"They'll be here in about an hour," Logan said after ending the call. "The Rex's name is James O'Meara."

"King James." I chuckled, walking into the kitchen to start coffee. "How long has the son been missing?"

"Since Saturday."

Dane cleared his throat. "I didn't see one, but I'm pretty sure I smelled lion on a couple of women at Dreamland Saturday night."

I fought a scowl. "So we were right there, again, when someone was nabbed."

"Looks that way." Logan leaned on the breakfast bar. "Is this going to be a problem with Mr. Whitehaven?"

"Nope." After the adoption ceremony and returning to work, I'd had a talk with the boss. My contract specified no freelancing, and that specification was there for a reason: to protect me.

Well, to provide what protection being in Mr. Whitehaven's employ could offer. Now that I had supe friends and was part of the tigers' clan, I had responsibilities to them. That meant using my abilities, as I had in the past to help Logan stop the attempts to kidnap Terra.

It also meant using them to help the clan's allies, when and if necessary. Mr. Whitehaven confirmed that, so while I'd update him, I didn't need his permission to act. He'd basically told me that it was my call, because anything I chose to do outside of official cases would affect my new "political standing" in the supe community.

Helping my clan's allies put a shine on my reputation. Not helping would tarnish not only my reputation, but the clan's too.

I wasn't willing to risk that, but it was nice that the first time a clan ally needed help, it tied into an official case. Two official cases, I amended while pouring coffee for everyone. Thorandryll was a client now too.

"Anything I need to know about O'Meara before he gets here?"

"He's tough, but fair. A good leader, and nice enough, unless there's a threat to his Pride."

"Pride as in his group, and not his "pride" pride, right?" I went to the fridge for breakfast makings, having gone to the store the evening before. None of the restaurants delivered out this far.

"Right."

"I'm not supposed to bow or anything, am I?"

"No, only his people do that sort of thing. Just," Logan shrugged. "Treat him like a client."

"Okay. Dane, would you let the big dogs in?" I needed to feed everyone and clean up before the Rex arrived.

James O'Meara, Rex of the Santo Trueno Pride, wasn't an imposing figure. He was my height and in good shape, but rather slender for a shifter. I knew right away that he was worried about his missing son, because the skin under his bright blue eyes looked faintly bruised. His hair was bright too, a coppery red that bordered on orange.

O'Meara hadn't come alone. The man with him was younger, taller, and looked as though he'd spent his entire life lifting weights. Though his skin was darker, that gorgeous clear brown some mixed-race children are blessed with, he had the same bright blue eyes as O'Meara, and his close-cropped, tight curls were a darkish red.

"James, this is Discord Jones, our newest queen," Logan said while leading them into the living room. I didn't have furniture for my office yet.

"Pleased to meet you, Miss Jones. Thank you for seeing us so quickly." O'Meara had a nice smile. "This is my eldest son, Tanner."

His son merely nodded, crossing his arms as he stood next to the chair his father chose. The arm crossing looked awkward, because

Tanner's arms were huge, and his chest was broad and bulky with muscle.

"You're welcome, and I'm pleased to meet you both." I was on the couch, Leglin lying at my feet, Bone and Diablo snoozing on either side of me, and had the Chihuahuas dozing in my lap. I'd had a talk with the dogs about their barking habits over breakfast.

Logan rested his hands on the back of the couch, evidently preferring to stand. Dane was sitting on the hearth.

"What's your other son's name?"

"Connor. He didn't return from his night out. We found his car in the parking lot of..."

"A club called Dreamland." When O'Meara nodded, his gaze sharpening, I said, "We've been there. Other people have gone missing from there over the past couple of weeks."

"I see."

"Prince Thorandryll hired us to look into the matter, and so did the mother of one of the missing men. We're already on it."

Tanner frowned. "Then why have us come here?"

I looked at his father, who reached into the pocket of his dark blue suit jacket. "For that."

Logan had remembered to ask the Rex to bring something belonging to his son. O'Meara leaned forward to place a gold chain with a small, black stone dangling from it on the coffee table.

"To bring that? Why?"

"Miss Jones is a psychic." O'Meara straightened, and for a second, his composure slipped, his calm expression tightening. He was prepared to hear the worst. "Please, if you would."

Speck's thin legs wind-milled when I moved him off my lap and next to Diablo. Squishy grumbled, but quickly curled up next to Bone and returned to sleep. I scooted forward to reach for the necklace. "I have to warn you that this doesn't always work immediately."

"I understand." The Rex's gaze tracked my hand when I picked up the necklace. From the corner of my eye, I saw Ginger gliding down the visible portion of the stairs. Diablo let loose a loud snore. I fought a giggle, closing my other hand around the lower half of the necklace and the stone.

Loud music, steamy heat, and a pretty brunette's smile. Shouting and a pissed-looking Tanner. Ripping into a deer, blood and meat hot as it slid down his throat.

Eww. I replaced the necklace on the coffee table, creating a new mental folder to tuck Connor's golden shimmer into. "He's alive, but that's all I can tell you right now."

The wave of relief O'Meara felt would've knocked me down if I hadn't been sitting. His voice gave no hint of it though. "That's enough to know for now. Thank you."

"You're welcome." I scooted back, trying to pretend I couldn't see Ginger prowling around Tanner. Her ashy gray hands trailed over the big shifter's body, and I mean, all over it. "We're going back to the club tonight, to see if we can't figure out how this is happening. One of us will keep you informed."

Tanner dropped his arms, his mouth opening, but his father stood. "Of course. I sincerely appreciate your assistance with this."

"We're allies. We'll do our best to bring him home," I promised. "Be careful driving."

Logan showed them out, and I caught a hard, thin-lipped glare from Tanner before he walked out the front door. I petted Squishy, who'd crawled back into my lap, and waited for the front door to shut. "He's really controlled."

"He has to be. Lions aren't like us. A Rex doesn't stay king if he's careless. It's not a position that passes down in a particular family," Dane said.

"It will be if James has his way." Logan dropped into the chair the Rex had used. "And I'm not looking forward to Tanner taking his place."

"Why not?"

"Tanner doesn't like allying with anyone he thinks isn't as strong as the Pride."

"Oh." I gently rubbed Squishy's belly. She still had the soft, pink skin of a puppy, but the vet had estimated her age to be two. "He thinks the clan's weak?"

"Going by numbers, we are compared to the Pride."

"I could take him." Dane's confident declaration put a grin on my face. "He thinks being big is what matters. It helps, but it's not the only thing that counts."

"I think I made him mad."

"Don't worry about it. You didn't offend James. He wants Connor home. Tanner, on the other hand," Logan waggled his hand.

"Yeah, I got a flash of them arguing. Tanner and Connor, I mean. Connor's the baby of the family, huh?"

Logan nodded. "Spoiled rotten, but he's a good kid in spite of it."

"Cool." I checked the time, which was four-seventeen. Late nights were becoming a habit. "Dreamland opens at seven. I'm going to do some more unpacking upstairs."

"Okay. Need any help?"

"Nah. I'll start dinner in a couple of hours. You guys do whatever."

Ginger followed me upstairs. Eventually, I'd have to figure out what to do about her.

When we arrived at Dreamland, Angel Elf notified Merlandon, who wasn't happy to hear someone else had gone missing. "I'm going to be relegated to cleaning the stables," he moaned, wringing his hands as he led us to the break room. "Prince Thorandryll does not look kindly upon failure."

That's the punishment he was so afraid of? Having to clean horse poop? My earlier sympathy for him took a healthy nosedive. "I'd be more worried about what's happening to the missing people."

Merlandon had the grace to look embarrassed. "Oh, I do worry, Miss Jones. I hope they're not injured. The guests here are my responsibility, after all."

Uh-huh. "We'll be circulating, keeping an eye out. Mind if we use a locker again?"

"Of course not. Help yourself." He hurried away, the tips of his ears bright pink.

"Okay, he's kind of a jerk," I said, shrugging out of my coat.

"He's an elf." Dane opened a locker. "Did you really expect different?"

"Cut him some slack. I wouldn't be looking forward to centuries of cleaning stalls either." Logan hung his leather jacket on one of the hooks inside the locker. I handed him my coat and purse. I'd switched to the one I thought of as my "case" purse, a largish, black messenger-style bag.

"Whatever. Okay, troops, eyes and ears open. Let's see if we can't manage to catch a clue tonight."

A clue wasn't in the cards right away. Instead, I caught a mild case of panic upon spotting Nick out on the dance floor half an hour into the evening.

There's nothing quite like seeing an ex when you aren't remotely expecting to. Nick was dancing with a tall blonde, and he certainly didn't look mopey.

Fortunately, I was alone when I saw him, and he didn't see me. I ducked out of sight behind one of the columns surrounding the dance floor. The club's décor had changed to some freaky version of Dante's Inferno, all black and red, with flames flickering on the walls. There was even a fiery waterfall. Or firefall. Whatever.

My attempt to quell the instinct to get the hell out of Dodge wasn't completely successful. I wanted to be gone before he saw me. Particularly before he might see me with Logan.

Not that leaving was an actual option, since we were working on a case. People were missing. That was far more important than a potential scene between Nick and me.

My stomach disagreed, flip-flopping violently, and Ginger chose that moment to materialize in front of me. I closed my eyes to block out her grisly grin, and flinched as I heard a familiar voice.

"What a coincidence. Psychic Girl at the very club I finally manage to drag my little brother out of the house to."

I opened my eyes in time to watch Patrick walk right through Ginger, and for a second, seriously considered throwing up on him. That would be certain to wipe the smug look off his damn face.

Instead, I hissed, "What the hell, dude?"

"You tell me. You're the psychic."

Gah. "I'm working."

"Sure." Patrick's grin widened. "You just happen to have a case that's resulted in your showing up at the college I attend, and the club I brought Nick, the guy who loves you, to."

Had I thought something earlier about not believing in coincidences? I was beginning to, and they could kiss my butt. "Yes, that's exactly what's going on. I can't leave, so you have to."

He laughed. "No way. I think maybe Fate's taken a hand in this. Maybe the old hag thinks you two belong together."

"Dude, I swear..."

"Cordi?"

Oh, damn. I turned around. "Hi, Nick."

His face lit up, a big smile following. "Hi. What are you...?"

And of course, that's when Logan walked up to join us. Nick looked at him, his smile gone, and his eyes narrowing. "Oh, you're on a date."

"No, we're on a case," Logan said. "I'm helping out."

Bless his gorgeous green eyes. "Yeah, we're working. Sorry, but I kind of don't have time to chat right now. Bye."

I managed a smile, grabbed Logan's arm, and dragged him along as I speed-walked away. I didn't stop until we'd gone around the dance floor far enough to change directions and hit the bar. "Holy crap."

"Can I have my arm back?"

"Sorry." I let go, and Logan rubbed his arm. "That was awkward."

"Kind of got that impression."

"Thanks for bailing me out."

"No problem." He ordered an ale when the bartender stopped to see what we wanted. I passed, climbing up on a stool. "Are you okay?"

"I don't know." My hands were shaking. I clasped them together and dropped them in my lap.

Logan noticed. "If you still have feelings for him..."

"No. I mean," I bit my lip. "I kind of used him, and I feel awful about it. Plus, he's been jealous of you since we met, and he pretty much accused me of breaking up with him because of you."

"Oh." Logan accepted his drink and tipped the bartender before resting his elbows on the bar. "What do you mean by 'kind of used him'?"

I sighed. "Remember the day you washed my car, and I babbled about rushing things?"

"Yes."

"I got together with him because I was lonely, and there was a freak-out involved, too, the day he and I met. I mean, I didn't like, plan it, but it did happen. Us hooking up, no prior dating."

"So you feel guilty."

"Big time. That's a horrible thing to do. And then the ring thing, and...well, everything. It's a mess."

"Compounded by my asking you out."

Maybe I did want a drink. "Yeah, I guess. Not really, but kind of, because if he hears we're dating, he'll think I lied to him."

"Instead of believing you broke off things because the two of you weren't working out."

"Right."

Logan nodded and drank some ale. I ordered a mojito. Talking had calmed my stomach.

"You're not responsible for what he decides to believe."

"I know, but jeeze. I already hurt him, and don't want to make it worse. You know?"

"Yeah."

"The only way to keep him from believing you're the reason I broke up with him is to tell him the truth, and that's a truly crappy thing to hit him with. 'I was lonely, and you were available'." I drained half my freshly delivered mojito. "But I don't want him mad at you either."

"I can handle it."

"You shouldn't have to. Man, this being an adult thing is hard."

Logan chuckled. "My suggestion is to not worry about it. We haven't had an official date yet, and I'm not about to rub Nick's face in the fact we've talked about it."

"You sure you still want to? I'm doing a lovely job of causing you trouble and unpacking all my baggage on you. If I were you, I'd find a girl who's less of a pain the butt."

"You're not a pain in the butt."

"Thanks. I hope you keep thinking that."

"Pretty certain I will." Logan gazed at me for a few seconds. "I really don't mean this to sound pushy, but I like you. I'm attracted to you, and I want to see what happens with us, since both of those things are reciprocated. Okay?"

Afraid my response would be a squeak, I nodded.

"Good. I'm going to get back to work. Yell," he tapped his temple with a finger. "If you need me."

He left me with plenty to think about.

I spent the rest of the evening avoiding Nick and Patrick while trying to watch my assigned third of the club. For most of it, I seriously thought Nick had cloned himself. He seemed to be everywhere I looked, but at least he didn't attempt to corner me for a talk.

About one-thirty, I met Dane and Logan at the bar. "Any luck?"

"No weirdness, and I haven't heard anyone mention a friend disappearing." Dane polished off his ale and immediately ordered another.

"Same," Logan said.

"Let's stake out the exit," I suggested. "We'll leave if nothing happens there."

"I just ordered a drink."

"We'll grab the coats," Logan told him. "But head that way when you get it."

"Okay."

In the break room, as Logan unlocked the locker, I laughed. "You know what this reminds me of?"

"What?"

"School. If you had a boyfriend, you shared each other's lockers."

He pulled out my coat. "Did you have a boyfriend?"

"No, I was too shy in tenth grade, and then the Melding happened, so you know, Snoozeville." I slipped into my coat as he held it for me. "I missed out on all that stuff."

"What else did school girls do when they had boyfriends?" Logan retrieved his jacket and handed me my purse.

"Tried not to get caught holding hands or sneaking kisses in the hallways."

He grabbed Dane's jacket, shut the locker, and looked at both doors.

"What are you doing?"

"Seeing if the coast is clear." He grinned and quickly kissed me. "There. We didn't get caught."

"Nope." Maybe one day, I wouldn't respond to a kiss from him with my dopiest grin.

"Want to see if we can get away with holding hands?"

"Sure." The warm tingle returned as we fitted our fingers together. We were so busy smiling at each other while walking to the door, we failed to realize a giant clue had appeared in front of us.

One second, we were in the break room, the next, we were falling into coldness.

THIRTEEN

"Ow." I landed on my side in a few inches of snow, which wasn't enough cushion for the frozen ground beneath it. About eight feet overhead, the circle of light we'd fallen through winked out.

Logan landed in a crouch, and immediately helped me to my feet. "You okay?"

"Yeah." I slapped snow from my coat. "Guess we know what happened to the missing people now."

"Uh huh." Logan shoved Dane's jacket at me. "Hold this. I don't like the looks of that."

"Of..." Then I saw the tall, white figure loping toward us, something flapping from its shoulder. "Oh, that. What is it?"

"Golem."

"A what?" I asked, but he was moving, charging toward the golem. "Dude!"

"It's ice," he called back. "I've got it."

"Okay, I'll just stand here looking stupid," I muttered, watching as the distance between them narrowed. "I mean, it's not like I could melt it or anything."

If I had, I would've missed the chance to admire Logan's fighting moves as he efficiently took the golem down in a fast series of whirling kicks. A few "oohs" and "ahs" may have escaped as I walked closer. "Ooh, big strong tiger man beat down the bad monster. Not that it had much of a chance. You are fast, dude."

"Thanks. Can you melt the pieces, before," Logan stomped on a hand that tried to skitter away. "They pull back together?"

"Oh, yeah." I called on my pyrokinesis, and in short order, was melting the various shards as he tossed them in different directions.

When we'd finished, he dusted off his hands. "Now we need to get out of here."

"We can't. This is our best..."

"I meant out of this area. It's not dead, but it'll take a while to reform."

"Oh. Frickin' golems."

Logan laughed. "Come on. Let's put some distance between it and us."

"Okay." I picked up the leather bag the golem had been carrying, which was what I'd seen flapping behind it. "This is a big bag."

"Yeah." We started walking, and I loosened the drawstring to look inside.

"Looky what I found." I showed him the strips of black cloth. "I'm going to guess the golem collects visitors."

"Then we're on the right track." Logan pointed to the imprints in the snow ahead of us.

"Yay. We're so awesome at this stuff." After putting the strips and Dane's jacket in the bag, I held it out to him. "Carry this, please?"

"Sure."

I looked around as we walked. Mountains rose on either side, and they weren't very far away, but a thick line of trees hid the bottoms of them from sight. We were walking down a clear, flat plain of snow, unbroken other than the golem's footprints and our own. The plain was somewhere between a quarter and half a mile wide.

"Tell me about golems."

"Magical constructs. We're lucky that one was made of ice. Those made of earth or rock are a lot harder to put down."

"If it's a magical construct, that means there's a magic user around here." Who had to be our bad guy, since it definitely appeared the golem had been sent to grab anyone who dropped in. I giggled. "Dropped in."

"What?"

"Nothing. Hey, maybe this is Narnia?"

Logan shook his head. "We came through a portal, not a wardrobe."

"Lewis could've changed the details. It was a series for kids."

"You have a point."

"I know, and it's a great point, because it leaves the option for this being Narnia wide open. How cool would it be if our magic user turned out to be the witch?"

"More cool than we'd like. Didn't she freeze people into statues?"

"I'll freeze her first." I wiggled my fingers. They were cold enough that it kind of hurt, and I shoved them into my pockets. We kept walking for what felt like a couple of hours, until it began to snow.

Logan muttered, "Shit."

"I was just about to say that." He glanced at me with a raised eyebrow. "Okay, I wasn't. We can still see them."

"For maybe ten more minutes." He kept walking. So did I, until the falling snow concealed the golem's tracks.

"Now what?" I covered a yawn, wondering what time it was. My cell phone was dead when I pulled it out to check. "My phone's not working. I charged it before we left the house."

"I doubt this place has wireless or electricity." Logan blew out a misty breath. "We better find some shelter."

"Think there's an empty igloo around here?" I was much colder than I had been, thanks to stopping, and tired enough to feel a little punchy.

"Don't know. I do know that I don't want that golem sneaking up behind us."

"But then I'll get to watch you karate kick it to bits again. That was cool." I wiped snowflakes from my eyelashes.

Logan smiled. "I didn't think you were impressed by that sort of thing."

"Are you kidding? I can't do those kinds of kicks, dude. I've fallen on my butt every time Jeff's tried to teach them to me."

"Who's Jeff?"

"Ex-Marine who teaches self-defense." I made a face. "I'm like his worst student. My coordination's not great." Or maybe I didn't practice enough, which is what Jeff constantly told me. Busy Discord was too busy to fit in extra practice time. I also didn't care to sweat a lot, because eww.

"Golems aren't intelligent."

"Huh?"

"If we move away from its path, we should be okay," Logan said. "The question is: right or left?"

"We could choose by the time-honored method of Eeny Meeny. There's even a part about tiger toes."

Logan focused on me. "You're tired."

"How'd you guess?"

He touched my cheek, and his fingers felt hot. "And half-frozen."

"Yep, that too."

"All right, shelter's our top priority. We'll go right."

"Sure thing." I followed him as he turned right.

"Cordi."

"Huh?" It was a struggle to open my eyes. Logan began chafing my hands.

"You have to keep moving."

"I'm not moving?"

He peered into my eyes. "No, sweetheart. You stopped walking."

"Oh, sorry." I couldn't feel my lips.

"Come on." Logan hooked his arm through mine. I stumbled alongside him, my feet not sending any information up to my brain. I looked down.

"My feet still there?"

"Shit," Logan murmured before assuring me they were.

"Okay." I took his word for it and looked up. "Oh."

"What?"

"It's Aslan. I knew it." I tripped, my bleary eyes snapping shut. "Oh, no, gonna fall."

"No, you're not." Logan kept me upright. "And that's not Aslan. It's Connor."

I managed to open my eyes for another look. The huge lion paced toward us, and shook snow from its black mane. "Nope, that's Aslan."

"Okay, it's Aslan. Keep moving. Maybe he's found some shelter."

"Told you it was Narnia. Because that's Aslan. And it's winter. See the snow?" I mumbled.

"Yes, I see the snow. Hard not to."

"Hah. I'm right."

"You're right," Logan agreed, but for some reason, I thought he was arguing with me, and went into a long, mumbling tirade about all the ways I was right about the place being Narnia, and the lion, Aslan.

"Is she going to be all right?"

My eyes crossed, honing in on the tip of a nose.

"If we get her warmed up. More wood, kid."

Darn, it really wasn't Aslan. I felt cheated as the nose retreated, and my eyes slowly uncrossed. "Uh."

"Hey." Logan bent over me. "How are you doing?"

"You liar. That's not Aslan."

"Better. That's good. I told you it was Connor, but you wanted to argue." He touched my nose. "Can you feel that?"

"Yeah." My eyes drifted shut.

"No sleeping." Logan hauled me into sitting position.

"I'm freakin' tired."

"I know, but you need to get warm first." He moved me around and then sat behind me to keep me from lying down.

I blinked. "Pretty fire."

"Yeah it is, if I do say so myself." Logan rubbed his hands together before pressing them against my cheeks.

"You're squishing my face." My words came out sounding like "Oor skithin mah faith" and I started giggling.

"It's for a good cause. You don't want it falling off, do you?"

The fact I had to think about it made me realize I might be in trouble. I dredged a couple of words out of the slush my mind had become. "Frost bite?"

"I think we got you under shelter in time. Shifters aren't susceptible to it, and I don't know what it looks like. I've only heard of it."

"Oh."

Logan dropped his hands and hugged me. "But you do have a healing ability. You'll be okay. I just need to keep you warm."

"She's coherent now?"

"Mostly."

"Great." Connor dumped his armful of wood by the fire. He proved to be the spitting image of his father, aside from his skin being the same beautiful, clear light brown as Tanner's. He wore Dane's jacket, which was too big in the shoulders for him.

Kneeling beside us, he smiled at me. "Hi. Sorry I'm not Aslan."

" 'S okay."

"You did make a good argument for it. I mean, the whole lion in winter thing? I'd probably think it was Aslan too." He picked up one of my hands. He felt as hot as Logan did. "You take the chilling out thing way too seriously."

As he began gently rubbing my hand between his, I wondered how big of an ass I'd made of myself. I couldn't remember much from first seeing him to being here. Wherever here was. I blinked a few times, and finally looked around. We were in a cave. "Ow."

Connor stopped rubbing my hand. "Does that hurt?"

"Pins and needles."

He grinned, not at me, but Logan. "That's a good sign."

"Yeah." Logan hugged me a little tighter.

I woke up nice and toasty, due to sleeping between two huge, fur-covered bodies. Those same bodies presented a problem because I needed to locate the closest approximation to a bathroom, having just woken up.

Once I made it clear they were in danger of getting wet if they didn't immediately rise and shine, the guys took my trip outside as an opportunity to shift and put their clothes back on. Even though I hurried to avoid freezing my delicate bits, I missed out on the chance to admire Logan's chest. Dude could dress faster than he could kick an ice golem to bits.

"Let me see your hands."

I held them up for inspection. Logan pinched the tip of each of my fingers after inspecting their color. "I'm fine."

"I'm hungry." Connor patted his stomach. "Haven't found a damn thing to eat except snow."

"Lucky you." I pointed to my over-sized purse. "I have some breakfast bars in there."

"You just became my most favorite person in the world."

"There's a bottle of water too."

"Marry me."

Logan rolled his eyes at the other man. "When did you start carrying food in your purse?"

"After I turned into a giant crankypants because I kept forgetting to eat while we were looking for my mom." Those hadn't been my finest moments. There'd been screaming and tears and I vaguely remembered threatening to stake Derrick "where the sun don't shine". Or maybe it had been Stone? One of them.

Connor picked up my bag. "May I?"

"Yes, and pass a couple over here."

We munched strawberry-filled cereal bars and sipped water. After Connor finished his, he asked, "What's the plan?"

"Try to pick up the golem's trail and see if we can find the others who were nabbed. Unless you want us to take you home first?"

"Well, I hate worrying my parents, but are you certain you can get back here?"

Good question. "I've been able to teleport into a sidhe when I want to, and I teleport into the Barrows a lot." But the Barrows were mostly public spaces, and for all I knew, Thorandryll could have given me a free, anytime pass into his sidhe. "But honestly, I don't know."

"Okay, I can wait."

"Are you sure?"

"Yes," he said. "I don't want to be the reason the others aren't found."

I had already liked him for the not-being-Aslan apology. Now I liked him more. "Okay, we have our plan."

Plans were great to have, but not knowing important information tended to throw giant wrenches into them.

Connor hadn't seen the ice golem, or any other living thing during the two days before our arrival. All we'd seen was the ice golem and him. Though we were alert, we weren't actually ready when the first attack occurred, not long after we left the cave.

"What the hell?" I yelped as the ground around us erupted, spewing forth a few dozen short, grayish white creatures. None of them were over two feet tall, but they all held long, sharp icicles, which they quickly proved unafraid to use.

"Snow gremlins." Logan kicked one away after slapping aside its frozen spear. The gremlin shattered when it struck a half-buried rock at landing.

"Ow, you little," I shook my hand and kicked the gremlin who'd poked it. The satisfying thwock of boot connecting to face meant my retribution hit its intended mark. Another one poked me in the leg. "Okay now, that is not nice."

There were too many of the snaggle-toothed little freaks for us to keep them away. I called up my pyrokinetic ability, and started blasting them with fire.

Connor cheered, before he and Logan began tossing the gremlins around, trying to keep them off of me and break up the clumps they gathered into. I kept blasting away, while dodging the little critters' increasingly violent stabs.

"Last one," Connor said, planting his foot between the gremlin's legs to heave it into the air. I hit it with a ball of flames. "Done!"

"Good, let's get moving again." Logan picked up the leather bag. "How are you doing, Cordi?"

"Not too tired yet." I was hungry though. One little package of breakfast bars didn't last long, but we only had three packages left.

"Okay, forward march, people."

Connor and I obeyed, following him. We took a break about an hour later, and had a brief discussion before deciding to eat one bar each. They came two to a package, so we'd still have something for later.

Break over, we began walking again, and the ground before us trembled, then snow flew as more gremlins leaped into view.

So much for my paltry lunch. "This is not a friendly place."

"It does kind of suck." Connor scowled at the advancing gremlins. "Okay, let's do this."

Logan looked at the sky. "We're going to run out of daylight if this keeps up. I want to find shelter before dark."

"Well then, gents, step back. I'll handle these guys. You can get the next batch." I eyed the gremlins. They were scurrying forward, sticking close to one another. Tapping into my telekinetic ability, I let it build up before throwing out both of my hands. "Cordi smash!"

Gremlins flew backward, their icicle spears shattering. Quite of few of them also shattered, but the rest climbed to their feet. More than one shook its head before they began running toward us again.

"They just don't give up," I complained. "Fine. How about a welcome bonfire?"

I created a wall of flame, and the gremlins ran right into it. None of them tried to avoid it at all. Their high-pitched screams of rage hurt my ears, but the sounds faded quickly as the little creeps melted. "There."

"Awesome." Connor held up his hand, and I high-fived him. When our palms met, he flinched. I looked down at the same time he did, to see the sharp, icy point jutting from the left side of his stomach.

Logan whirled around, kicking the gremlin away before stomping it to pieces. I tried to keep Connor upright, but he was too heavy. I did keep him from slamming to the ground as he passed out. "Logan!"

"Right here." He pulled the melting spear out of Connor.

"I don't know about you, but I'm kind of ready to go home, and see about coming back with an army of elves."

Logan checked Connor's side. "I'm good with that. At least we found one of the missing."

"Okay. Here we go."

Logan took hold of Connor's hand, and mine, when I held it out. I teleported us, and we hit something in between, bouncing off it and appearing in mid-air.

"Holy…"

We landed in a snowdrift, creating our own shower of the white stuff. It was also dark, and I wondered if we'd teleported into the future or something. "Crap."

"You all right?"

I sat up and wiped snow from my face. "Yeah. Are … uh-oh."

Logan sat up, looking where I was. "Is that…?"

The hound growled.

"Nope, not mine." I scooted forward. "We're friendly, just lost. If you could maybe give us directions, we'll go away."

"Hold, Leandra." Thorandryll stepped out from under a tree. At least, I thought it was him. The bow and arrow pointed in our direction made me take a closer look. Same golden hair, same face, but his eyes were dark instead of pale. "Who are you?"

"Discord Jones. Why do you look just like Thorandryll?"

The elf lowered his bow a few inches. "He is my brother. You're human."

"That's what I keep telling everyone."

"What is a human doing in the company of two shifters? And in Unseelie lands?"

"Freezing my butt off at the moment. Mind if I stand up?"

"Slowly." He watched me, while his hound watched Logan and Connor.

"Thorandryll's never mentioned a brother." I dusted snow from my coat. "What's your name?"

"Kethyrdryll. How do you know my brother?"

"He hired me to solve a problem."

Kethyrdryll stared. "He hired a human to handle something for him? How do I know you're telling the truth?"

"Why would I lie about that? He gave me a hound, too."

"Which hound?"

"I don't want him here until I need him. Wherever here is. Unless this is your sidhe?" Had we made it home after all? "Wait. You said Unseelie lands. Who or what are they?"

Kethyrdryll raised his bow. "How can you know my brother, but not who the Unseelie are?"

"Because I apparently didn't read enough fairy tales before the Melding. Would you please put that bow down before someone loses an eye or something?'

"No. You are the first people I've seen in," he hesitated. "Quite some time, and you are not Unseelie."

I sighed. "I asked nicely."

"You did," Logan agreed.

"I've blown up a god. You're not going to be much trouble, dude. Put the damn bow down, now." I glared at the elf. The hound crept forward. "Stop right there, pup. I don't want to hurt anyone, but I will if you try to hurt us first."

Leandra froze and sniffed several times. *"She smells of my son."*

"You're Leg... uh, his mother?"

"Who are you talking to?"

"Your hound. Long story, but I can understand dogs. And hounds." How could she be Leglin's mother? "He said he was three..."

Kethyrdryll lowered his bow. "Hounds are quite intelligent, but they aren't skilled with tracking time."

"Oh."

"You said something about the Melding?"

"Yeah." I glanced at Logan and Connor. "We're cold, hungry, and he's injured. Do you have shelter nearby? I'll be happy to answer what questions I can, once we're out of the cold."

"What's the name of my brother's personal healer?"

"Alleryn, and he's my friend. A good friend."

The elf nodded, putting his arrow away. "Follow me."

FOURTEEN

His camp wasn't far away, and was surrounded by a tall, thorny barrier. When Kethyrdryll touched it, the vines or whatever parted, forming a tunnel.

"I offer you hospitality," he said. I glanced at Logan, who nodded. Connor was still out, and Logan had him over one shoulder.

"Thank you." I followed the elf into the tunnel. It wasn't long, maybe six feet. His shelter was a pavilion, divided into two parts. One had hangings across the door, the other didn't.

A white horse stood in that side, covered with a blanket and eating hay.

"Where'd you get hay?"

"I always travel prepared." Kethyrdryll pulled back one of the door hangings. "Please come in."

We did, and I blinked, because the pavilion was definitely bigger on the inside. Elves apparently knew a few Time Lord tricks. Or maybe Time Lords had learned elf tricks. Or elves were the seed idea for that series? I shook my head. *Focus, Cordi.* "Nice place."

"Thank you." He gestured to an opening on the left. "You can lay your companion in there. He is healing?"

"Yes, thanks." Logan carried Connor through the opening and I followed to look. It was a room with a comfy-looking cot. Logan bent, easing Connor onto it; I stepped forward to help remove the younger shifter's boots and jacket.

"How long before he's better?"

"Pierced some organs. Maybe a day."

Kethyrdryll brought in a tray. It held a bowl of steaming water, some clean cloths, and a glass jar. "The salve will help."

We cleaned Connor from the waist up and Logan applied the salve. After he was done, he laid the last clean cloth over the wound and I covered the younger man with a blanket before we left the room.

"If you wish to wash, the bathing chamber is through there." Kethyrdryll gestured to the back of the pavilion, past the short, rectangular table and chairs in the center of the main room. "Clean clothing will be waiting."

I noticed four chairs. Had there been four when we had first walked in? "Bathing chamber? Like, a tub with hot water?"

He smiled. "Yes."

"Oooh." I took a step before looking at Logan. "You go first."

Logan shook his head. "I can wait."

"Are you sure?"

"I'm sure. Go ahead."

"Thanks." I untied the belt of my coat and shrugged out of it. Logan took it, and I hurried to the section of hangings Kethyrdryll had indicated. Slipping through them, I had to stop and stare. It was a smallish room, but there was a large, raised, blue marble tub, a toilet behind an ornately carved wooden screen, and a counter with a sink, its marble matching the tub. A towel and the promised clothing waited. I liked the elven idea of camping a lot right that moment. "Jackpot."

Kethyrdryll pulled out a chair for me and I sat, feeling like a princess in the red dress I wore. My feet were warm for the first time since we'd arrived in the wintry realm. The thigh-high stockings were nice, but I really loved the soft, over-the-knee, dark green boots. "Thank you."

"Wine?"

"Um. Do you have hot tea?"

"Of course." A teapot, delicate china cup, and sugar bowl appeared on the table before me.

"Is the food magic?"

Kethyrdryll chuckled quietly. "No, but it has been magically stored to ensure it does not go to waste."

"Oh." I poured and added sugar, taking a sip before saying anything else. "All right. Who are the Unseelie?"

He sat down at the head of the table, to my right. "Our people are divided into two courts, Seelie and Unseelie."

"Light and dark, good and evil?"

"Life is never that simple, Lady Discord."

I nearly choked on my tea. "I'm not a lady with a capital L. Alleryn calls me Cordi."

"What does my brother call you?"

"Miss Jones."

His lips twitched. "I see. The Unseelie are the dark to our light, but they are not evil. They tend to certain... unpleasant matters. They handle duties that are necessary, but distasteful."

"Ah. They're the folks that get the job done, whatever it is. Okay." I tilted my head. "They're not dark elves, though?"

"The dark ones were annihilated centuries ago, and they were renegades from both courts who turned to forbidden magics." He paused. "How do you even know of them?"

"Your annihilation missed one. Dalsarin. He's dead now. We helped your brother hunt him down. He was in cahoots with a god, Apep. That's the one I blew up."

Kethyrdryll blinked. "Interesting. You mentioned the Melding?"

"Yes, that's what the breaking of the Sundering is called." My turn to pause. "Uh, how long have you been here, and why are you here?"

"I was sent to discuss a sensitive matter with the Unseelie Queen. I did feel the shift of magical energies, but... it is always night here, and always winter. That makes it difficult to judge the passage of time for those of us who aren't Unseelie."

My eyes had gone wide. "Dude, the Melding happened almost eight years ago. You've been stuck here all that time?"

"Apparently so." Kethyrdryll shrugged it off with a faint smile. "The more important questions are why it closed the portal, and why no one has come to meet me."

My brain had quit at the knowledge he'd been sitting in one spot for years. I blinked. "Not everyone's territory came through, but the people did."

"Not the Unseelie," Logan said as he left the bath chamber. "Or if they did, they've been silent."

Kethyrdryll gestured at the chair to his right, and Logan sat across from me.

"Does that mean we're stuck here, too? Forever? I don't want to be stuck in an endless winter night forever. My dogs need me. The clan needs you."

Logan held up his hands to stop my babbling.

"You're tired."

"Yes, but I'd be panicking even if I wasn't."

Logan smiled. "Don't panic. We have towels."

I had to laugh. "Right. Everything will be fine because we have towels."

"I'm afraid I don't understand why towels are a source of comfort," Kethyrdryll said, and I began laughing again.

Once started, it took me a while to stop, and the elf's concerned questions about hysteria and other ailments didn't help. Neither did Logan's fight to keep from laughing with me, as his face contorted into expressions that tickled my funny bone even more.

At last, I managed to stop, wiping my eyes on a linen napkin as exhaustion weighed down my body. "Sorry. Had to vent."

"It's okay. Feel better?" Logan asked.

"Yes and no. I could sleep for days, but that's not going to help anything." I took a deep breath, and it escaped as a giggle.

"Perhaps a meal and rest is in order for all of us." Kethyrdryll snapped his fingers and dishes of food began appearing on the table. My teapot slid backward and a plate, fresh napkin, and silverware popped into existence in front of me. A bowl of broth appeared, too. I breathed in the steam, appreciating its garlicky fragrance. "Mm, real food."

"Is there another kind?"

"Yeah, it's called 'junk food'. I'll introduce you to it when we get home."

Logan aimed a smile across the table. "There's the Cordi I know."

"A hot meal is guaranteed to bring her out," I said. We began eating, and my stomach jumped for joy at being filled with something besides breakfast bars.

"Is my brother doing well?"

I swallowed. "As far as I know. He's healthy and irritating. Elves played a major part in talking sense to everyone after the Melding."

"What was it like?"

"No clue. I conked out at midnight and was in a coma for three years."

Kethyrdryll's gaze sharpened. "You slept that long?"

"Yes."

"And you gained much power."

I finished my soup. "How do you know that?"

"The Sundering drew most magic away from the human realm, but there were humans who were born into magic. You're descended from one of those families if you slept and woke with power enough to 'blow up a god'."

"Oh." Made sense. "I'm not the only one."

"Of course not. It's highly unlikely those families would all have died out, as often as humans breed. But did any others sleep as long?"

"I hold the coma record, as far as Alleryn knows. He worked at the hospital, and helped me a lot after I woke." Which reminded me I had a lot of questions about that for the mahogany-haired elf.

"And you're one of my brother's people."

"Uh, no. I'm one of his." I tilted my head toward Logan. "People. The clan adopted me. I work for your brother sometimes, when he needs a private investigator."

"She's employed by Lord Whitehaven," Logan said.

"Ah. I begin to understand. Interesting. And she is a queen of your clan, as well." Kethyrdryll's dark blue eyes twinkled. "I'll wager that discomfits my brother greatly."

The soup bowls disappeared, replaced by some sort of baked fish drizzled with a pale red sauce. Wine-based, I decided after trying a bite. "Thorandryll thinks I'm stupid."

"Beg pardon?"

"He keeps trying stuff." I wasn't going to admit I still had to fight the hazies around the Prince. "People don't try to overwhelm other people unless they want something."

"You're wise for someone so youthful."

But not brave enough to have a private "come to Jesus" meeting with Thorandryll. Yet. It would happen one day. Maybe even one day soon. "More like I don't think a mere human can compete with his high opinion of himself."

Logan snickered and the elf chuckled. "My brother can be a bit, ah, arrogant."

A bit? Oodles. I concentrated on the fish and its rather spicy sauce.

"Hey." Connor staggered out of his room. "There's food."

Logan jumped up to help him over to the table. Connor kept his hand over his side, grimacing as he sat in the last remaining chair. "Who's he?"

"Our host, Lord Kethyrdryll."

"Oh. Thanks for the bed." Dinnerware appeared in front of him, and Connor sniffed the fish. "And this."

"You're quite welcome."

Kethyrdryll hadn't behaved like I would have expected of someone who looked so much like Thorandryll. I watched him separate a piece of fish from the serving on his plate and give it to Leandra, who'd lain by his chair at some point. She took the tidbit as gently as Leglin always did.

I missed my hound.

The elf was being much nicer to the two shifters than I'd ever seen Thorandryll be. Even Alleryn used a snooty tone when speaking to Logan. Maybe Kethyrdryll was glad to have company, and didn't care who it was?

Connor looked up from his plate. "How'd we get here? What happened after that thing stabbed me?"

"Logan tromped it." I grinned at him. "Then I tried to teleport us home, but we kind of hit something and came out here. Well, not here, here, but not too far away."

"Here is good for now." Connor speared the last of his fish.

"We're in Unseelie land," Logan said.

The other looked up at him. "Here is not good. We weren't invited."

Kethyrdryll spoke. "I was, and since the lady undertakes certain tasks for my brother, I'll claim responsibility for you all. Of course, no one has come, and I don't think anyone will."

I stopped Connor by raising my hand. "We're saving discussion for tomorrow, after a good night's sleep. Tonight's plan is to eat and rest. There's a bathroom. With a tub, in case you need help with that."

Dinner over, we retired to separate rooms. Mine looked exactly like the one we'd put Connor in: smallish, and furnished only with a cot. The lighting was magical, because I couldn't find a source by scanning the ceiling. The only obvious difference was a folded nightgown at the foot of the cot.

I changed, and Ginger startled me by walking through the outer wall. We stared at each other for a long moment before I sat on the cot. For the first time outside of nightmares, I spoke to her. "Where've you been?"

She cocked her head, her gaze dropping to my lips. "You missed all the fun."

Maybe the cold had kept her away. No, wait, she hadn't had any trouble appearing outside while I drove around the city. Boy, that felt like ages ago. "What do you want? An apology?"

Ginger squatted, still staring at my mouth. Would an apology send her away? Apologizing hadn't worked when I was asleep. "I thought I was doing what you wanted. I didn't know he made you tell me all those horrible things. If I could take it back, I would."

She shot to her feet and began capering around the room. I watched her for a few minutes before muttering, "So much for that idea."

Ginger continued her wild dancing as I slipped into bed, and the light slowly dimmed down to full darkness.

I really was losing it.

FIFTEEN

"I was leaving the restroom." Connor helped himself to another slice of ham.

"And we were about to leave the employee break room. Now we know the portal thingy doesn't have a fixed point in the Dreamland pocket realm." I made a note on my legal pad. It and a couple of pens were items I'd decided to keep in my case purse. There'd been too many times I'd needed to jot something down to keep from forgetting it, and had nothing handy.

"Okay, how did you get here? You said you were invited."

Kethyrdryll nodded. "Yes. I entered through the arch in the gardens."

"In Thorandryll's sidhe?"

"Yes."

Now I knew where it led. I'd seen it during my first case for his brother. That had been one of the things I'd meant to ask about, and had forgotten. "I know where it is."

"It's not the only entrance to the Unseelie realm. It is, or was, our doorway. A few days after I arrived, it closed." Kethyrdryll paused for a drink of juice. "I check daily to see if it's reopened, which is why I was there when you three arrived."

"And you've been here, alone, for eight years."

The elf stroked his hound's head. "I haven't been alone, with Leandra and Selwin as my companions."

Selwin was the horse's name. Check.

Connor reached for another slice of ham, and I frowned at him. "Dude, slow down."

"There's no need to worry about supplies. My pavilion's well-stocked."

After eight freaking years? I wanted some of that magic for my new kitchen. Connor stuck his tongue out at me, and I said, "Brat."

Looking at my notes, I said, "If no one's come to meet you, something's happened to them. Have you tried to find out what?"

"The inner defenses are still in place. Invited or not, I'm not allowed to pass them freely, and the first isn't one I felt I would be able to safely defeat without assistance."

"Okay." I sighed. "This is what we know. The Unseelie realm went into lockdown mode when the Melding occurred. You haven't seen hide nor hair of any of them since you got here. Did you ever have to wait on prior visits?"

"Not longer than a day."

But he'd waited a few days this time, and ended up stuck. "I'm thinking something must have happened right before the Melding, which kept the Unseelie busy."

No one disagreed with my assessment. Cool. "Next item is that Santo Trueno is having its first real winter in years, and people started going missing. And both of those things tie into Thorandryll's club, Dreamland. It's new, it's a pocket realm, and it's where the people, including us, went missing from."

I paused for a drink of my tea, wishing for coffee. "Third item we now know is that the Dreamland pocket realm has an intermittent connection with another one."

"You mean the Unseelie realm." Connor raised his eyebrows when I shook my head.

"I don't think so. We weren't here. We were...on the other side of the mountains from here, and I think it's a different pocket realm. I mean, there was nothing alive there, except the golem and those snow gremlins. One was sent to grab drop ins, and the others apparently wanted to kill anyone or anything that intruded."

Logan nodded. "A buffer zone."

"Yeah. I think maybe it's part of the lockdown mode. Whatever happened must be really bad, if a large number of elves couldn't handle it. And we have to find out what happened, if we want to go home."

Kethyrdryll lifted his hand from the table to get my attention. "I mentioned the security measures are still in place. They are the reason I've always waited for an escort. Even should we successfully pass them, the castle itself will oppose our entry."

"One problem at a time. First problem: an escort. Problem solved, because we're it." I smiled at him. "How far do we have to go?"

His gaze fell to the table top and he frowned. "I'm not certain. The last time I visited, it was a matter of a few hours to reach the castle, with an Unseelie escort."

"You said it's always night," Logan said. "Does that mean the moon doesn't move?"

"I've never seen it change position."

"Then it's a fixed point of reference. Do you know which direction we have to travel to reach the castle?"

Kethyrdryll's frown had faded. "Yes."

"So we have a compass." Logan looked at me. "And you're the backup compass."

"If my tracking ability cooperates."

"You're a Tracker?" the elf asked. "That's an extremely rare power."

"I prefer to call them abilities. Sounds less magical. And I don't know if it's the same thing you mean. I sometimes see colored threads that led me to useful clues, or lost objects and people."

"Yes, you're a Tracker." He studied me for a moment. "Exactly how many pow...abilities do you have?"

"More than I know what to do with, and enough to make things confusing."

Kethyrdryll chuckled. "I do not ask in order to pass the information on. We discussed the families I knew of last night. Each had certain specialties. I'm curious which family you're descended from."

"Oh." Now I was a little curious too.

"Can you call fire or ice to hand?"

"Both."

"Wind?"

I blinked, reassessing my aerokinetic ability. "I can thicken air. Never thought of trying to create wind though."

"Hear the thoughts of others, or feel their emotions?"

"Both."

Kethyrdryll's gaze sharpened, and he leaned forward the tiniest bit. "See the past or future?"

"The first, a lot, but the second, only once that I'm certain of."

He smiled. "Do you have visions when you touch objects or people?"

"Yes."

"Can you call lightning?"

"Yeah, and that one's new."

"Move objects?"

"Yes."

"You're a Tracker and can teleport." Kethyrdryll gave a slight shake of his head. "You are truly remarkable, Lady Discord, and quite right to be wary of my brother's interest. You're descended from each of the great families who were natural mages."

"I'm a psychic, not a mage. Or a witch."

"That may well be what humans call you, but your kind were known as natural mages in the past. You don't need spells, potions, or the favor of gods to work your magic. Yours comes from within."

My mouth felt dry. "Psychic sounds a lot less scary."

Kethyrdryll laughed. "Legends would have it that your kind are the children of the gods."

Okay, now he was trying to put one over on me. "Yeah, right."

"Have you heard of Herakles?"

"Hercules? Yeah, he was the son of Zeus and," I paused. "He's just a myth."

"No, he was quite real, and he was a natural mage."

Whoa. Me, descended from gods? My turn to laugh. "If what you're saying is true, it's been thousands of years since all that god and human hanky-panky was going on. Pretty sure any god blood would be way diluted by now."

"Yet, you have many abilities." The elf's smile disappeared. "Have you died?"

I had to clear my throat as cold spread down my spine. "Once."

"Your injuries heal more quickly than other humans." It wasn't a question.

"Yes."

"I now have far more confidence we'll survive the trek to the castle," Kethyrdryll said.

And I had a bad feeling I'd just learned the reason why Sal had begun visiting me.

"Are you sure she can carry us both?" I petted Selwin's white neck.

"For hours and hours." Kethyrdryll tightened the cinch. "Give me a moment to break camp."

"Sure." I walked over to Logan and Connor, who were both going to travel in their animal shapes, and had already shifted. Logan could handle the snow and ice, but Connor had admitted to feeling a little cold. "Let me check the straps."

The lion chuffed, holding still while I looked over the straps and buckles holding the horse's blanket in place. "I hope you're toasty."

He coughed. I mussed his mane and moved to Logan's side. "Are you okay?"

I'm fine. You?

"Great." The elf's invisible servants had provided warm clothing in the form of boots, thick socks, and leggings that felt like silk, but were thick and waterproof. I also had a long shirt of the same material, a handy leather belt, and gloves. My tiger coat covered most of the outfit, but that was okay. It'd cover most of Selwin's rump too, and hold in the heat she generated.

I turned around as the elf spoke a few words, and my jaw dropped as the pavilion collapsed. It folded itself into a neat, extremely small square. The thorn barrier was shrinking and contracting, to become less than a handful of tangled, dried brown vine.

Kethyrdryll picked them both up and dropped them into the pouch at his belt. "Are you ready, Lady Discord?"

"Sure." I'd tried to discourage the "Lady" business, but he insisted.

He mounted the horse, freed his boot from the stirrup, and leaned to offer his arm. My ascent was easier than I expected, but I did have to make a few minor adjustments to the skirt of my coat once behind him.

Leandra fell in beside us as Kethyrdryll nudged the mare into a walk. Connor and Logan trotted past to take the lead. We were on our

way to find the Unseelie, and I had to grin
My life was just one giant adventure.

SIXTEEN

Bright moonlight and a lack of clouds meant Connor stuck out like a sore thumb on the snow. It was obvious Logan had loads more experience in snowy terrain and at night, from the way he moved alongside the trail, under the shadows of the trees.

There were times I couldn't see him, even though his fur was mostly black and should've been more noticeable against the blue white of the snow.

However, Connor was watching the older shifter, and learning as he went. I liked the guy. He wasn't saddled with a giant ego. We rode for a few hours before coming to a wide, slow-moving river. Kethyrdryll brought his mare to a halt. "Our first obstacle."

"How deep is it?"

"I don't know. I chose not to attempt crossing due to the inhabitants." He raised his voice. "I wouldn't venture too close."

Logan and Connor veered away from the riverbank, and came to join us.

"Okay, what are we up against? Cold water piranhas? Ice sharks?"

"Winter drakes. Fortunately, the wingless variety, but they're vicious beasts."

"Oh. Um, what's a drake?"

Kethyrdryll threw his leg over the horse's neck and slid down. "I'll show you."

My dismount wasn't as graceful, but I didn't fall on my butt. The elf walked to a point about thirty feet from the river's edge, and bent to dig around in the snow. He straightened with a fist-sized rock in his hand. "Watch."

When he threw the rock, I followed its path and jumped as a large, pale blue head shot upward from the water to catch it. The drake's head was easily as long as I was tall, with a mouthful of sharp teeth.

It smashed the rock to bits before turning to strike at us. Kethyrdryll had judged the distance well, so its attempt fell a good five feet short of us. It had flippers instead of legs. The front half of its body hit the bank, making the ground shake.

"Too heavy to move well on solid ground," he said as the drake whipped its head back and forth, its flippers sending snow and other debris flying. The drake had a hard time pushing itself back into the water.

I nodded, watching its long-snouted head slip under the water. "Okay. My first thought is to teleport, but considering what happened last time, I'd rather not risk it."

"Spells of transport do have a way of going awry in this reality."

"Next would be telekinesis, but," I squinted at the far bank, "I've never tried to move anything that far."

"Ice."

"Yeah." I sighed. "I'll try to freeze a bridge across it."

It would be tricky. The "bridge" needed to be thick enough to hold us, and to keep from breaking under the weight of an attacking drake. It would also need to be wide enough for us to stay out of reach while crossing.

The river was a half-mile or more wide. I was going to have to freeze a lot of water. "Is there a spot where it's not so wide?"

"I'm afraid not, however, I may be of some assistance. My spell repertoire for ice and water isn't extensive, but I can distract the drakes."

"Okay. You do that and I'll work on bridge building. I don't know how long it'll hold, though."

He studied the river's flow. "Take yourself, Leandra, and your companions across as soon as it's ready. I'll ride."

I knew from experience elf-bred horses were fast, and agreed. "There's our plan, then."

We'll mark where the sides should be, Logan said. I nodded.

"It might take a while. I've never tried to freeze anything this big. I'll hurry as much as I can."

"Leandra, stay with Lady Discord," Kethyrdryll ordered. The hound responded with a single nod of her head.

"All right, guys, let's do this." I waited, chewing my bottom lip, while the three men moved into position, Kethyrdryll leading his horse down to the bank. Tiger and lion coughed and chirped until they'd found the right spots, about thirty feet apart.

The elf climbed on his horse and rode another thirty feet past Logan. He was too far away for me to hear his incantation, but I could see his hands move. A whirlwind grew into existence, sucking up snow, which became clumps. With a swing of his arm, the elf directed the whirlwind toward the river. He began calling a second one as the first flung snowballs over the water.

The river churned, drakes rushing to the disturbance. I waited until it calmed in the correct area before beginning to concentrate.

Was six feet of ice thick enough? I had no clue, and was acutely aware our lives depended on my getting it right the first time. There wouldn't be a do-over.

The water froze along the bank. I turned from side to side, making certain it reached both shifters, then froze another line against the first. Then another and another and another, before moving a few steps forward. The first six feet weren't bad, because of the slope of the riverbed.

It would be easier if I could touch the water. I glanced at the elf and the frenzied mass of drakes. There were a dozen or more of the creatures. All of them in this section?

No way to tell without scanning telepathically, and I'd already broken a sweat.

"Screw it." I walked down to the bank and tested the ice with one foot. It held firm. "Okay, Cordi, you can do this. Just a few fingers in the water."

Stripping off one glove, I went to my knees, then my stomach, stretching my arm toward the edge of the ice.

My fingers went numb the second I put them in the water. "Argh! That's frickin cold."

I took a deep breath and pushed with my cryokinetic ability in four directions. Both sides, down, and forward. The ice began to spread, and I closed my eyes, trying to envision what I wanted to build. I had to grit my teeth against the burn in my fingers as water froze around them.

After a few minutes, I opened my eyes to check my progress. It wasn't bad, about a third of the way across.

Kethyrdryll was continuing his job of keeping the drakes busy. I climbed slowly to my feet and started walking in wide circles, shaking my fingers to restore circulation.

Logan's voice sounded in my head. *Do you need us to keep marking the edges?*

"No, come on out. Be careful, though." If my bridge broke under their weight, at least they had a chance to make it to safety before the drakes noticed.

Reaching the edge of the river again, I knelt and put my fingers back in the water.

Even with contact, it was using a lot of energy to freeze so much water. I began sweating in earnest.

By the time the shifters reached me, I'd frozen the second third of my bridge. "We might need to camp early. This is wearing me out."

Logan purred, stepping close as I stood up. *Need a lift?*

"Thanks, but I'd better walk ahead and test." My incomplete bridge was swaying slightly right, with the current. "And I need to hurry, before the middle breaks off."

Okay. He said something to Connor in big-cat speak and the lion nodded. They followed me at a distance of ten feet as I jogged forward.

"Final phase." I knelt and touched the water again, hoping I didn't end up with frost bite.

Dizziness struck when I rose, and I staggered forward, wishing I were home in front of the fireplace, with a big mug of hot chocolate with tiny marshmallows floating on it. The shifters caught up with me. I threw an arm over each pair of shoulders. "I'm tired."

They kept me upright, walking me the rest of the way and a safe distance from the bank.

I'll be back, Logan said, and trotted away.

Connor purred as I pulled on my glove while leaning against him. We watched Logan as he stopped where Kethyrdryll would notice him. The elf sent a final snowball-laden whirlwind over the river and turned his horse before urging her into a gallop.

He'd reached the middle of the bridge when Logan yowled, drawing the drakes' attention. A few swam over to try to attack the tiger, but the rest disappeared under the water.

I focused on the elf. "Come on. Go faster."

The mare stumbled three quarters of the way across when a drake slammed into the ice bridge. She skidded forward on her knees, back legs slowing.

Kethyrdryll didn't miss a beat, throwing the reins over her head and leaping out of the saddle. The ice bridge shuddered under a second impact, and a drake lunged out of the water, snapping at the elf.

Ice groaned, creaked, and cracked under the pair.

"Crap!" I tried to refreeze that section, but the drake's ungainly thrashing caused more cracks. "Run!"

Kethyrdryll snatched hold of the reins and pulled. Selwin lunged to her feet, blood dripping down her forelegs.

She tried, but her stiff-legged jog wasn't fast enough as the cracks spread. Kethyrdryll hauled on the reins, pulling her as the drake wallowed closer.

I hit it with a blow of telekinesis, knocking its head away so it missed the mare's hind quarters by inches.

Logan rushed past us, turned, his hind paws skidding, and bounded out onto the ice.

The cracks were spreading. The horse stepped in one with a hind hoof, her head jerking up and yanking Kethyrdryll off his feet.

A second drake surged out of the water, and ice broke under its weight. The mare's hind quarters slipped into the water, and the elf howled her name.

I ran, concentrating, and lifted her to more solid footing. Logan reached them, snarling and rearing to slash at the drake's face. He scored and the beast roared.

"Come on," I yelled, blinking at the bright dots threatening to blind me. Leandra barked, cutting in front of me, and I tripped over her to face-plant in the snow.

It knocked the breath out of me. The hound grabbed the hood of my coat in her jaws and dragged me away from the riverbank. I managed to roll over and saw Kethyrdryll coaxing his horse the final few steps.

Logan was backing up, his tail lashing. I closed my eyes for a second, dragging in a painful lungful of air before re-opening them.

Just as the center of my ice bridge broke and a third drake shot out of the water on the far side. It landed right behind Logan, breaking the ice underneath them.

Drakes and tiger fell into the water.

The elf yelled out an incantation, dropping his reins and rushing back toward the riverbank. Connor roared as he ran past. Leandra kept dragging me backward. "Let go."

She ignored me. I spotted Logan's head as it broke the surface, and an arrow flew over it, landing in a drake's eye as the monster loomed over the tiger.

"Swim!" I screamed and tried to gather enough energy to use my telekinesis. Kethyrdryll was firing arrows one after another, each thunking into the drake's face.

Connor roared, trying to distract the drakes while standing at the river's edge.

Logan reached a chunk of ice and clawed his way half onto it.

All I could manage was a wimpy TK boost, lifting him fully onto the ice chunk. But it wasn't too far from the river bank. He'd have to jump.

Logan crouched, his ears flat, and a breath later, leaped. At the apex of his jump, a smaller drake burst out of the water and nabbed him.

Both disappeared and I lay there, unable to process what had happened for a second.

I sat up, frantically searching the river's surface. Connor retreated, slinking toward me with his mouth open, deep moans rolling out of him.

Kethyrdryll was looking too, and still firing arrows at the drakes showing their heads above the surface. One by one, the creatures retreated, sinking below the water.

Everything was quiet.

Logan was gone.

"Cordi." Connor squatted down and held out a steaming mug. "Soup."

"Thanks." I burned my tongue on the first sip. "How's the horse?"

"Kethyrdryll is wrapping her legs, says she'll be fine in a day or two."

"Good." We could stay put until then, in case Logan came back. I stared at the river and shivered.

"You should come in where it's warm."

"Can't move. My legs went to sleep ten minutes ago." I petted Leandra's head, and she responded with a faint tail wag. The hound lay across my thighs, and my back was against the trunk of a tree. I had a great view of the water as it sparkled under the moonlight between breaks in the clouds.

Connor quietly said, "I'm sorry. This is my fault."

"No, it's not. You weren't the only person we were looking for, and none of us chose to get swallowed by that damn portal."

He turned and dropped onto his butt, to look at the river. "You think he's alive."

"I'm not going to believe he's dead unless I see his body." Or parts of it. My stomach considered returning the soup. I convinced it not to, because the rest of me really needed food. My headache had faded, thanks to a draught of some pain remedy Kethyrdryll had on hand.

The elf had dropped to one knee and kissed my hand for helping to save his horse. She'd been one of only two friends he'd had for eight years.

I thought he'd say something more, but he'd risen and set up camp, leaving the thorn barrier open on its river-facing side. He'd also brought me a leather cloak and a cushion to use while I kept watch.

"If there's anything left to see, it'll come up miles downstream." Connor's hands flexed on his legs. "Do you want me to go look?"

The first fat snowflakes began falling while I considered his offer. I looked at the sky, filling up with dirty gray clouds, and shook my head. "I promised your dad I'd bring you home. Be hard to do if you fall into the river in the middle of a blizzard, or freeze to death."

"Be hard to do if you sit out here and freeze to death," he said. "You should come inside."

"In a little bit." I drank more soup, and kept watching the river until the snowfall grew too heavy to see that far.

Leandra stood and shook, snuffled at my face, and left us for the pavilion. Connor had to help me to my feet. He grabbed the cushion and cloak before putting an arm around my waist. My legs wobbled the first few steps, feeling heavy and useless before blood began circulating. "Ow, that hurts. Don't let a hound use you for a pillow."

"Can't say I see it happening."

We stopped to peek in at the horse, who raised her head from a big pile of hay and softly nickered, stretching her neck to hold out her nose for us to pet. "I'm glad you're okay."

A few more pats and we went inside. Kethyrdryll was sitting at the table, gazing into his bowl of soup. He looked up and jumped to his feet when he saw us. "Are you injured?"

"No, Leandra's heavy and used my legs for pillows. I'll be fine in a few more minutes." I patted Connor's hand and hobbled to the table under my own power. "The soup's good. You should eat yours."

"Of course." The elf sat down again.

"If no one minds, I'm going to take a bath," Connor said. We didn't mind and he left the main room.

"There's no sign of him?"

I shook my head. "Not yet. Can I ask you a question?"

"Certainly."

"Why are you nice to them? Your brother likes to pretend they don't exist, and Alleryn's kind of snooty to them."

"They're people."

"I don't think Thorandryll thinks so."

He half-smiled. "My brother has a fragile ego."

That pulled a laugh from me. He didn't join in. "Wait. You're serious?"

"Thorandryll appears confident, but appearances can be deceiving. He dislikes shifters because when he was young, not even into his third decade, a human woman he fancied chose a shifter over him."

"Ouch. And then his wife," I hesitated when Kethyrdryll raised his eyebrows. "He told us about Dalsarin and her."

"I'm surprised."

I leaned back to untie the belt of my coat. "And then there was Carole, but you can ask him for details. All I'm going to say is she did him dirty."

Kethyrdryll shook his head. "He's been singularly unlucky in love. It's why he ... 'does stuff,' I believe was the way you put it."

New view of Prince Snooty Pants, and I wasn't sure I liked it. "He'd be more likeable if his ego weren't in overdrive."

"Perhaps. Selwin will be healed and ready to travel in roughly two night's time. I must ask what your plans are now."

I took a deep breath. "We keep going. If Logan ... he'll find us when he can."

"You care greatly for him."

"He's my friend, and clan."

"More than that."

"Yes." I had no intention of elaborating because I'd think about our lunch, and the kisses, and start crying. If I cried, I'd be admitting he was dead.

Logan hadn't given up on me when Dalsarin had turned me into a dog, or when Merriven tore my neck open. I wasn't giving up on him. It had been a smaller drake than the others. Maybe a baby or a runt adult. Shifters were tough, and Logan was strong.

Kethyrdryll gazed at me for a few seconds before changing the subject. "More soup?"

SEVENTEEN

I expected a visit from Sal once I'd gone to bed and fallen asleep, but he didn't drop in, and that was worrisome. The little god always showed when a case led to mortal peril.

Instead, I dreamed of walking around the empty rooms of my new house, and of climbing the ladder to the attic. The attic was gone, and I stood there with my head just above the river's surface, face to face with a drake. Its breath smelled like rotting fish, and fresh, bloody furrows marred its snout and neck.

"Where is he?"

The drake opened its mouth wide, and it made all the sense in the world to climb in. Once I had, the creature closed its mouth and swallowed. I went rushing down its throat, which felt and looked like one of the covered slides at a water park. The slippery ride ended when I landed on a concrete floor in front of Logan's car.

The headlights came on, and the engine purred. I stood and realized the car was empty, but the driver's door was open in silent invitation. No sooner than I slid behind the wheel, the door slammed shut and the car was driving across snow-covered terrain, more snow falling from a dark sky.

"He's dead, Miss Jones," Thorandryll said. I glanced over to find the elf in the passenger seat. He wore all black. "We will mourn the passing of the black tiger in due time."

"The car knows where he is. The drake told it."

"Hungry mouths spew lies." Thorandryll had a dagger. He sliced the dash and blood spilled from the cut. "You should be more concerned about the darkness."

"The way is lit," I said, looking out the front windshield at the twin beams of light. "There's always light at the end of tunnels."

"Unless it's night." Thorandryll made another slice in the dash, freeing more blood. "This is perpetual night."

"You carry your own light, Discordia," Mr. Whitehaven said from the back seat, his eyes glowing red in the rearview mirror. "Your own fire."

"You're going to get yourself killed." Nick leaned forward from his seat beside my boss. "How many have to die before you understand?"

"Understand what?" I shivered and looked down at the floorboard. Blood covered my feet and moved higher.

"People like you need cages."

"I won't live in a cage."

"A cage will keep you from hurting others." Nick sat back and faded from sight.

"How many have you hurt?" Thorandryll asked, carving more lines in the dash. "How many have died because of you?"

"She wanted to live. To be young and beautiful forever," Merriven whispered in my ear. I looked in the rearview mirror to meet Mr. Whitehaven's gaze.

He smiled. "You can control the very elements with naught but a thought. Hear and influence the thoughts of others. Rather terrifying, isn't it?"

The blood had reached the tops of the car seats, starting to creep up my thighs, and it was freezing cold.

"It's because of you I live in fear." Betty had taken Thorandryll's place. "You're dangerous. My children are going to die because of you." She stabbed the dagger into the dash. "I'm going to die because of you."

"No, I won't let that happen." Dark shapes appeared, running beside the car. Wolves.

"How's the maze-building going?" Jo asked, and walls of ice shot up on either side of the car's path. The wolves edged closer, their eyes gleaming gold and orange and yellow.

Mr. Whitehaven was gone. My witch buddy grinned from the back seat. David sat beside her with his nose buried in a book.

"Have you been practicing?" Jo waggled her eyebrows, then lifted a cup from our favorite coffee shop. "New blend."

The hot scent filled the car, nutty, rich, and slightly sweet. I looked down to find the blood had reached my waist. "We're going to drown."

"Drowning's better than being eaten by wolves," David muttered, pushing up his glasses. "Look at those teeth."

The car turned right, fishtailing around the corner. Its rear panel struck a wolf, knocking the animal into the ice wall with a sickening thump.

"Nasty creatures, they are. Vicious and greedy." Thorandryll had returned. Betty was gone. "You can't trust those who wear two shapes."

A steady sound came from outside, not quite a flapping noise, but close. I leaned forward to peer through the windshield at the sky. A large, pale shape flew above the car.

"Dragon," David remarked. "Interesting creatures. Not many of them left."

The dragon flew higher, disappearing from sight, and the car slowed to a halt. I sat back, blood rippling from the movement. It was chest-high now.

"You have reached your destination. Please exit the vehicle and have a nice night," a robotic female voice said. The wall in front of the car had a door set in it.

"What are you waiting for?" Thorandryll asked, holding out the dagger. "Take this, Miss Jones. You'll need it."

"Thank you." The blade was warm and pulsed in my hand. "It's alive."

"Not for much longer," Jo said. "Better hurry, Cordi."

Wolves swirled around the car. "Are they going to kill me?"

The car door opened and the blood poured out. My head turned and I met the amused gaze of a green-eyed man with antlers rising from the top of his head. "The Hunt can't begin without you, child. Come with me."

"Where?" I climbed out of the car, ignoring my blood-soaked clothes and the circling wolves.

"Through the door."

I was in front of the door without having walked to get there. "What's on the other side?"

"I don't know," Cernunnos replied. "Strange. I should know."

The door knob was silver, and warm to the touch. I opened it. There was nothing on the other side except darkness.

"Ah." Cernunnos chuckled. "You have to jump."

Clutching the dagger, I peered into the darkness. "There's nothing there."

"Of course there is. The night hides many things."

Someone grabbed my arm, pulling me away from the door. Nick stared at me, his eyes golden. "Things that want to kill you."

"All that live, die, and death clears the way for new life." Cernunnos threw back his head and bugled. Nick released his hold on me, turning into a wolf. "You're running out of time, child."

"Okay." I turned to face the doorway. "I can do this. I just wish I knew what 'this' was."

"Dummy," Ginger whispered. "You do this all the time. You did it with me."

My heart froze. "Did you want to die?"

She smiled, her skin turning gray, and collapsed into a pile of ashes.

"No time to waste." Cernunnos pointed at the doorway. "Choose to jump or choose to die."

The snarling of wolves filled my ears. I took a deep breath, two steps, and jumped. No ground met my feet. Wind howled. I fell and fell and fell.

Something brushed against me; light flickered. I saw tigers, prowling in a circle around me as I kept falling. "I'm clan. Help me."

They purred, the sound rising and falling. I slowed until I was floating. One by one, each tiger left the circle to look into my eyes.

"Human."

"Clan."

"Save her?"

A tiger snarled, breaking from the circle and rushing toward me. I held up the dagger and it veered away.

"Too human."

Another tiger left the circle, a white one with pale green eyes. She padded toward me. I let my arm drop.

"Become," she murmured before lunging. I fell backward as she struck and went through me.

No. Not through, but inside. My body twisted, my front paws hit first as the river appeared. I landed on the bank.

"You're not a normal girl, are you?"

I stretched, my claws extending, and yawned.

Mike the EMT stepped out of the shadows the trees cast. "You have really weird dreams, Discord Jones."

"Tell me about it." I started walking. He jogged to catch up.

"Got the call, but my ride is buried in a drift. Did you know there's things in the water? One ate my partner. Gobbled him right up."

"They do that."

"It's messed up. Don't let them gobble me."

"I won't."

We walked in silence for a minute or two, before he asked, "Why are you a tiger?"

"The ancestors are helping me because I'm clan."

"Helping you do what?"

"Find him."

"The guy we got the call about?" He stumbled and caught his balance. "It's too late for him. We came to pick up the body." Mike waved his arm. "The cold finished him."

"I still have to find him. We're clan." Far ahead I saw something dark lying partly in the river. "There he is."

"I'm not going that close to the water. You'll have to get him."

"Fine." I broke into a run, slowing as I reached the shape. Logan's eyes were closed, his body spattered with too-bright blood. I could count the holes left by the drake's teeth.

He didn't move when I nuzzled his shoulder. Walking to his other side, I opened my mouth and closed it gently around the back of his neck.

It felt like forever before I'd dragged him to the safety of the trees. Mike opened his bag and pulled out a stethoscope. "One of those things got him, huh?"

"Yes." I watched him move the stethoscope around.

The paramedic looked at me, his eyes wide. "I'll be damned."

"What?"

"He's still alive. Don't know if he'll stay that way for long. I'm not a vet."

"What do we do?"

Mike shook his head. "Try and warm him. I don't have a blanket big enough. He's a shifter. As long as he's warm and not hurt too much, he'll heal. It's cool how they can do that."

"Yeah." I lifted my forepaw and placed it on Logan's shoulder. He slowly shifted to human form. "Blanket?"

"You're really not normal." Mike pulled out a silver square from his bag. "Move."

He spread the blanket and rolled Logan onto it. "A shifter burrito. We need a source of heat."

I edged forward and lay next to Logan.

"Hugs make people happy." Mike faded away.

I pulled Logan closer with my paws, tugging him under my furry body.

"May all your hunts end so successfully." Cernunnos stood over us. "What are your intentions?"

I moved my head, tucking Logan's head between my chin and neck. "To save lives."

"Then you can't stay here. There are many lives at stake. You need to wake the Unseelie, and soon."

"I can't leave him."

The Horned Lord snorted. "I admire loyalty. I'll send another to watch over him."

"But..."

"I have spoken, child. You must wake them, before the others break the spell. Seek what's missed."

"Rico and the others."

"Not only those. Now. Wake." Cernunnos touched the tip of his forefinger to the spot right between my eyes.

My eyes popped open and I listened, hearing nothing. I was hugging a pillow and my head hurt. "Frigging gods."

Yet the dreams when Sal visited weren't ever chaotic or weird. Maybe it was just a dream, one my brain vomited out to soothe my guilt. I released the pillow and rolled onto my back. *Logan.*

No response. Blowing out a huff of air, I sat up to rub sleep from my eyes, the dream already fading. The hanging to my room rustled and moved. Kethyrdryll looked in, his face pale. "Selwin is gone."

We stood in the pavilion's doorway, watching the snow fly sideways as the wind whistled and moaned. The thorn barrier was barely visible, but we could see enough to know it wasn't open.

"If you have to open it, I don't see how the horse could get out,"

Connor said. "There's no blood. Nothing came in to attack her."

"Yet she's gone," the elf said, letting his side of the hanging fall. He touched Leandra's broad head and the hound whimpered. Patting her, he added, "We won't be able to travel as quickly now."

I left the doorway, Connor following. "Won't be going anywhere until this blizzard stops. We can't see the moon."

"She wasn't injured badly enough to die." Kethyrdryll crossed to the table and sat.

"There'd be a body." I dropped into my usual chair at his left, and massaged my temples. My headache was slowly improving.

"No, she would fade to nothing."

"Oh." A new bit of info I didn't care to learn. "Do hounds do that too?"

"Yes."

"How long do they live?"

"A very long time," he replied. "One of the oldest in our pack counts more than five centuries, now."

"Wow, Leglin's not even, oh, crap." My hand flew up to cover my mouth. I moved it enough to talk. "I wasn't calling him. It only works if I'm actually calling him, right?"

"They should only appear when intentionally called, yet you've gone missing. He may have heard you."

"Double crap." I scanned the room. "He's not here. Damn it, what if he did and he's stuck on the other side of the mountains?"

"You've called him once. Call him again. And a third time. If he responded, you don't want him crossing the river, and it'll bring him past if your second call doesn't."

I looked at the elf. "Do you know that for sure?"

"No more than I'm certain he heard you at all."

Argh. I hesitated, worried my hound was stuck somewhere, that I might dump him in the river, or bring him when he was safe at home because he hadn't heard me.

"Three is a magical number," Connor said. "Go ahead."

"Leglin." We all looked around. No hound. "Okay, one more time. Leglin."

Nothing happened. I sighed and reached for the waiting teapot. "He can't hear me. Good."

"Good? Wouldn't having another hound be better for us?" Connor sat down.

"He's safe at home, and he takes care of the other dogs. I like knowing he's safe."

"There is a bonus."

"What?"

Kethyrdryll smiled. "You're bound to him and he to you. As long as the jewel on his collar reflects that bond, others will know you're alive."

"They'll keep looking," Connor realized. "Yeah, that's a bonus."

"Can you bind a hound to more than one person?"

The elf shook his head. "No, but some do listen and respond to others they are fond of."

That was a new thing I didn't mind learning. "We should eat. Be ready to go in case the snow quits soon."

The snow didn't stop until much later, while we slept after a day spent fighting cabin fever, because we were all anxious to get away from the place of our losses.

EIGHTEEN

"What the hell is that?" I watched the creature strip another limb from a tree and stuff the greenery into its car-sized mouth. Crunch, crunch. Splinters and slobber sprayed. "It has perfectly awful table manners."

"A yeti."

"Oh. Now I know why they call it the Abominable Snowman." The yeti blinked its huge yellow eyes and smacked its rubbery lips, reaching for another limb. It resembled a gorilla in the face, with similarly long arms, as well. "Don't suppose it only eats trees?"

"Has fangs," Connor pointed. "It'll eat meat if it can catch some."

We all looked at the mile-wide, flat expanse before us, and then to either side. I sighed. "Guessing more yetis either way. Fun, fun, fun."

"Glamour."

"Huh?"

Kethyrdryll smiled. "I can create a glamour to hide us, though it won't hide our scents."

"It's a mile." Connor began undressing. "I can run that far, carrying you both, faster than Cordi can cross it on her own."

The elf nodded. "Physical contact will make holding the glamour in place less difficult."

Look at us, coming up with a simple sneaky plan. I kept my mouth shut, determined not to jinx it. Connor stripped, and I rolled his clothing together to make it easier to carry.

He shifted and laid down. I climbed on, holding his bundle of clothes in one arm, and burying my free hand in his mane.

"Wait until I say," Kethyrdryll cautioned him while sliding into place behind me. He didn't speak a spell, or even wiggle his fingers, but stayed still for a good five minutes. Finally, Kethyrdryll put his arms around my waist, and took hold of the lion's mane. "Go."

Connor slowly stood and began walking, Leandra pacing him. Within a few paces he was trotting, and a few more, he began to run, his body elongating and contracting under us. The hound had no trouble keeping up.

Grinning, I managed to keep from laughing, knowing the yeti would hear.

I was riding a lion in winter.

The crossing of open ground went as planned, to my surprise. I wondered if it was because I hadn't made or helped make the plan in any fashion. Connor passed through trees and I blinked. "What the ...?"

We were back where we started, in the far tree line, the yeti on our left enjoying his meal of tree limbs. The snowy expanse was clean, no sign of paw prints from our crossing.

"You've got to be kidding me. Game reset. Who does that?"

"The Unseelie," Kethyrdryll muttered. "We'll have to think of something different."

We slid off Connor's back, and I kicked at the snow.

"Bright side," Connor said after shifting back. I shoved his bundle of clothes at him. "Or maybe bright side. If their enchantments are working, doesn't that mean the Unseelie are still alive?"

The elf smiled. "Yes. Or at least some of them are."

"Great. It'd be nice if somebody noticed us and came to see what we want." I leaned against a tree trunk. "What are our options?"

"It's too big to kill." Connor had finished dressing. "Wounding it would probably make it angry."

"Right." We didn't want an angry yeti chasing us. "Do you have a spell to put it to sleep?"

Kethyrdryll shook his head. "No, but you could attempt that."

"Me?"

"Yes. You did say you feel what others feel, and can hear thoughts. Tell the yeti he's tired, and make him feel it."

"I've never done that before."

The elf regarded me. "You've never encouraged another's thoughts or emotions?"

I hedged. "Well ..."

"Lady Discord, I do appreciate the fact that you're young, and have only had your abilities for a short time. But the young have a tendency to be curious. To test things."

"Okay, fine. I've encouraged a few people not to be afraid. To be brave. But," I lifted my hand. "I only did it to get them out of trouble, and they wanted to be braver, less scared."

The men exchanged a look I didn't quite understand before Connor said, "That yeti looks exhausted to me."

"You better hope it's tired, because I don't know if I can make it do something it doesn't want to." I tightened the belt of my coat. "I have to get closer. Stay here."

I didn't worry about the yeti hearing snow squeak beneath my boots while I marched its direction. The creature couldn't hear that noise over its crunchy meal. Yet I did my best to stay out of sight and not make any louder noises. Once I'd drawn close enough, I sat under a tree and closed my eyes, needing to calm myself before touching the yeti's mind.

My nervousness wouldn't help. Neither would my doubt. We needed across, so I had to do this. After a few minutes of slow, deep breathing, I opened my eyes and a small window in my mental maze. The window belonged to the room where I'd housed my empathic ability.

Sal had given me some great advice, and I'd experimented, discovering it was a lot easier to use my active abilities if I compartmentalized them. Then I didn't have to worry another ability would jump in.

I let a tendril of empathy escape, and guided it toward the yeti.

The creature was content. Plenty of food to eat, no others to fight for the right to eat it, and no man-things had come in a long time, to poke sticks or make their shrill sounds that hurt its ears.

Fascinated, I added a touch of telepathy and gently dug into its memories. That took several minutes, but I found one where it hadn't attacked intruders.

Yay, I had a backup plan for us.

Carefully leaving its memories, I focused on my own and gathered a few of various times I'd been spectacularly tired. The yeti stopped chewing when I began to filter my remembered exhaustion into its mind. It began chewing again when a few seconds passed, but more slowly.

More chunks of wood and mashed pine needles fell from its mouth. The yeti swallowed and swiped the back of its hand across its mouth.

I increased the strength of my memories, upping the speed I sent them into the yeti's mind.

It made a weird sucking noise, and I grinned when I realized it was yawning. *That's right, you're really, really sleepy. A nap is a great idea.*

About ten minutes passed before the yeti lay on its side, snoring away. I punched the air with both fists before standing to hurry back to the others. "Okay, let's go."

We began walking across the open stretch and I kept glancing at the yeti. It continued snoring away, a few globs of mostly chewed food clinging to the corners of its lips.

Not a cute sight, but a reassuring one.

I bumped into Connor, and turned my head to see what he was staring at. Another yeti was ambling toward us from the opposite direction. "Keep walking."

"But ..."

I pushed him. "Keep walking. Don't run."

"We're going to die," he muttered, but began walking again. Kethyrdryll did too, Leandra beside him.

The hound's hackles were raised and quivering.

"No, we're not. Don't run, and don't attack it. Just keep walking." The second yeti was nearly on top of us. I raised my arm and yelled out the word I'd "heard" in the other yeti's memory.

It lifted its hand and stepped over us. Kethyrdryll laughed. He kept laughing until we reached the tree line, and there he bent over, really letting his hilarity flow.

"What's so funny?" I couldn't keep from smiling. Connor was chuckling.

Kethyrdryll looked up and gasped, "You told it 'hello' in Elvish, and it didn't attack."

My giggles bubbled up. "That was the secret password? Hello? Seriously?"

The elf caught his breath. "I'm certain our lack of panic was of assistance. That was brilliant, Lady Discord. Absolutely brilliant."

"Thank Sleepy, not me. He has pretty clear memories, and those are where I learned it from." I wiped my eyes, which had gone damp from suppressing the urge to laugh. "We still have to see if it worked. Come on."

We tramped ahead, and saw nothing but trees and more snow. "No reset. Awesome."

"Two challenges down."

"How many more?"

"At least one, and of course, there's the castle itself."

"Okay." We saved our breath for hiking after that.

The next challenge didn't present itself before I began stumbling. We'd walked for hours and miles, slogging through snow and ducking the occasional falling clump from overburdened tree limbs.

"Cordi needs to rest, and I'm hungry," Connor finally said. "We should make camp."

"Of course. We need to find a clear space."

That took another hour or so, and by then, my stomach was growling. At least making camp didn't take long. Kethyrdryll only had to put the pavilion square and little knot of dried vine on the ground, and "Abracadabra". We had shelter and a line of defense.

"Seems to me the Unseelie could've made things a little easier for people coming to try and help." Connor removed his coat and went to the bath chamber.

I dropped my coat and gloves in my room before going to the table. "I don't know. The yeti was pretty easy."

"I doubt they expect assistance," Kethyrdryll said. "Our arrival will be a surprise."

"As long as they recognize you before they turn us into pincushions." I took my turn to wash up as Connor left the bath chamber. Dinner was being served when I returned. Must be nice not to have to shop and cook yourself.

"If no one is standing guard, the castle will be extremely difficult to gain entrance into." Kethyrdryll fed Leandra a slice of roast.

"If no one's standing guard, it'll be because they're busy in the castle, or can't," Connor said. "Either way, can't say I'm looking forward to that part."

"Well, we have to find out what happened before we can figure out how to get home. I still need to find the other missing people too."

How long had we been gone? I tried to count, but the elf was right. It was hard to keep track when it was always night. "I hope we haven't missed Christmas."

"Christmas?"

"Humans celebrate that instead of Winter Solstice now. It's a religious holiday celebrating the birth of Jesus Christ, the son of God," Connor explained.

"Which god?"

"God, god," I said. "We date time B.C. and A.D. That means 'Before Christ' and 'Anno Domini', or after Christ's birth. We're in two thousand seven A.D. unless it's two thousand eight now."

"Interesting. Perhaps it's the One God you speak of that some humans believe created the world. We heard of them before the Sundering."

I nodded. "That's Him."

"The world existed before those humans latched onto that idea. Not that their 'One God' doesn't exist, but if he caused the creation of the world, he left it alone afterward for millions of years. I believe it unlikely he'd return and the other gods wouldn't know it."

"How long have elves been around?"

"Far longer than humans, as have most races. Only shifters are younger than humans."

"Cool. So did you see us crawl out of the ocean, or did we just appear out of nowhere?"

"Those are the theories?" Kethyrdryll chuckled. "Well, neither is correct. The first humans came from the stars, delivered from a great ship by strange beings of light. Humans were little more than animals then, but evolved as did other animals, at least to a point. Then they surpassed the animals and at that time, we began our acquaintance with them."

My mouth had fallen open. I closed it. "Mind blown. We're aliens?"

"If that means beings not natural to this planet, yes, though now, millions of years later, I suspect present-day humans cannot be considered 'aliens'. Your species has been here too long to not be a part of the natural order of this world."

Connor snickered, and we looked at him. "I'm going to guess there were some romances way back when, because elves have treated humans as near equals for as long as shifters can remember."

The elf shrugged. "Possibly. All of that occurred well before the birth of any elf currently living. The eldest elves we have are merely in their fifth millennia."

Elves were supposed to be immortal, but I'd seen one eaten by a god, and knew they could be killed. Logan had told me that beheading worked on most supes. Plus, elves had done their best to eradicate dark elves. "How long can elves live?"

Kethyrdryll's expression brightened. "We don't know. Historical records indicate some of our ancestors lived nearly a million years— and by the way, we did crawl out of the ocean, Lady Discord. Or some groups of us did. Others stayed, evolving differently. It's all quite fascinating."

"Yeah, it is." My head was spinning, trying to fit his information into place with what I'd been taught and what humans had believed for so long.

Though there was a group that believed we'd been planted here by aliens. They called it the "Seeder Theory" or something. Apparently, they were right.

"Can you explain what magic is in terms that won't make my head explode?"

"Energy. Some of us have always been attuned to it, and others have become attuned to it. Those who are attuned can use that energy to manipulate the world around them."

My head didn't explode, because his explanation was simple and made sense. "But not everyone can just do it. Witches..."

"Like much of life, there are levels to magic. Some require aids, others do not. For example, I must visualize or focus by using words. A witch must do the same, but needs the assistance, or favor, of a god to achieve results."

And psychics?"

"Far more attuned. You think and do. You're natural energy conduits, hence the term 'natural mages'. Though of course, even your kind has levels, those who can conduct more energy than others."

All of it actually made loads of sense, and sort of chilled the "it's scary" feeling I'd had since waking up from my coma. But it raised a huge question. "If we're natural conduits, how come the Sundering stopped us from being able to do anything?"

"That was the genius of Olven's spell. It drew all of the energy we're able to manipulate, and wound into a...well, a ball. That ball," the elf smiled, "Bounced a bit out of step with the world."

I had to think about that for a minute. "So all the magical energy was out of sync."

"The majority of it, yes. I said all, but some had to tether the rest to the world."

"Okay." That explained the brownie excursions. "I guess the Melding was because the ball stopped bouncing? Came back into sync?"

"Yes. Nature doesn't enjoy being divided in such a manner for long. Olven's spell was a masterpiece. There were many discomfited that a human was the solution to saving our world."

"I'll bet." Olven had been human. Another thought occurred to me. "Um, the demon realm didn't sync completely."

"As it should not. Different energy, though similar in some respects. It bounces at a slightly faster rate, and always has."

"Oh." Did "faster" mean David's theory that demons saw time differently was right? "When we get home, I want you to meet a friend of mine. His name's David, and he's a witch. He's really smart. I think you two will like each other."

"I'll be honored to make the acquaintance of any you call friend."

I didn't know how to respond to that, and decided to smile and concentrate on eating dinner.

NINETEEN

Before bed, I wanted a soak in hot water, but had barely slipped into the tub when a howl sounded.

Leandra howled in the main room, and I climbed out, grabbing for a towel. The hangings between the bath and main chambers fought my attempts to go through. The howl sounded again, closer, and I stopped to listen.

I knew who was howling, and couldn't believe it. "That's Leglin."

The hangings finally cooperated, letting me through. Both men looked at me. Connor grinned. "You can't go outside in a towel."

"Don't leave without me." Ducking back through the hangings, I found clean clothes waiting. After drying and dressing, I went back out to grab my gloves and coat. The guys were suited up and ready to go.

Out we went, into a light snowfall. Kethyrdryll opened the thorny barrier and we heard Leglin howl again. Leandra howled back and ran ahead, disappearing from sight before anyone could call her back.

"Uh-oh."

We ran after her, following her paw prints in the snow. The two hounds traded howls, locating each other. By the time we caught up with Leandra, she and Leglin were bouncing around each other like a couple of puppies, their tails blurring the air.

"Leglin!" I ran a few more steps, and my hound spun around, his ears perking.

"*Mistress!*" He came to me, and I bent to hug him.

"Are you okay? I didn't mean to call you here."

"*I am well. I heard your calls, but this is a strange realm. I cannot travel as I should be able to.*" Leglin licked my cheek, his tail thumping the ground. "*You found my mother and her master.*"

"Sort of."

"*I found someone too.*" Leglin turned. "*Here they come.*"

"Selwin," Kethyrdryll said. "She has a rider."

Connor jogged away, going to meet the horse. "It's Logan!"

Logan was barely conscious, half-frozen, and wearing the horse's blanket as he clung to her neck. We hurried back to the pavilion, the hounds leading the way. After they helped Logan off the horse, Kethyrdryll took Selwin into her stall, and Connor carried Logan into the pavilion.

"Put him in my room." Logan's guestroom didn't exist right now. I went in first, to pull the covers back and helped Connor untangle Logan from the horse blanket. We tucked him in, propping him up with pillows, and Connor moved the brazier closer to the bed.

Logan slowly blinked. There were still punctures across his stomach and back. They weren't bleeding. I bit my lip. "Maybe we should put him in the bath. It'll warm him faster, and we can clean him up at the same time."

"Okay." Connor hauled Logan upright again, ignoring the older man's groan. "You'll feel better soon."

I forgot Logan was naked until we lowered him into the tub, and I stepped away for a second to stretch my lower back. He was relaxing, his arms uncurling, his back and legs straightening, so I was treated to a full frontal view. If not for the puncture wounds, the view would've been amazing, and I may have blushed more than I did.

Because of the holes, I focused on business, instead of drooling over him, and grabbed a couple of towels. Logan began shivering as I knelt beside the tub. Dropping one towel in the water, I put the other behind his neck and head. The second towel had soaked up water, sinking below the surface.

I tried not to look or touch while spreading the towel out and tucking one edge under his butt. Connor smirked at me while tucking the towel on the other side. "Humans think about sex too much."

"You can shut up now."

He laughed. "You do. Must be because you wear clothes all the time."

"Probably." I picked up a bathing sponge and wet it to wipe Logan's face.

He mumbled and opened his eyes. I smiled. "Hey."

Logan mumbled again, his eyes slowly closing. I glanced at Connor. "What did he say?"

"I think it was 'my queen'."

"Poor guy's delirious. Must think I'm Terra." I finished cleaning Logan's face.

"Guess so."

"How long should we leave him in here?"

Connor put his hand on Logan's shoulder. "Until his temperature's normal."

"What about the bite wounds?"

"They'll heal without help, once his temp's normal and we get some food into him."

"Okay."

Kethyrdryll slipped through the hangings. "How is he?"

"He'll be all right," Connor answered.

"How's Selwin?" I asked.

"She is well. Her injuries have healed and she's eating."

"Good." I made a note to take her a couple of apples. "Her blanket's in my room."

"Thank you." He left.

"I'll see about feeding the hounds. Yours is probably hungry."

"Thanks. I'll uh, make sure Logan doesn't drown." Connor left, and there I was, alone with someone who could accurately be described as a wet dream. Even if it wasn't exactly what "wet dream" really meant, and there were holes in him that shouldn't be.

I wiped down his neck and shoulders next. Logan's eyes opened again, and his lips nearly formed a smile. "Are you in there?"

He blinked, and responded in a hoarse whisper, "Barely."

"Coherency. Yay." I patted his cheek, scruffy with a lack of shaving. "I bet you're starving."

"Could eat."

"As soon as you're warm." His cheek felt chilled. I wet the sponge again, and wiped his face, as well as those bits of him that were exposed above the lightly steaming water. "They thought you were dead."

"You didn't?"

"No," I agreed. "I didn't. You have nine lives, remember? Though you're down to six now, by my count. Need to quit spending them so fast."

Logan chuckled. "Sorry."

"You should be." I leaned forward and kissed his forehead. "Quit scaring me, damn it."

"Saw you."

"What?"

He shivered. "Pulled me out of the river."

"Um, no..." Was he delirious? "I haven't seen you since the drake snatched you in mid-air."

"I saw you," he said, his voice firmer and less hoarse. "Couldn't pull myself the rest of the way out. You came."

"Logan, I swear," I paused, something trying to surface. "I didn't... wait. I had a dream that night."

"White Queen." He blinked. "You were a White Queen."

Chills ran through me, lifting every tiny hair on my arms and the back of my neck. His words triggered a clear recollection of hanging in darkness, a circle of tigers around me. "I think I was a tiger in my dream."

"You pulled me away from the river and helped me shift. Warmed me. Then you were gone and the horse was there."

I can't leave him.

I'll send another to watch over him. You need to wake the Unseelie, and soon.

Water splashed as Logan began to sit up. I planted my hand on his chest. "What the hell do you think you're doing?"

He subsided. "You looked scared."

Of course I did, finding a mostly forgotten dream had been real. "Did you see anyone besides me?"

"No."

"And I was a tiger?"

"A White Queen with green eyes."

"My life is unbelievably strange."

He blinked. "It was you."

"Apparently so." I frowned, trying to remember more of the dream. "We wanted to look for you, but the horse was hurt and a blizzard started. When I went to sleep, I was in my house. The river was in the attic. There was a drake, then I found your car and it took me for a ride. Really weird stuff went on. But the weirdest is I dreamed of becoming a white tiger and found you on the river bank, and you frigging saw me."

"Gods?" Logan had some color in his face.

I shrugged. "No clue. Whatever it was, the important thing is that you're alive and back with us."

"Because of you." He smiled. "Always one-upping me."

I returned the smile. "You're definitely feeling better."

"Yeah."

I touched his shoulder, then his forehead. Both felt cool, but not chilly. "Okay. I'll send Connor in to help you out and into some clothes. Dinner and bed after that."

"I might still be cold." He shivered, but the corner of his mouth quirked.

Tapping his nose with my finger, I looked him in the eyes. "If you want snuggling, say so."

"I want snuggling."

"Then there will be snuggling." I stood and grinned. "May take a little while to convince Connor, though."

"I can get out of the tub."

I laughed and hurried out. "Connor, would you please help Logan?"

"Sure, but the snuggling thing isn't happening."

"Oh, come on. Cats love to snuggle." I blinked, realizing the hounds were lying in front of a fireplace, and that wall of the pavilion had turned into stone. "We're redecorating?"

Kethyrdryll came in from outside. "I thought it would be useful to have a larger source of heat this evening."

Connor wiggled his fingers. "Magic."

"Right. Good idea."

TWENTY

Not too long passed before Logan had eaten his fill. I insisted on wrapping his wounds, even though nothing had begun leaking out of them. "Sorry, but they look yucky, and I really don't want open wounds on my sheets."

"Yes, ma'am." He cooperated, lifting his arms to let me roll the linen bandages Kethyrdryll had provided around his middle. Done, I called Leglin to follow us; we went to my room. The other two had already gone to bed.

"Redecorated in here, too." A large, rectangular cushion was in one corner, and my hound went to it. My cot had disappeared, replaced by a queen-sized bed on a wooden frame. A nightgown lay across the foot of it. "I'll go change."

"Okay."

When I returned, Logan was already in bed with his eyes closed. I quietly slipped in next to him, and the magical lighting began to dim.

I rolled onto my side and found his hand under the covers.

"Not exactly snuggling," he said when I put my hand over his.

"You have holes."

"They're healing." He turned his head to look at me. "Just don't touch them."

"You really want snuggles, huh?"

"Yes, please."

"Okay." I scooted closer and he moved his arm. A minute of arranging, and I was mostly against his side, my arm across his chest, my head on his arm and a pillow. "Better?"

"Your knee's poking me."

I bent my leg and let it rest on his. "Now?"

"Much better." He kissed my forehead. "Here we are, in an elf's bed again."

"Guest bed."

"Guest bed," he repeated. "I'm curious."

"About what?"

"If we'll ever be in one of our beds together."

I felt my face grow warmer. "Well… We're breaking the snuggle barrier tonight, so no telling what the future might bring."

"That's a maybe. Right?"

More like a definite yes, but I didn't want to say that because I wanted to do things without rushing into anything. "Right."

"Maybe's good," he said. "I like 'maybe' when you say it under these conditions. I like that we're breaking the snuggle barrier, too."

Boy, so did I. He'd warmed up nicely, his skin a few degrees hotter than my own. Perfect snuggling partner for winter.

"Are you sleepy?"

"A little." Not really, since the image of him naked in the bath was on a loop in my mind.

"I'm not. Think I was out of it too much." He moved his free arm and put his hand on mine. "Are you cold?"

"No. Just human temp."

"Right." Logan was quiet for a minute or so. "Do you think we can do this? Find a way back home?"

"Absolutely."

"Good. I don't like this place. Don't like being so far from the clan. Especially from Terra."

I gave a slight nod. "She's going to need you around for a while yet."

"Yeah, but I won't be as busy."

"No, you won't."

"Does Arcane Solutions have room for another employee?"

"You'd have to ask the boss, but I'd say chances are good."

Logan's hand moved, his fingers sliding down my forearm and back. "I'll ask, unless you don't like the idea."

My skin was tingling under the slow sweep of his fingers. "I've grown up a little. Enough to admit backup isn't the same thing as having babysitters. I don't need a babysitter. But backup? Oh, yeah. Definitely need that."

"Okay. I'll have to run the idea by Terra first." He wiggled. "They're itching."

"Sorry."

Logan laughed. "You didn't make them itch. Why do humans apologize for things they didn't do? It happens all the time."

"I don't know. Maybe because we can't think of something else to say?"

"Guess that makes sense." He sighed. "Not sleepy yet."

"I noticed."

"I'm keeping you up."

"I don't mind. Rambling Logan is fun." I liked listening to him, and yeah, liked the way he kept caressing my arm.

"Rambling? Guess I am. The queens' council kind of upended my life."

"In a good way, though, right?"

"Yeah. I just wasn't really expecting to be let off the hook so soon.

Or mostly off the hook. Now I need to figure out things I wasn't expecting to have to face for a few more years."

"Oh."

"I wondered if living with the clan would be a problem once Terra didn't need me as her Protector anymore. If it would interfere with her leading them, especially if we disagreed about something." He tapped my arm. "What do you think?"

"Me?"

"You're clan," he pointed out, beginning to stroke my arm again.

"Well, yeah, but like, the newest newbie."

"New or not, I value your opinion."

Dang it, now I had to say something. "Well, I don't see you causing a ruckus. You'd talk to her privately."

"True," he agreed. "It's important to present a united front."

"Right." Whew. I'd said the right thing. "She's not mean or stupid. Maybe inexperienced, but I think she's been doing great so far."

"She is."

"Then don't worry about future differences of opinion. At least, not right now." We had to get back before that sort of thing could happen.

"I have to worry about the future. It's part of my job description."

That made me laugh. "Yeah, guess it is."

"You worry about your future."

I worried about staying alive. Pretty much the same thing. "Yes. I guess everyone does."

"I want to say something, but I don't want it to sound pushy," he said.

"Go ahead."

"I want you to be a part of my future. A part you already are, but there's a part I hope you'll be."

I couldn't not ask, because I wanted to know. "What part is that?"

"Clan, friend...lover."

Oh, my God. Something about how he said "lover" sent a spike of heat right into my heart. I wanted to giggle like a maniac at the idea, but he might think I was laughing at him. Instead, I responded with something guaranteed to knock my giggle urge over the head. "Not wife?"

"That option's open for future discussion. When it seems like a viable option. I think we probably have a lot of ground to cover before that happens."

"Yeah." Relief, excitement... I didn't know which felt better to me. "Hey."

"What?"

"Since we're having a kind of heart-to-heart here, I want to ask you something."

"Okay."

"Do you want kids?"

Logan chuckled. "I'd love to have kids at some point."

My heart sank.

"But it's not going to happen."

"Why not?"

"Black tigers can't father children. We're sterile."

"Seriously?"

"Yes. No one knows why, but there's never been a black tiger who's sired children, doesn't matter who they were involved with."

I blinked, not quite stunned enough to keep from thinking "no more condoms," even though that situation wasn't in our immediate future. "Oh."

"And adoption's out, because orphaned cubs go to the closest family members," he added. "I'm resigned to being an uncle."

"Do you have brothers or sisters?"

"A brother, Ryan. He's five years younger and lives with our old clan."

"Are you close?"

"No. I wish we were, but being chosen as Terra's Protector..."

"I get it." And it made me sad for him. "But you're not like, um, not friends?"

"No, we get along fine. We just haven't gotten to spend much time together over the years." His shoulder twitched. "That's why I worry about Terra so much. She's the only family member I'm really close to."

I tilted my head and meant to kiss his cheek, but the angle was wrong and I kissed his jaw instead. He sucked in a breath. "What was that for?"

"I'm trying to be a sympathetic friend but my aim was off."

"Oh. Thank you."

"You're welcome." Could he feel the blush covering my entire head?

"For future reference, that's a good spot to kiss if you have different intentions."

"I'll remember that." I wanted to sink through the mattress into the ground. Good thing people couldn't die of embarrassment.

"Please do. You're blushing."

"Gah. You're not supposed to notice."

"Sorry."

"It's okay. God. I don't know why you'd consider dating me. I'm a complete doofus."

Logan laughed. "No you're not."

"I flail through life."

"You have a good, kind heart. That's what I like best about you. Doesn't hurt that you're also smart and strong."

He hadn't said a word about my looks. I decided I liked that. "I've done bad things."

"Sometimes life forces us to."

"Did you take a class in how to always say the right thing?"

"They have classes for that?"

We both laughed.

"So... you're not interested in me for my body, but my heart and brain."

"Well, those are considered delicacies. Ouch," he said when I pinched his chest. "I'm kidding."

"Better be."

"Did you want me to only be interested in your body?"

"Body does factor in, huh?"

"How people look is the first thing you tend to notice. You didn't answer my question."

"No."

"Good. You're attractive outside, but it's what's inside that's most important. At least to me." He paused. "Feel free to overshare like I have. Any time."

I had to laugh. "You want to know what I like best about you?"

"Love to."

"You're compassionate. You care, even about people you don't know, like Zoe and Tonya. You have a good, kind heart, too." I hesitated. "Maybe it's weird, but I pretty much liked you the moment we met."

"Same here." Logan moved his hand from my arm to cover a yawn.

"Oh, now you get sleepy."

He chuckled. "I'm warm, I have a full stomach, and am having a good, quiet talk and snuggle with one of my favorite people. It's cozy and relaxing."

"I'm one of your favorite people?"

"Yes."

"Who are the others?"

"Terra, Soames, Moira, Alanna. My dad."

Sounded like I was in excellent company, and that maybe he was a little on the choosy side when it came to picking favorites. "Cool. Cuddle with Dane a lot?"

"Once. We were out hunting in winter and a storm hit. Spent two days curled up together in a snow den."

I smiled. Good to learn he didn't instantly equate cuddle with sex. Not that I had a problem with cuddling before or after, but sometimes just cuddling was nice. "Neat. What about the others?"

"Terra all the time. She was a demanding little thing. I don't think her feet touched the ground her first two years of life. My dad cuddled us a lot when we were small."

Was he avoiding Alanna and Moira? Did it matter if he was?

"Alanna is a cuddler. You have to realize a lot of us were pretty young when Terra was born. We shared a room the first few years, and slept in groups of three or four."

"My little brothers sneak into each other's rooms a lot so they can sleep together."

"They're cute kids."

"Yeah." I missed them a lot right then.

"Moira didn't join our clan until later," he said. "We were together for a while, but decided it wasn't working out."

Ah hah. "I like her."

"She's a good person. She likes you, too. If she didn't, you wouldn't be clan." He winced. "That sounded wrong."

"Nah. I get it. She's like the spiritual leader, right?"

"Yes. By the way, she wants to talk to you sometime, about what you saw during the ceremony."

"I saw them again, in the dream. One, I don't know, jumped into me. That's how I turned tiger."

Logan hmmed. "Maybe she can figure out why you saw them. It won't be weird for you, will it? Knowing that she and I were lovers and being around her?"

"Maybe a little, but I'm glad you told me so it didn't come out later as a big surprise." I wondered if he'd loved her, or still did. What if they'd been doing friends with benefits for years? "Um, how long ago was it?"

"We called it off about three years ago, and it lasted about that long, too."

Yikes. They'd broken up about the same time I'd decided to stop being a virgin. "Now it's weird."

"Why?"

"My longest relationship was six whole months."

"If it makes it better, my shortest was two months," he said.

"Mm, yeah, that does make me feel better."

"We should probably get some sleep."

"Yeah, probably. Does it bug you that I'm six years younger?"

Logan countered with, "Does it bother you I'm six years older?"

"You know my mom's more than ten years older than my dad, right?"

"Actually, no, I didn't. Now that I do, I'm wondering whether you prefer younger men."

I laughed. "I'm twenty-three, dude. I can't like much younger men or people would call me nasty names. Besides, I do like somewhat older guys."

"Am I in the 'somewhat older' category?"

"We've kissed, I'm snuggling with you, and none of it's been icky, so, yes."

He laughed. "Then I won't worry about the age difference if you don't."

"Okay. Good night." My aim was better. I kissed his cheek that time.

"Night." We snuggled closer and I closed my eyes.

TWENTY-ONE

"Lady Discord."

I groaned and tried to pull the covers over my head, but Logan's arm pinned them to my waist.

"Lady Discord?"

Why was Logan's arm on my covers? I cracked one eye open to find a lovely view of Leglin's nostrils. Didn't move away, because I couldn't. Logan's arm was on my covers because he was behind me. Right behind me, as in, we were spooning. I was Little Spoon. He was a purring Big Spoon.

"Lady..."

"I'm awake," I said, wishing the elf hadn't decided I should be.

"Very good. Breakfast is being served."

"Okay, thanks." I touched Leglin's cold nose. "Good morning."

Thump, thump, thump.

"I missed you bunches. Are the other dogs okay?"

"Yes, mistress. Soames has tended to us since you disappeared."

I made a note to do something really nice for Dane. "What do you know about what's happened?"

Logan woke, his purr trailing off. "Morning."

"Did you sleep well?"

"Yes. You?"

"Like a log."

"We make a good snuggling team."

I smiled, scratching my hound's chin. "It was pretty epic snuggling."

"I thought so too. Did someone mention breakfast?" Logan rolled over onto his back. I could feel him stretching.

"It's on the table." I patted Leglin's head. "You can tell me everything you know while I get dressed."

"Dane's informed everyone we disappeared," I said while joining the men at the table. "And Damian was one of the people he contacted first."

Logan looked up from his plate. "The time-lapse spell?"

"The time-lapse spell. They know about the portal. Thorandryll's closed the club, and has people going over it. He even has a," I had to fight a smile. "An extraction team on standby, waiting to rescue us once the portal opens again."

"But they'll be on the other side of the mountains, in that other realm," Connor said.

"We'll talk about that in a minute. Kate and Damian are part of the extraction team. Dane too." My partner had told Leglin everything, in case I called the hound. I even knew that Alanna would take care of my other dogs when the extraction team made it through the portal.

"Who are Kate and Damian?" Kethyrdryll asked.

"Witches, two from the most powerful coven Santo Trueno has to offer. The cavalry's on the way, guys." I grinned, but put on my serious face after a few seconds. "Now for the other realm thing. I'm wondering about something. You said the Sundering sucked all the magical energy and shaped it into a ball. One that bounced out of sync with the human world."

"Correct." The elf put his fork down.

"And the Melding was supposed to put the supe realm back in sync. Which it did, except for this part, the Unseelie realm."

Kethyrdryll glanced at Logan, who said, "That's what the humans call all of us: supes. It's short for supernaturals."

"Ah. Then, yes."

"Okay, so what we have, or I think we have, is three different realms basically operating at different frequencies. Human realm, the outer one surrounding the Unseelie realm, and the Unseelie Realm. Where did that outer realm come from?"

"I thought we decided it was part of the Unseelie lockdown plan?" Connor scratched the side of his head. "Didn't we?"

"I think we did, yeah. Anyway, here's what I think: that outer realm is actually an extension of this one, a failsafe to keep something or someone from getting out of here. It shouldn't be operating at too different a frequency as the inner realm, because someone sent that ice golem to pick up people."

All three were staring at me. I hoped they thought I was making sense. "That outer realm has managed to hit the same frequency that Dreamland operates at, because that's where it's been opening."

"So if you'd tried to teleport us home when the portal was open?" Logan asked.

"We probably would've gone home, because Dreamland operates

at close the same frequency as the human realm, and so do I. But the portal wasn't open. We bounced off the outer realm, and I guess that might have changed our frequency, at least for a few seconds, because we landed here. In the inner realm." I waved my hands. "That's not the best part though. Or maybe the worst part. I think the outer realm is matching Dreamland's frequency more often, because Nature doesn't like being divided."

"Coming into sync." Connor grinned. "But that means we'll be able to go home for sure."

"Yeah, but what's going to go home with us?" No one had an answer for that. "What I also think is that since I've been here for a few days, maybe I'm attuned to the frequency now. I mean, the Unseelie realm one."

Logan tapped his fingers on the table's edge. "How can you find out?"

"By doing this." I teleported to the pavilion's door. The men jumped to their feet. "Over here, guys."

They settled back down, but Logan frowned at me. "Warn me next time. What if that hadn't worked?"

I walked back to the table and retook my seat. "I'd be in the outer realm, unless the portal was open. I'd teleport again, and get bounced back here."

His frown deepened. "Exactly where, here?"

I waved his question away, because I didn't know and was really glad my spur of the moment test had worked. "I can teleport again. I'm pretty sure I can teleport over the mountains, if I'm right about the realm frequencies coming into closer sync. Which means I can bring the extraction team back here, to help us get to the castle and find out what the hell's going on with the Unseelie."

"You mean, we can bring them back," Logan said, his frown turning into a scowl as I shook my head. "Why not we, instead of just you?"

"Because there's at least eight elves, Damian, Kate, their familiars, and Dane. That's a lot of people to transport, dude. I'd rather not sprain my brain doing it by adding you three, both hounds, and Selwin."

"Oh." His scowl faded. "What if they're not there?"

"I'll wait."

Connor snorted. "What about the gremlins? Or that golem?"

I smiled. "I'll stay close to the trees. None of them went close to the tree lines."

The men wanted to discuss it further, and we did, but in the end, everyone agreed that I should at least try. They didn't want me to go alone. Kethyrdryll had to stay with the pavilion—some magical bonding thing. Logan wasn't fully healed, and since we were supposed to get Connor home safe, that only left Leglin.

Logan was waiting outside my room after I grabbed my coat. "Hey."

"Hey."

"You're going to be careful."

"Absolutely," I promised.

"Good. Would it be all right if I kissed you?"

"Yes, please." I hoped it was a super, duper good one. Just in case my plan went up in flames and I dumped myself in the river with the drakes.

"Great." He slung his arm around my waist, pulled me close, and buried his other hand in my hair. I nearly missed the chance to put my arms around him, and let out a squeak of surprise. Then his lips were on mine.

The best kisses are those that make you forget everything but the person you're kissing. I hadn't experienced many such kisses, and that one blew those few others off the playing field entirely.

It was a serious freaking kiss, one that sent my pulse soaring. When Logan ended it with a final, firm press of his lips, my eyes fluttered open. "Wow."

A slow smile spread across his face.

"I may have forgotten my name."

"You're going overboard."

"Not really."

He hugged me, his fingers slipping from my hair. "Don't be gone long."

"I'll try not to." We walked outside hand in hand, where Connor and Kethyrdryll were grooming Selwin. Well, the elf was. Connor was watching.

Kethyrdryll stopped to hand me a small, leather pouch. "Emergency tent. It will provide shelter, warmth, and food. There's also a barrier ring. Simply place both on the ground. Once the others arrive, one of them will break camp for you."

"Thank you." I tied the pouch to my belt.

"Fair travels, Lady Discord."

On impulse, I pecked him on the cheek before turning to give Connor a hug. "You guys stay out of trouble."

"I have so had my fill of trouble. You don't even know," the younger shifter said.

About to laugh, I didn't as a vision flashed across my mind. *Terra's pale head, his bright one bent close, their arms around each other.* "No, you haven't."

"What?"

I shook my head. "Nothing. Gotta get moving."

Logan hugged me again, and whispered, "You saw something, didn't you? What was it?"

"Something that points to us getting home."

"Okay." He released me, and I called Leglin to my side.

"We're off." I took hold of the hound's collar, and teleported.

Not far, just out of sight of camp. I'd decided to take it in stages, in case something went wrong. Maybe then, I wouldn't end up bouncing wherever, but actually land somewhere relatively familiar.

My second teleport did land me somewhere familiar: At the edge of the yeti challenge. "How did you pass him?"

"The yeti ignored us, mistress."

"Huh. Hey, do you love me?"

My hound gazed up, his ears perked. *"Yes."*

"I love you too. How about you call me Cordi instead of mistress?"

Leglin's tail began to slowly sweep side-to-side. *"You will allow me to use your name?"*

"That is what names are for. Plus we're family and pack."

Faster wagging. *"Thank you...Cordi."*

I bent down to hug his neck. "You're welcome. Ready for another jump?"

"Yes."

About three jumps later, I stared at the mountains, wondering if we'd make it over them, or bounce off and land God knew where. "All right. Here's our moment of truth."

Tucking my fingers under Leglin's collar again, I hesitated. Had our cavalry made it through yet? I didn't really want to be stuck over in the buffer zone for a long time. "Quit procrastinating, Cordi."

My hound looked up. *"What is that?"*

"Procrastinating? It's putting off doing something you need to. Which I'm going to stop doing right now. Here we go." I took a deep breath, closed my eyes, and visualized the cave we'd spent the night in. My stomach flip-flopped as we hit something, but it gave way instead of bouncing us. A stale odor of smoke told me the last teleport had been successful before I opened my eyes. "Yay, we're here."

I knew the way from cave to tree line, and that we needed to travel left from there. Once out in the open, just out from under the trees, I concentrated on making short hops. Teleportation was much faster than slogging through ankle deep snow, though I had to be careful not to overdo it.

Didn't matter which ability I used, they all took energy. I didn't want to be too tired to make it back as quickly as possible. A rest would be necessary anyway, before trying to transport as many people as there were supposed to be coming to save our bacon.

Mm, bacon. It and coffee were two items Kethyrdryll didn't have in his invisible kitchen.

My plan to stick close to the trees seemed to be working. We hadn't seen any snow gremlins or the ice golem. The only problem I had was that I'd been out of it for part of the way, and didn't know exactly how far to go.

Which was why we were making short hops. Probably why, after about an hour, I saw some figures not too far ahead. "I hope that's our cavalry and not bad guys."

"*Do you wish me to scout ahead?*"

I scratched Leglin's neck. "Not yet. Let's get a little closer, see what we can see first."

Two more hops, and I knew it was the expected arrivals, because Dane was running toward us. He grabbed me into a bear hug, smooshing all my air out. "Ungh."

"Sorry. Where's Logan? Did you find Connor or any of the others? Don't worry about your dogs, and I've kept the boss, Terra, and Sunny updated. I knew you'd call for Leglin sooner or later." Dane finally released me, stepping back with a huge smile on his face. "So?"

I sucked in air, holding my finger up for him to wait. "Logan's safe, we found Connor, Leglin told me, and I'm glad to see you too."

TWENTY-TWO

"You're not planning to camp here, are you? Because there's a oh, you met the golem." One of the elves dropped the golem's head into a leather bag as Dane, Leglin, and I walked up. "But there's snow gremlins too."

"We've spelled the ground." Kate waved. "Hello, Jones. Strange choice for a vacation."

"Unfriendly too."

Thorandryll stepped out of the wine-red pavilion they'd set up. "Miss Jones. I'm pleased to discover you're well."

"Thank you."

"Now that I'm aware of the issue, your services are no longer required."

"Maybe you don't require them, but I am working for another client whose case involves your issue."

He shook his head. "We'll find the missing and return them safely home."

"It's like he doesn't know you at all," Dane said.

"The missing are now a matter of police business." Damian had come over from helping bag golem pieces. "And Cordi is one of our valued civilian experts."

"Basically, you're not allowed to blow me off." I gave Thorandryll my brightest smile. "Sorry, dude."

"I'll remember to keep my concern for your safety private from now on."

"Right." Like he really cared. If he did, Thorandryll would've been honest about his stolen grimoire. However, I did want to speak to him privately. My personal opinion of him being a total jerk aside, people deserved privacy when being given certain information.

Our discovery of his long-lost brother was that sort of information. "I need to talk to you alone."

Thorandryll's normal, arrogant expression faded. His lips tightened, and faint lines appeared on either side of his mouth. "Of course. Please come inside."

I followed him into the pavilion, working hard to keep a straight face. He obviously expected bad news. "Ooh, is that coffee?"

"Yes. Please take a seat." Thorandryll poured a cup and placed it before me. He then sat down next to me. "You found something."

I did consider drawing it out, but noticed how white the corners of his mouth were. "Kethyrdryll is alive."

His eyes closed, and his entire body sagged as his face softened. I had to smile. It was good to see his brother meant a lot to him.

Opening his eyes, Thorandryll smiled too, right before leaning and planting a kiss on my lips. "Dude."

"Thank you for bearing such welcome news to me."

I decided to let the kiss slide this time. "You're welcome. Now it's time for the bad news."

"That's what we know so far," I said, reaching for my coffee cup.

"You would have to fall into a mess hundreds of elves couldn't handle." Kate's brow creased. "Is it hundreds? Or thousands?"

None of the elves bothered to answer her, too busy trading meaningful glances and touching their weapons. More than one wore smiles. Life in the real world must've been boring them, judging by the flickers of excitement tapping against the walls of my mental maze.

Great, all we needed were some trigger-happy elves to round things out.

"If you're correct about this frequency idea, how are you going to teleport all of us into the Unseelie realm?" Damian patted Illusion's back. The husky was gazing at me with his head cocked. "Wouldn't this many people operating at a different frequency cause a problem?"

"No problem." Startled, we all looked at Percy, who was perched on the back of an empty chair. The parrot stretched his wings wide. "Make bubble. Cordi's aura."

"What?"

Thorandryll nodded. "Yes, that's possible."

"What's possible?"

"You have a strong aura, Miss Jones. With the right encouragement, it should be possible to cause it to expand enough to encompass all of us."

"A Cordi aura bubble." Damian smiled. "Yes, that would insulate us and prevent interference."

I looked around. There were nine elves, each partnered with a hound, my three friends, Leglin, Percy and Illy. What would expanding my aura to allow all of them inside of it do? Would there be side effects, like elf residue smeared all over it? "I don't know if I like this plan."

"Me neither." Dane frowned. "It sounds invasive."

"Our auras touch all the time," Kate said. "They're not static second skins. They spin, pulse, and trail tendrils constantly. There's no danger to Jones in this idea."

That made me feel better. She'd been careful to keep Thorandryll from getting hold of my hair and blood, so the elf couldn't use them for any nefarious purposes.

"Nefarious" meaning things I didn't want to think about most of the time. The golden-haired prince had snuck a macking in on me once, while I was caught in a porno vision starring him. I suspected him of using glamour on me a few times as well, and knew he had a problem being truthful.

He was well over a thousand years old, maybe even over two thousand. A little up there to be sincerely interested in an often immature, twenty-three-year-old human for romance.

"Are you sure?" I didn't know enough about auras. "It won't break or crack or something?"

"Auras are elastic, Jones. Yours will return to normal once we're done," she assured me.

Dane still wore a frown, but I nodded. "Okay. What do I need to do?"

I should've realized my witch buddies had no intention of allowing Thorandryll or any other elf to handle the aura stretching. It actually required two spells: One to make my aura visible, the other to allow them to reshape it.

Having never seen my aura before, I was dismayed to discover it wasn't a single color, or even a pretty rainbow of bright ones. Instead, it was a swirling mess of fifty-fifty, bright and dark. "Is it supposed to look like this? That much black isn't good, right?"

With Damian and Kate busy pinching and pulling at my aura, Thorandryll answered. "Each color represents different experiences, emotions, and bonds. Yes, black is typically considered negative, but no one travels through life without encountering situations that affect them negatively."

"Oh."

"The green, brown, and orange represent your bonds to the earth and your clan."

"Neat." There were healthy amounts of each. "What about the red?"

"Violence and/or passion."

Way too much red, and I was certain most of it was due to violence. I wondered how red my aura would be if I lived to be eighty. "I should work on that."

The elf chuckled. "Our auras are the history of our lives."

"Mine's hard to read." I could pick out hints of gold, silver, purple, blue, and even rose. There were lesser amounts of other colors present, but it became difficult to see them as the witches stretched my aura thinner.

Damian stopped pulling to ask, "Any discomfort, Cordi?"

"Kind of beginning to feel a little itchy."

He nodded. "This is far enough. Everyone inside."

They all gathered inside my stretched-out aura. "Discord Airlines is now boarding. Please secure your hounds, touch your fellow travelers, and keep all feet, paws, tails, and hands inside the aura bubble at all times. The emergency exits aren't something you'll want to use."

I waited until everyone was in contact.

"We will be making more than one stop on our journey today. Please do not leave your assigned seating unless the captain okays it." I flashed my toothiest smile around. "We wouldn't want to leave anyone behind. Everyone ready?"

Everyone was. "Great. Here we go."

Taking a deep breath, I teleported to the spot where Leglin and I had first been able to see them. After a quick check to make certain I hadn't lost anyone, I teleported again. Being able to skip across miles of snow sure beat slogging on foot.

Upon reaching the end of the line—which was near the trees close to the spot Connor had been stabbed—I took a really deep breath. "Next stop: the Unseelie realm. You may feel a little pressure this time."

My warning was a teensy bit off. It felt like trying to push through partially chewed taffy. We appeared roughly three feet above ground level, and not everyone managed to keep their holds.

I fell on my butt, and a steady thunder of pain filled my head. "Sorry. Oh, my head."

"That's enough for now," Thorandryll said. He'd landed on his feet. He bent, taking hold of my arms, and pulled me to my feet. "Set camp immediately. Alleryn, you'll attend to Miss Jones."

"I can do one more."

"Not until we redo the spells," Damian said. "That last teleport snapped your aura back in place."

Sure enough, the thin bubble was gone. "Oh, okay."

It didn't take long for the pavilion and thorn barrier to supersize. Alleryn hustled me inside, clucking like a mother hen. "You really shouldn't tax yourself."

"I want to get back, do what we have to, and go home. And get Rico and the others back where they belong."

He patted my shoulder before pushing me down into a chair. "I know, but how are you going to do it if you're exhausted? Cordi, you have to take care of yourself. It's comparable to airline attendants instructing parents to put their air masks on first, before doing it for their children. You have to take care of yourself before you can take care of others."

"I do take care of myself."

Alleryn snorted. "To a point, but when on a case, you have a tendency to overdo when it's not exactly necessary."

I didn't argue. He was actually kind of right, and any future downtime I needed could keep me from being involved in whatever planning was possible. The elf patted my shoulder again before going into one of the side rooms. Alleryn returned with a small, dark blue bottle. "Drink this, and then I want to you to lie down for a while."

"How long is a while?" I took the bottle and uncorked it for a sniff. "Does it taste bad?"

"It's the same headache remedy I always give you. Drink up."

I obeyed, because it didn't taste awful. It didn't really taste great either, but "not awful" worked. "How long of a nap do I have to take?"

"A few hours. You can use that room." He pointed to a section of hangings, next to the room he'd retrieved the bottle from. "Go."

"Okay, okay. I'm going." I removed my coat as I went, dropping it over the footboard of the bed inside the room. Much fancier bed than the one in my room in Kethyrdryll's pavilion. This one had a canopy. I sat down to pull off my boots, and then lay down as ordered. The drum contest in my head was still going when I dropped off to sleep.

A low murmur of voices woke me, and my head no longer hurt. I opened my eyes while rolling over, and saw the door hangings move. The tip of Illy's tail whisked out of sight.

I sat up, but couldn't see any dog hair on the crimson coverlet. Weird. Illy had spent the night with me several times, and he'd always slept on the bed with me.

Oh, well, maybe he'd only come in to check on me. I stretched before scooting to the edge of the bed and reaching for my boots.

Out in the main room, lunch had been served. An empty chair waited at Thorandryll's right. He indicated it, and I knew he'd been watching when I came out. "Join us."

"Thanks." I sat. We were having stew for lunch. "I'm fine now. We can keep going once everyone's finished eating."

He nodded. "Excellent."

I teleported to just beyond sight of our camp. "Okay, it's like a five minute walk from here, and no monsters. Everyone out of my aura bubble."

People let go of each other, and the hounds, stepping off as directed. I flinched as my aura retracted, even though I didn't actually feel anything. "Not you."

"I beg your pardon?" Thorandryll paused to look at me, his nose rising a centimeter higher in the air.

"We're going ahead." I held my hand out. *Logan.*

Hey, good to hear you.

Same here. Ask Kethyrdryll to go outside, please. I have someone who wants to see him alone.

Will do, Logan said, and a second later added, *Okay, he's going out.*

Thanks. I wiggled my fingers. "Come on. Your brother's waiting."

A surge of eagerness threatened to overwhelm my mental maze's walls as Thorandryll took my hand. I teleported us inside the thorny barrier, and pulled free of his grasp as the two elves caught sight of each other. They simply stared for a moment, before hurrying toward each other.

I smiled as they hugged. Facilitating reunions was one of my favorite parts of my job.

TWENTY-THREE

"Elven magic is freaky," I whispered to Kate, who nodded. They'd added their pavilion to Kethyrdryll's, and the pavilions had knitted together to form a larger one. Instead of a main room, we had a banquet hall. With a U-shaped table, which meant we could all see each other.

There were two bathing chambers on the wall opposite the entrance, their doorways separated by a long fireplace. Bedrooms lined each side of the long sides. Hounds lazed in front of the fireplace. They'd already eaten.

I was full too, and wondering if the elves planned to party all night. They were celebrating Kethyrdryll's return. Not something I had a problem with, but I'd done a lot of teleporting and it felt late. My grasp on time had failed me, with the endless night thing.

Percy side-walked toward my plate, his head turned in order to keep one eye on me. "What?"

The parrot balanced on one leg and snatched a piece of melon off my plate. "Cordi not eat?"

I'd been picking at the food remaining on my plate, but now that he'd stuck his scaly foot in it, wouldn't be anymore. Pushing the plate toward him, I said, "You can have the rest."

"Thank you." He began gobbling down the bits of fruit with a vengeance.

As far as I was concerned, it was time to excuse myself and go to bed. There was a slight problem with that plan, because I didn't know which of the rooms was mine now, with all of the magical rearranging.

Kethyrdryll decided to stand up and clear his throat at that moment. Everyone quieted to listen to him. "I've immensely enjoyed our reunion, yet it is late, and we face challenges unknown if we are to find our way home."

"Of course," Thorandryll agreed. "We should retire."

That broke up the party nicely. I bumped Logan when we stood up at the same time. "Oops, sorry."

"My fault. Ah," he bent his head, lowering his voice. "Any chance you're in a snuggling mood?"

I suddenly was, looking into his eyes. "Yes."

A smile curved his lips. "I hoped you would be."

"I have an ulterior motive. I'm hoping you know which room is mine."

"I do. It's the one closest to the ladies' room."

"Awesome. Meet you there in a few." I needed to visit the ladies', and noticed Kate and Alleryn whispering to each other when I turned to head that way. They were probably planning to meet too. I thought Thorandryll already knew about them dating. Maybe he didn't.

I was brushing my teeth when Kate came into the bathing chamber. "Are you two still secret?"

She raised her eyebrows. "Sorry?"

"Oh, come on. He must've told you I found out."

She gave up with a shrug. "Yes, he did. Habit reigns supreme."

"After the book thing, I'm pretty sure Thorandryll knows too." Alleryn had loaned her a history book to help solve a problem. Or shed light on a motive. Same difference.

"Probably. I'm more interested in what you and Logan were discussing out there."

I couldn't prevent a grin. "We're snuggle partners."

"Oh ho. Just snuggling?"

"Yes. For now." I left the bathing chamber, her laughter following me out. Entering my room, I found Logan pulling off his boots, and a fresh nightgown lying across the foot of the bed. I grabbed it. "Be right back."

"You can change in here. I'll close my eyes."

"No peeking?"

"No peeking," he promised, and turned away. I hurriedly changed, a little disappointed he didn't try to peek. Who knows where peeking may have led to?

Then again, the walls were soft material and not exactly soundproof. Plus, I was tired. "Done. How's your owie?"

Logan turned around and took off his shirt. "Almost healed."

The holes were gone, pink spots marking where they'd been. "Nice."

We slid under the covers from opposite sides. I snuggled up to him when he lifted his arm. "I like snuggling with you."

"That makes two of us."

"You like snuggling with yourself?"

Logan squeezed me. "I meant with you."

"Oh, good, because it would be weird the other way." I muffled a yawn. "I'm tired."

He chuckled. "I can tell. Good night."

"Night." Closing my eyes, I dropped right off.

At some point, I grew conscious of dreaming, but it wasn't anything to write home about. Nothing but a jumble of memories from after I'd woken from my coma. Then it changed to the New Year's Eve of the Melding. I listened to the distant pops of firecrackers, and my parents' soft conversation. They looked so happy.

The sky lit up with multicolored sparks. I blinked at the brightness, and found myself standing in a line of people in long, white hallway. Tapping the shoulder of the man in front of me, I asked, "What are we in line for?"

Damian turned around. "I don't know."

"Can you see anything?"

"People, and I think there's a door ahead."

I leaned to look past him, and the people in front of him. There were about a dozen between us and the door he'd mentioned. "If this is a party with alcohol, I'm not old enough to go."

Damian laughed. "I don't think it's a party. How old are you?"

"Fifteen." Time skipped, and we were closer to the door. By peeking around Damian, I was able to see a man standing inside the door. There were three women in the room beyond, sitting behind a long table.

The man listened to something the women said, and gestured the man in front of Damian inside. He then sent him out of sight to the left.

It was Damian's turn, and the man sent him left too.

My turn. The man looked at the women, who whispered to one another for a long time. Their quick glances made me feel uncomfortable. "Did I do something wrong?"

The women stopped whispering, and one of them nodded to the man. He pointed to the right, where a door waited. I went through it.

"Cordi, are you home?"

I stepped out onto the back porch of my new house. The air smelled of pine and honeysuckle. Logan jumped over the stairs, landing in front of me. He picked me up and swung me around. "Come see the babies."

Holding hands, we ran through trees until we reached a grassy clearing. A lion lay dozing in the sun, and a pale-coated cub batted at his twitching tail. Not far away, a white tigress held down a second cub, washing its face while it mrowed protests.

"Twins," Logan said with a proud smile. "Healthy twin boys."

"They're..." I was alone, standing on the edge of a cliff. Far below, a sea of dark fog churned.

"You have to decide," a voice boomed. "You must make your choice."

"What choice?"

"Cordi." My eyes shot open, and I sat up.

"Easy." I was awake, Logan sitting beside me, and we were in my room in the pavilion. "You were talking in your sleep. Are you okay?"

"Yeah, just some weird dreams." My hair was sticking to my cheeks. I swiped it away, and realized I'd cried in my dream. "I have to go to the bathroom."

"Okay."

I left the bed and slipped through the door, right out into the frozen night. "What the hell?"

"It's been difficult to reach you," Sal said. He appeared a dozen feet away, his slight figure translucent in the moonlight.

"It's about damn time you showed up."

"I had to request a bit of help. You need to get your butt in gear, young lady, or a lot of people are going to die."

I stomped toward him. "I have an idea. How about a little help instead of criticism and vague-ass warnings? Like, I don't know, maybe tell me exactly what the hell's going on here?"

"Cordi?" Turning, I saw Logan step out of thin air. His eyes widened as he looked around. "Why are we outside, and who is that?"

"Sal, my fairy godfather."

"Oh." Logan walked across the snow to my side. "Hello."

"Well, well. This is interesting." Sal regarded Logan with a smile. "You shouldn't be here."

"My apologies, sir."

"A polite young man. What a refreshing change." The little god shot me a reproving look. "You could learn something from him, girl."

"Yeah, yeah, missing people?" I prompted. "Come on, give me something useful."

"She's pushy."

"It's in her job description," Logan said, earning a chuckle from Sal.

"I suppose I can bend the rules a bit, since someone else is breaking them. The Unseelie are prison guards, and one of their prisoners is trying to make a break. He hasn't been entirely successful yet. It's not as though the Unseelie are idiots, you know. They had a failsafe."

"We figured that much out." At least the failsafe part, and that it was to keep someone in.

"A failsafe doesn't last forever, and he's gotten some help. He knows how to destroy it now."

"Argh." I threw my hands in the air. "I'm so sick of this always being the thing. Because it's a sacrifice thing again, isn't it? The missing people?"

"She's quite astute when she tries," Sal told Logan, who responded with a tiny grin that disappeared when I glared at him.

"How do we stop him?"

"Wake the Unseelie. They may need a little help, and you'll want to go with them anyway, to collect your missing humans."

"Okay, how do we wake them?"

Sal snorted. "You have all sorts of useful people in your group. Figure it out."

"Gee, thanks."

"You'd better hurry, because you don't have much time left. Maybe a few days, tops." His dark gaze slid away for a second. "It's a messy, painful way to go."

Logan asked, "What exactly does the spell do?"

Sal studied Logan for a moment. "Destroys the Unseelie realm and looses the darkest things in all of creation upon the world."

"End of the world, blah, blah, blah. We get it," I said.

"Good, now go stop it." Sal stepped forward, lifting his hand. He touched me between the eyes. "Now wake."

I woke, with a major headache, and groaned. "Frickin' gods."

"At least we know what to do now." Logan rolled and propped his elbow, to rest his head on his hand. "I guess we're done snuggling for the night."

"Wait, you were really...? Dude." I wasn't sure how to feel about him being in my dreams. I mean, in my dreams and conscious of being in them. Things could become highly awkward in the future.

"Should I apologize? I don't even know..."

"No, it's okay." I sat up, drums pounding in my head. "Holy crap, my head's killing me."

Logan left the bed. "I'll wake the others, and see if Alleryn has something for a headache."

"Thanks." Wow, Logan had been in my dream and met my irritating fairy godfather.

The weirdness never ended.

If I'd learned anything since becoming a psychic, it was that people—regardless of species—tend to give dreams far less credence than they did when you changed "dream" to "psychic vision". Even diehard skeptics were more inclined to listen then.

Not that there were any skeptics in the crowd gathered around me, but I started with a lie. "I had a vision, a precog."

Logan didn't even twitch. Mentioning an unknown god had given me advice didn't seem like a solid plan with a bunch of elves around. One of them, or all of them, would want to dissect and speculate, and we didn't have time for that.

"It's a prison break."

Thorandryll gave his brother an epically dirty look. "You're not supposed to know about..."

"Hello, psychic here? On a case? I find stuff out, dude. It's my job. Anyway, the prison break's not complete, though he did knock out the guards. I mean, the Unseelie. He's going to sacrifice the missing humans to crack the failsafe." I hesitated. "When he does, it's going to blow this realm to hell and let a lot of nasty things out into the world."

"You saw this?" Thorandryll's eyes were narrowed.

"Yes." Not a lie. I had an imagination, and it had offered up a few images while Sal talked. "We're running out of time to stop him. We need to get to the castle and wake the Unseelie."

Illusion, Damian's husky familiar, was staring at me with his head cocked. He suddenly bared his teeth and hid behind Damian. What was his problem?

"Very well. Ready yourselves," the prince ordered. "We march in less than an hour."

I loved it when people didn't question me about important stuff.

"You take the horse," Kate insisted. "I want to ride the lion."

Since elves and shifters could move faster, and keep going longer, it had been decided the three of us would ride. I was aboard tiger Logan's broad back, watching my witch buddies argue.

"Why do you get to ride the lion?" Damian pulled on his gloves.

"I weigh less. Besides, Percival is already on him." The parrot was half-buried in Connor's mane.

"Oh, all right." Damian walked over to Selwin, Illy on his heels.

"Hah, I love winning." Kate pointed at Connor. "You, down."

I'd never seen a lion roll his eyes before, but Connor obeyed to let her climb onto his back. Once seated, she smiled. "The lion and the witch. All we need is a wardrobe."

Logan chuffed as Connor rose to his feet. I was hoping I wouldn't fall off, since he didn't have a mane for me to hold onto.

The elves had finished breaking camp by then, and Thorandryll issued orders to form a column, with the three of us directly behind Kethyrdryll and him.

Turned out a tiger's jog wasn't all that hard to get used to.

We ran into the third challenge about the time my stomach decided it was tired of being empty. The gurgling growl it made turned Logan's head. "Sorry. Also, holy freaking crap."

Off in the distance, the Unseelie castle stood on a snow-covered hill. Its black walls were speckled with faint twinkles of light, matching the night sky.

Between it and us was a vast maze of ice, sharp points lining each and every wall. We weren't high enough to see a way through.

I slid off Logan's back, slogging through newly knee-deep snow to where Thorandryll and Kethyrdryll stood. "That's not going to be easy."

"No, yet if one person successfully navigates it, the challenge ends," the prince replied.

"Are you sure about that?"

"There are rules, Miss Jones, and certain 'shortcuts'," Thorandryll turned around. "We'll camp here, and discuss the available options."

I swallowed a bite of stew while letting what Thorandryll just said sink in. "Wait a minute. Someone can just carry like, a hair from everyone?"

"Yes, or drops of blood. Any physical representation should work," the prince agreed.

Kate and Damien were nodding, but both wore expressions I knew preceded objections. Kate was the one to voice theirs. "Of course this presents a problem. Willingly handing over a piece of yourself gives the receiver power and permission."

"We all wish to return home, Miss Smith," Thorandryll said.

"True, but that doesn't mean I trust you any further than Jones can toss you with her telekinesis. There's history to support my lack of trust." She used her chin to indicate me.

"I have paid for my past misjudgments."

Kate sniffed. "Doesn't erase them."

"I'll do it." Everyone looked at me. "Well, it makes sense. I don't have a clue how to use blood or hair against people."

That wasn't true in the strictest sense, because I could use both to find people, or find out if they were alive. But I couldn't do spells with it.

Plus, I trusted Kate, and she'd always been careful to keep Thorandryll from obtaining my hair or blood. Leglin had once told me he'd witnessed the Prince do "terrible magic" with those things. "Come on, I'm the most logical choice. I'll burn everything once I'm through the maze."

"What's to prevent you from removing an item once out of sight?" an elf asked from across the table. He had long, silvery-blonde hair, and a pleasant, not suspicious, expression on his face.

"I wouldn't but if anyone's worried, we can tamper-proof whatever's used to hold the stuff. I'll wait to destroy it after, until everyone's seen it and verified I haven't opened it."

"Satisfactory solution," he said with a nod.

"We don't know what lies in the maze, Miss Jones. It would be safer for a warrior to undertake this venture." Thorandryll inclined his head. "I mean no disrespect by that statement."

"Hey, I'd be happy to sit here, sipping hot chocolate and eating bonbons instead of freezing my tootsies off. But I've actually spent some time studying mazes recently, and I'm a Tracker."

The prince glanced at his brother, who smiled. "Be that as it may..."

"Lady Discord is the reason we've passed the first two challenges," Kethyrdryll said. "I have faith she will successfully complete this one as well."

"We trust Cordi," Damien said.

"So do we," Dane waved his hand to indicate Logan and Connor.

"We trust our prince's decision upon this matter," the silver-haired elf said.

"Cordi won't require charms or potions," Alleryn remarked, and Thorandryll side-eyed him.

I returned to eating my stew and trying to decipher which herbs had been used in it. My name was in the hat, and everyone could argue pros and cons all they pleased.

Which they did for over an hour, before deciding one representative from each of our groups would go.

Me for the humans, Logan for the shifters, and Thorandryll for the elves.

All I could think was, "This will be fun. Not."

TWENTY-FOUR

I tucked the little, clear glass bottle into my shirt after pulling the leather thong it was attached to over my head.

The bottle held a hair from each shifter, both witches, Illy and Leglin, as well as the tip of one of Percy's feathers. Kate had corked the bottle and sealed its top with wax.

"Not that I mistrust you," she'd said, and I'd nodded.

Thorandryll had a similar bottle, full of hair from each elf and their hounds. Logan wanted me to carry his, Connor's, and Dane's hairs, in case he had to shift.

"All right. Wait here until the way is clear," Thorandryll said.

"Twenty-four hours and no word, come find us," I whispered to Kate. She patted my arm.

"I'll be on the lion."

"No, it'll be my turn," Damien said before hugging me. "Be safe."

"That's the plan." I left them arguing in murmurs over Connor, to give him and Dane hugs. "We'll see you guys."

"Better. I don't want to have to tell the boss I misplaced you." Dane made a face. "Or tell Terra that I lost both Logan and you."

"Yeah, wouldn't want that." I laughed and walked over to Leglin. "Keep an eye on them for me."

"*I will,*" the hound promised. "*You will call if you need me?*"

"Yes." I hugged him too. Illy, I skipped, because the husky was watching me from the cover of the pavilion's entrance. Percy was in the pavilion, perched by the fire. They were kind of hurting my feelings, avoiding me the way they had. Maybe I smelled funny, or perhaps it was the frequency thing.

"We're ready, Miss Jones."

"So am I." I joined him and Logan, and we walked down the incline that led to the maze's entrance.

The elf didn't hesitate, striding right into the passage, which was wide enough for us to walk side by side.

Walls of seamless ice, too thick to see through, created the passageway It didn't take long to reach the first turn, and not a few minutes later, we had a choice to go left, right, or straight.

"Okay, thoughts?"

"Right would put us heading toward the castle again," Logan said.

"The most direct route isn't always the correct one."

"Guys, stop. I'm not going to listen to the two of you argue all the way through."

Thorandryll sniffed. "Which passageway do you suggest?"

"Straight first. If we hit a dead end, we'll back track and go left next." I walked ahead, and pulled out the dagger Kethyrdryll had given me to scratch a one on the wall of my chosen passageway. "Come on, speed's a priority."

We went straight at every opportunity. I scratched a one on a wall at each juncture, until we hit a dead end. "Crap. Okay, let's go back."

Ten feet back, we turned, and Logan said, "Um, Cordi?"

"What?"

"Your mark's gone."

I closed my eyes. "Of course it is. Why did I think that would work?"

"We can retrace our route, Miss Jones. By memory and," Thorandryll gave Logan the slightest nod. "By scent."

"Great. Lead on, fellas." I followed them until they stopped short several minutes later. "I don't want to know why we've stopped, do I?"

"Scent trail's gone."

"We did not pass through here."

"Grr." Pushing between them, I looked left then right. My sense of direction had given up trying to keep track some time before. Not that it mattered if the maze was changing. "Let's go left."

Hours later, I regarded the smooth wall of ice ahead of us. "Well, isn't this just perfect? Another friggin' dead end."

"We have two choices," Thorandryll said. "Attempt to retrace our steps again to take a different route, or go through."

"By 'go through', I'm guessing you mean I melt a hole in it." When the elf nodded, I scowled. "Isn't that against the rules?"

"Possibly, yet as you've continually reminded us, we are under a time constraint."

"A maze this size, we could wander for days," Logan added. "Unless you have any psychic leads that help us through faster."

"Nothing yet." I'd been hoping for my tracking ability to kick in. It would make things so much easier. "But I don't want to try melting a hole and have the whole damn thing decide to bury us."

"Retracing our steps it is," Thorandryll muttered, turning around. I traded an exasperated look with Logan. The elf was getting on my nerves. He'd suggested I use my telekinesis to lift him, so he could see where we were. I'd tried that, and the walls had grown taller.

We'd taken a break for some rest and food after that, and had to listen to him bitch under his breath until I was ready to try catapulting him with my TK. Imagining him smacking face first into a wall had nearly given me a case of the giggles.

The fact that I knew we were running out of time kept me from giving in to them.

Another thirty minutes passed before we found ourselves at a new juncture. The maze had changed again. I wasn't the only one growling choice words as we looked down each passageway.

"Which way now?" Logan's teeth were showing, and his eyes had lightened.

"Give me a minute, and hey, calm down."

"I hate this. It's a giant trap. A cage."

I patted his shoulder, and caught a glimpse of something from the corner of my eye. Ginger was standing in the left passage. Pre-vampire Ginger, not rotting or covered in blood. She wore jeans and her favorite lavender tee with a white kitten on the front.

She smiled and beckoned before turning away and beginning to walk. I stared at her figure, not sure what to do. Ginger paused to look at me and make a "Come on" gesture before she turned right.

"Cordi?"

I looked at Logan. "Let's go this way."

"Are you all right? You look like you saw a ghost."

If only he knew. "I'm good. This is the way we need to go."

"Okay."

I led the way, hoping it wasn't a mistake. After all, why would Ginger, or her ghost, appear to help me? I had murdered her.

Or had Merriven been lying? I shivered, recalling thy slimy feel of him in my mind.

But why would he lie? He'd had me at his mercy, locked in his little pocket realm. The bastard had kept me from using some of my abilities. I had the sneaking suspicion he'd manipulated my anger and grief, and knew for certain he'd tried to lull me into accepting being turned.

Maybe he had lied. He'd gone spelunking in my memories. I wasn't certain which ones he'd accessed. The problem was, I'd never know if he'd lied or told the truth. Merriven was dead, beheaded by order of the council.

We'd reached the turn, and Ginger was waiting thirty feet ahead. She tossed a smile over her shoulder and began walking again. Looking at both men's faces as they flanked me, I could tell neither could see her. What if I were leading them straight into trouble by following my delusion?

I chewed on my bottom lip. We were running out of time. Maybe Ginger's image was replacing a tracking thread, because I was crazy. Or going crazy.

A crazy psychic might see ghosts. Or think she was.

I wished I knew what the hell was going on. Every other time I'd seen Ginger had been horrible. Why was this time different?

Logan caught hold of my hand, slipping his fingers between mine. I wondered what he'd say if he knew what I was really following. Things had been going so well between us. I didn't want to mess them up by sharing my fears about my mental health.

Instead, I gave him a quick smile and kept following Ginger as she led the way deeper into the maze. We walked for a few hours, without running into any dead ends. I'd nearly reached the point of stopping when she disappeared around a corner. Turning it, we saw the opening and beyond it, the dark, smooth wall surrounding the castle.

"Well done, Miss Jones," Thorandryll said before taking the lead. He didn't look at me. Probably couldn't stand the sight of me holding hands with a shifter.

As Logan and I cleared the maze after him, a faint grinding noise sounded. I turned around and stopped. "What is that?"

"We solved the maze. It is no longer needed, and is beginning to descend. Once it has, the others will be free to join us."

"Oh." I let Logan's gentle tug put me in motion, and we walked across the flat, snowy area to the recessed entrance in the wall. Up close, the stone walls weren't black, but a deep, dark blue. The outer wall stretched high over our heads, and the main entrance was blocked by thick, metal bars. "How do we open it?"

Logan peered through spaces in the barrier. "Why open them? You can teleport us inside."

"The castle is aware. We'll need its permission to enter, or it will attack us," Thorandryll said.

I turned around to check the maze's descent. "We'd better wait for everyone else."

"You did mention a lack of time. I'll attempt to gain our entrance while we wait." Thorandryll moved into the recessed entrance and put his hand on one of the stone blocks. He closed his eyes.

Nothing exciting to see there. I turned around to watch the maze sinking instead, and shivered. "This is pretty damn weird, even for me."

"Are you cold?"

"Little bit."

Logan came up behind me to share his cloak by wrapping it, and his arms, around me. "How's this?"

Standing cuddles. Definitely okay. "Better, thank you."

I had plenty of time to think about stuff while we waited. Stuff like how easily the two of us got along, how warm he was, and how much I liked him. Slightly problematic stuff, since I didn't know if I was ready to settle into a long-term relationship, if things did work out for us.

Logan had done a great job of making certain I knew he was seriously interested, without being super pushy. He'd become a lot of fun to daydream about as a possible future boyfriend.

Maybe what I needed to concentrate on was what I wanted. All advice from my mom and Jo aside, I'd yet to grow super comfortable with playing the field. Plus, it was hard to find a guy who didn't end up freaking out about my abilities.

They hadn't bothered Nick, but if I could be honest with myself about why we'd ended up together, I could also be honest about the two things I hadn't liked about him: He'd been too possessive and over-protective.

Logan didn't think I was a helpless idiot.

"Here they come," he said. "Maybe another ten minutes."

I nodded, trusting his eyesight, and kept right on musing. He was a great guy, and keeping with the being honest thing, the surety of no babies was a huge draw. Logan was older, and self-confident. He was willing to share a lot more about himself, his family, everything, than Nick had been.

Huh, maybe I was finally beginning to grow up. Here I was, thinking serious thoughts before things became serious, instead of rushing to the next step.

"You're quiet."

"Just thinking."

"Need a sounding board?"

"Not right now, but thank you for offering."

"Any time." Logan rearranged the front of his cloak, for a more secure grip on the edges.

Maybe I was overthinking. He was a good guy, person, and friend. Hell, we might not even survive to start officially dating.

Well, that was a dumb thought, because it triggered the urge to jump his bones so I wouldn't miss out on that experience if we died.

The rest of our group had come far enough that I could distinguish their figures from the shadowy landscape. I checked the sky. Yes, there were clouds, which probably meant more snow. "Hey, you having any luck over there?"

A grating noise responded, and we turned around. The bars were rising as the elf dropped his hand from the stone block he'd been silently communing with. "We have permission to enter, but if we cause harm to any Unseelie within, the castle will respond with extreme prejudice."

"We'll be really, really careful." I wasn't curious enough about what a building would consider "extreme prejudice" to risk finding out.

TWENTY-FIVE

The wall around the castle was perhaps thirty feet wide. It was hard to tell for certain because the entrance tunnel wasn't straight, but sort of S-shaped.

The far side opened unto a large open area that appeared to be a combination of court and stable yard. I could see a few horses in the stables to the left, their heads lowered and eyes closed.

Selwin whickered, but none of them responded to the mare.

I saw something else, and tugged on Logan's sleeve. "What's that?"

He looked at the shape crumpled at the base of one stall door. "A body."

Thorandryll sent two of his men over to check things out at the stables. They returned and reported what they'd found. "The horses sleep, but all the stable hands are dead. Long dead."

"They were human," Kethyrdryll murmured to me, and I nodded. Sal and Cernunnos had both said the Unseelie slept. Humans couldn't sleep for years without medical help. Or magical, but obviously the Unseelie or the bad guys had felt the need to assure... Wait a minute: "What were humans doing here?"

"Some swore their lives in service, and therefore stayed among us in spite of the Sundering spell," Thorandryll answered. "There are benefits, Miss Jones."

"What benefits?"

"Prolonged life for one."

I glanced at the shape I'd first noticed. "Uh huh, that worked out well."

Kate snorted. "Didn't it just? What are we looking at here? A Sleeping Beauty or Snow White spell?"

"I beg your pardon?" Thorandryll raised both his eye brows.

"One's a curse, the other is a poison," Alleryn said. "Curse is more likely. It'd be quite difficult to administer a poison to so many at once."

"Not if you poisoned the well," I shrugged. "If there is a well."

"Underground reservoir, which is connected to most rivers and lakes in this realm," Kethyrdryll said. "It would take barrels and barrels of poison to ensure a proper dosage, and likely would've affected every creature in the realm."

"No Snow White, check," Kate crossed it off an invisible list. "Sleeping Beauty?"

"I doubt they all pricked themselves on cursed spindles. " Alleryn waved his hand at the stone steps leading to the castle's heavy doors. "We need more information."

"Then let's collect it," she said. "Forward ho, and all that."

Forward ho we went, climbing the stone steps to a wide terrace. Crossing it, we paused at the doors. Thorandryll put his hand on one, and it opened about an inch. His brother helped him widen the gap.

I filed in between Logan and Damian. The warlock tapped me on the shoulder. "I've been meaning to ask you what you think of Tabitha?"

Nice to discover I wasn't the only one distracted by personal stuff. "I like her. Why?"

"Do you think she'd agree to a date?"

"That, I don't know."

"Well, of course you don't. You're not her. She's the only one who knows." Damian sighed as we stopped to check out our surroundings. "I'll have to ask her."

Fighting a grin, I patted his shoulder. "Yep, sorry."

A long hallway led to wide stairs, but there was more hallway beyond them. Doors or archways dotted the walls beginning about forty feet past the main entrance.

Dane and Logan exchanged a glance before Logan said, "Why don't you three stick with us? Let the elves lead."

"Why?"

"Because they're used to the sort of magic this place is made of."

"Oh, right." The elves might be able to avoid tripping any traps. "Okay."

Leglin pressed against my leg, and I scratched his shoulders. He managed to nearly knock Alleryn off his feet with the resultant tail wagging.

"Really, Leglin," the mahogany-haired elf muttered after regaining his balance. My hound responded with a doggy grin, his tail still sweeping the air.

I stifled a laugh. Leglin's habit of whacking people with his tail had become a source of amusement for me. Most of my friends had learned to stay out of range by now. Alleryn was officially a friend, but he hadn't exactly hung out with us.

"We'll set up camp here."

I looked at Thorandryll. "Camp? We need to..."

"I'm aware of our mission. My people and the hounds can search. They'll inform us of their findings." Thorandryll paused to listen to Kethyrdryll's whisper. He nodded. "It will be safer to remain here until we know where the Unseelie are."

I hesitated but then nodded. Exploring unfamiliar territory really wasn't high on my priority list after the things we'd already encountered. "All right."

The prince sorted his people into teams while his brother set up camp. Camp consisted of a pavilion along each wall, between the entrance and the first doors, plus a thorny barrier across the entrance and the hallway at the opposite end.

A narrow opening was left in that barrier, so the elves and hounds could leave. One elf and hound pair were assigned to guard the opening.

Kethyrdryll stabled his mare. The rest of us—three shifters, two witches, Thorandryll, three hounds, and me—went into Kethyrdryll's pavilion. The table had been set for dinner.

Looking over the beautifully glazed ham and assorted veggie side dishes, I felt sorry for the other elves having to work without a hot meal first. I loaded my plate and a goblet of chilled juice and carried it out to the guard. "I thought you might like something to eat."

The guard, an elf with white hair and blue-green eyes, gave me a startled look. "That's very kind of you, milady. Thank you."

"You're welcome." I handed the plate, silverware, and goblet over to him. "I put an extra slice on for your hound."

The hound's ears perked, and I realized it was Enid. "Oh, hi, I haven't forgotten about the steak. We'll have the cook-out as soon as it warms up, okay?"

She gave a small wag in response. I patted her broad skull and went back into the pavilion. There was a new place setting in front of my chair.

"That wasn't necessary, Miss Jones," Thorandryll said as I began to serve myself.

"Maybe not, but it was polite."

He stared at me. "Are you implying my treatment of my people is lacking?"

"Nope, I just felt weird eating while they didn't." Though if that's what he thought my act meant, maybe Prince Snooty Pants needed to do a little self-assessment. "That's all."

"I have found Lady Discord to be quite kind," Kethyrdryll said. "Kindness is an admirable trait."

"She does have a tendency to let her inner mushy show." Kate fed Percival a bite of apple. I checked the area in front of the fireplace. All four hounds and Illy were settled there with raw hambones. The bones had chunks of meat still attached.

"I'm not mushy. It doesn't cost anything to be nice to others." One of Mom's favorite sayings. Of course, it did cost time, but so what? A few minutes here, an hour there...better way to spend time than constantly worrying about stuff.

Like where dating Logan would lead, or what would happen if we couldn't wake the Unseelie.

Once I'd thought those things, I began to worry again.

One by one, the searchers returned with bad news. None had found a single Unseelie snoozing anywhere.

"Maybe I can locate someone with telepathy. I mean, it's worth a shot, right?"

"If you're willing to make such an attempt, please do," Thorandryll answered.

"Just be careful." Kate frowned. "You know what can happen when you make contact with old minds."

"They're elves, not vampires."

"Right. Instead of a massive attack of blood thirst, you'll acquire an ego the size of an ocean."

"You know, we are right here. Actually in the same room," Alleryn said.

She smiled sweetly, batting her eyelashes at him. "I'm aware of that."

"Okay, I think I'd better go outside, have all of you behind me." When I stood, so did everyone else. "I work better without a crowd watching, people."

Dane and Logan remained standing as everyone else sat down. I shrugged. "Okay, you two can come with."

The same elf I'd taken dinner to had stayed on guard duty. He allowed us out, and the guys took up positions on either side of the opening. Logan said, "We'll wait right here."

"Okay." I turned away and walked about ten feet before halting and closing my eyes. I concentrated to put as much juice into my mental shout as possible. *Anyone home?*

No response. I tried again. *We're here to help.*

I listened carefully, and though I heard something, maybe a faint whisper. *Hello?*

Dead silence. Shaking my head, I turned around and walked back. "Nothing."

"Hey, you tried." Dane grinned. "Don't worry, we'll find them."

"Before or after the big kablooey part?" I let Logan pull me into a hug when I was close enough. "You know, sometimes I dream of being a stripper."

That earned hoots of laughter from them both, and Logan squeezed me a bit tighter. "Why?"

"It has to be a far easier job than being a psychic."

"My question is, are you any good at it?" Dane waggled his eyebrows. "Oh, and what's your stage name?"

"Barbi Ella."

Logan chuckled. "Seriously? Barbarella?"

"No, I had to make something up because he asked, and that movie came to mind." My head was beginning to ache again, and all the worrying I'd been doing made it feel as though snakes of uneasiness were squirming around inside me. "I'm tired."

"Bet Logan will tuck you in." Dane hurried ahead of us to avoid the cuff Logan aimed at him. "Missed me."

"I won't next time," Logan promised. "Quit teasing Cordi. She's tired."

"Thanks for letting us out," I said to the guard elf, who nodded.

It sucked to have to shake my head at everyone's hopeful looks when we reentered the pavilion. Dane bent to whisper to Alleryn, who left his seat. "I'll bring you something for your headache."

"Thanks. I'm calling it a night." I glanced at Logan. *You're welcome to snuggle when you're ready to go to bed.*

He smiled. *Okay. I'll be in after a while.*

"Good night." I went to my room, and took my medicine when Alleryn brought it to me. I was asleep before Logan came in.

TWENTY-SIX

"Cordi, wake up. He's going to hurt your mom." Ginger shook my arm. "You have to stop him."

"What?" I rubbed my eyes.

"He has your mom, and he's a vampire. Get up," she pleaded, her hair mussed and tears rolling down her cheeks. We wore our matching, oversized purple T-shirts, and our Halloween costumes were hanging over my desk chair.

I groaned and rolled over. "I told you not to eat all your candy tonight. Now it's giving you nightmares."

"No, this is real. I went to get a drink of water, and he has her." Ginger pulled the covers off me. "Cordi!"

"Gah, all right. Jeeze, we'll go look." I knew she wouldn't leave me alone until we did. Sleepovers with Ginger didn't involve much sleep.

"Take this." She shoved something at me when I rolled over and sat up.

It was a stake. "What are you doing with this?"

"Hurry. He might already be drinking her blood."

"Yeah, right." Rolling my eyes, I slid off the bed. We crept out of my room and down the hallway to the living room. The light came on, and we shrieked.

Dad grinned. "Thought I heard something. Do you girls know what time it is?"

"She had a nightmare. Again."

"Did not. There's a vampire in the kitchen." Ginger shoved me. "There really is, Mr. Jones."

"Oh." Dad winked at me, and I winked back. "Well, we'd better go check things out."

We met him at the swinging door. Dad put his finger to his lips before pushing it open. The light was on, and when we looked inside, Ginger screamed. So did I, at the sight of a man with his teeth buried in the side of Mom's neck. Her eyes were open and vacant.

"Sunny!" Dad charged into the kitchen. "Get away from her!"

The man let go and stood, letting Mom flop to the floor. I stood there, open-mouthed and staring, as he hit Dad, smashing in the side of his head. Dad fell on top of Mom, and neither of them moved.

"Run!" Ginger yanked on my arm, and I dropped the stake. "Cordi, run!"

I shook my head, my gaze captured by the man's red eyes. He smiled, revealing bloody teeth. "What beautiful little girls."

"You're not real." Ginger was crying, begging me to run. I shook her off. "This never happened. You're not real!"

Silence fell. He smiled again. "I'm not, but she is."

"You should've run, Cordi."

I slowly turned around, the living room morphing into a shadowy cavern. Ginger's eyes were red, and she was all grown up. "First you didn't save me, and then you killed me."

I shook my head while backing up. She glided toward me. "You killed me, Cordi. Why?"

"I thought that was what you wanted. I didn't know it was him."

Ginger flickered closer, her gray face mottling with black veins. "You murdered me."

It hurt to hear out loud, and I flinched. "I did what you asked me to do. I didn't know he was making you say those things."

"You should've known," she shouted right in my face before swinging her fist. It struck my left cheek, snapping my head to the side.

I'd done enough to her, couldn't fight back as she hit me again and again, until I went down. Curled in a ball, my arms over my head, I did the only thing I could think of. "Leglin!"

Ginger screamed and screamed again, the second ending in a gurgle. I cautiously uncurled, searching the darkness, and swallowed a scream of my own as a shape slunk clear of the shadows. "*Cordi?*"

"Good boy."

Leglin's tail wagged. I sat up and hugged his neck once he was close enough. "I don't know where we are, or what happened."

"*I was chasing deer,*" the hound said. "*With a great pack. You called me.*"

Chasing deer? What...oh. "We're dreaming."

"*We are?*" Leglin sniffed the air. "*This smells real.*"

"The last thing I remember is falling asleep. Then I was here. We have to be dreaming." I paused. "They said we had to wake them."

Which meant we'd fallen under the same spell. But the elves hadn't found the Unseelie. Crap. Was someone dragging off all of us to wherever they'd hidden the Unseelie? I shuddered at the idea.

The bad guys had missed a beat, because being unconscious and at the mercy of others was a much bigger nightmare. I'd lost three years of my life with that happening while I was comatose.

Anger tightened my voice. "We have to find the others."

Leglin stepped back as I climbed to my feet. My nightgown flapped around my legs in a sudden breeze, and I looked to the side to discover old Henry advancing. Invisible moonlight shone off his straight razor.

For a second, I cringed. Only a second. "You're dead, dude. You're just a memory, and I am not a helpless girl."

Henry's maniacal smile wavered.

"Go the hell away before I blow you to bits."

The serial killer flickered, lowering his weapon, and faded from sight. I sighed. "Discord Jones, Dream Warrior."

The nightgown had to go. All my favorite movie heroines tended to dress way bad ass.

This was a dream, and thanks to Mom, I knew once you were aware you were dreaming, you could change things. It was called lucid dreaming or something.

"Wardrobe," I muttered and nodded as my nightgown became jeans, black combat boots, a black tank top, and black leather jacket. My hair rearranged itself into a ponytail. "Much better."

Ready to kick ass, I grinned. "This may turn out to be fun. Let's go."

"*Where?*"

"To find the others first, then we'll look for the Unseelie. Come on." I set off for the darkness with a confident step. Right now this was my dream. I could do anything I wanted to in my own damn dream.

A familiar place formed as we walked: The ravine where the dog fight and my first face-to-face with Dalsarin had taken place. As we neared the ring, transparent figures ran past.

One wasn't transparent. Logan ran ahead of us, his ebony, white-striped body straining for every step, as though he were running through quick sand.

I remembered nightmares like that, and stopped to watch for a second.

Bad idea. Dalsarin put two arrows through my doppelganger before the tiger broke free and leaped onto the dark elf. When Dalsarin shouted, flinging Logan away, the tiger couldn't escape the wave of green fire. I hurried forward, dropping into the pit. "Logan! It's not real!"

The tiger's writhing and roars of agony didn't cease. I had to put my money where my mouth was, running forward to grab handfuls of fur on either side of his jaws. "Dude, it's not real. Look at me."

No more tiger. A confused Logan peered up from the ground, his head at an awkward angle because of my double-fisted grip in his hair. "Cordi."

"Hi."

"Ouch. You're kind of pulling my hair a lot."

"Sorry." I let go and the surroundings disappeared, leaving the three of us in a spotlight circle of light.

"We're stuck in Dreamland. Or maybe Nightmare Land is more accurate."

"Oh." Logan sat up and climbed to his feet, smoothing his hair down with one hand.

I wondered if it was me in particular he worried about not arriving in time for, or if I'd just been a symbol for all those he cared about. Could've asked him, but I didn't want to tell anyone about my nightmare. Fair was fair. "I think we're under the same spell the Unseelie are. We need to find the others."

"All right, how?"

I shrugged, "We just started walking once I realized what was happening."

Logan nodded, "Okay, Which direction?"

"Have I ever said 'thank you' for how you just go along with my ideas?"

"I did argue once, and you took an arrow to the shoulder."

Hm, that was right. "I'll listen better the next time you argue."

He smiled. "Sure. Which way?"

"Let's go straight. That's how we found you."

"Have you tried waking up?"

"Nope. Sal said we didn't have much time to wake them. This is the first real opportunity we've gotten to do it." Besides, what if we did wake to find ourselves being dragged off? Someone would get hurt. Maybe even dead. "Let's take it."

"Okay."

Off we walked, into the darkness again.

"Look familiar?" I asked Logan as we stepped from dark to a sunlit meadow. He shook his head, scanning the immediate area. "I don't recognize it either."

"I smell blood," he and Leglin said at the same time.

"Lead the way." What would we find? Whose bad dream was this? I followed them through knee high grass, and stepped around Logan when they halted.

Thorandryll's face was hidden as he hugged the limp figure of an elven woman to him. It took me a second to realize the prince was weeping.

Bloody froth dripped from her lips. Her dark eyes were glassy and staring. The remains of a picnic were scattered about them, including an overturned goblet close to her lax hand. Thorandryll rocked her, still quietly weeping, and her dark brown hair swayed.

"Son of a bitch," Logan breathed. "She looked like you."

"I guess." She had to be his wife, the one who'd cheated on him with Dalsarin. "He poisoned her."

"Looks that way."

I took a deep breath, "I'm going to wake him."

"Okay."

Two steps, and Logan said, "Wait."

I turned around, "Why?"

"You're in a dress. Her dress."

Looking down, I discovered he was right. "What the hell?"

"I'll wake him." Logan walked past and stood looking at Thorandryll for a few seconds. He crouched down and grabbed the elf's shoulder. "Wake up."

The woman disappeared when Thorandryll lifted his head. He blinked at Logan, noticed me, and looked around as the scene faded from sight. "You will speak of this to no one."

Releasing his shoulder, Logan stood, "Didn't see a thing."

"I won't tell anyone," I said. "Wardrobe, damn it."

The long, blue dress turned back into my ass-kicking outfit. "Come on, we need to keep going."

"Where?" Thorandryll rose. "What is going..."

"We won tickets to Nightmare land. Aren't we lucky? Now move your butt. We have to find the others and the Unseelie."

"No, we should wake ourselves."

"Go right ahead. We'll wait." I was curious if we could.

Thorandryll frowned. "It appears I cannot."

One by one we found the others. Kate was wandering, calling "Daddy?" in a little girl voice, Percy asleep in her arms. Dane was in a cage, huddled in a corner, his expression lost and lonely.

Connor was arguing with a faceless woman, storming away from her as we approached. Alleryn stared out a window in his clinic, and I had no idea what his nightmare represented to him.

Damian knelt at the foot of a pile of bodies, Ily asleep beside him. Each body had a toe tag with a big red X – Unsolved Cases. Kethyrdryll's nightmare was familiar. We found him at his original camp, his mare asleep, and Leandra nowhere to be seen.

The rest of the elves' nightmares involved loss or failure.

Finally, we marched into a meadow full of hounds, many of them playing or eating from several deer carcasses. "That's way more than you came with."

"The Unseelie Queen's pack," Thorandryll replied. He spoke in Elvish, calling them to order. The meadow and deer remains faded away.

We were making good progress. "Okay, let's find her next if we can."

"This is Spot, her pack leader." Thorandryll gestured a hound slightly bigger than Leglin forward. "He should be able to lead us to her."

"Spot? Really?"

"Maeve has a strange sense of humor."

"Uh huh. Okay." I focused on Spot. "Please do your best to lead us to your Queen."

Spot sniffed. *"Humans do not order me."*

"I didn't order you, bub. I asked nicely."

The hound tilted his massive skull, perking his ears. *"You understand me?"*

"Yeah. I was a dog for a while, picked up the language," I said.

"*Interesting.*" His head straightened.

"I thought the same thing. Now, would you please lead us to the Queen? We're here to help her and the rest of the Unseelie."

Spot lifted his lips enough to show the tips of his fangs. "*There are shifters among you.*"

"Yeah, and they're my friends. No biting, or I'll have to show you how wrong you are about my being human," I warned him.

He sniffed, tilted his head and sniffed again, more deeply. "*You're not human. What are you?*"

"Hell if I know anymore. Chop, chop, Spot. The Queen needs us."

The hound growled, but he glanced at Thorandryll, and the elf nodded. "*I will obey the Prince.*"

I suddenly wondered why Thorandryll was the prince, and Kethyrdryll a lord. After all, they were brothers. Even if only one parent was royalty, wouldn't they both be princes? Unless they were half-brothers. Maybe that was the reason. A glance at them and I couldn't see that being the case. They were practically identical twins. Oh well, bigger fish to fry. I could ask about it later.

Spot turned and trotted away, the other hounds following. I hoped they could lead us to the Queen, and that we didn't run completely out of time before they did.

Quite a few minutes passed before Kethyrdryll asked, "Does anyone else hear that?"

"I do. Sounds like music." Logan stared into the darkness, his eyes paling. "There's light ahead."

"Yay. Go." I gave him a push and grabbed Kethyrdryll's arm. "Come on, people. Boots in motion. Hut, two, three."

A few minutes later, I could see the light and hear the music too. The end appeared to be in sight. Well, at least the end of looking for the Unseelie.

Between one step and the next, we went from gloom to a brightly lit ballroom. Elegantly attired dancers whirled in perfect time. Everyone wore masks, but their pointed ears made it clear we'd found exactly the people we needed.

A gorgeous woman dressed in a lacy, lilac ball gown sat on a white marble throne above the crowd, watching them. Her long hair was pale blonde, and a delicate crown of gold and diamonds twinkled on top of her head.

She saw us, and rose from her throne. The dancers split like a school of fish dodging a shark, clearing a path to the steps that led up to her throne.

"Come forth," she commanded. I decided to let the elf brothers lead. We walked between two lines of masked, staring dancers, which I didn't much care for.

Once we reached the foot of the steps, she smiled. "Welcome, my sons."

TWENTY-SEVEN

"She's your mother?"

"Yes."

Queen Maeve didn't look old enough to have two full-grown sons. Then again, elves didn't noticeably age. "Oh, cool."

"Who are these people?"

Kethyrdryll stepped forward and bowed. "Your Majesty, this is the Lady Discord. Her companions are Logan Sayer, Prince Connor O'Meara, Dane Soames, Miss Kate Smith, and Detective Damian Herde."

"Percival," Kate's parrot added, "And Illusion."

"Shifters and witches." The Queen frowned. "Except her."

She was looking at me. I wondered if I should bow.

"There's tiger in your aura, yet you're not a shifter."

I indicated Logan and Dane with a wave of my hand. "They adopted me into their clan."

"Hm. You're a natural mage."

I wasn't about to argue with her. "Looks that way."

She lost interest in me, looking around. "Where is this place?"

I let Thorandryll explain, watching as Maeve's expression turned hard and her blue eyes frosty. When he finished, she uttered one word. "Morpheus."

"Oh, I know that one. The god of sleep, right?"

"One of the gods of sleep and dreams," Thorandryll corrected me, gazing at his mother. "I wasn't aware you had him in custody."

"You're Seelie, It's not your place to know such things."

"Why would you have Morpheus in custody?" My question drew Maeve's attention back to me.

"It is the duty of my people to capture and hold those who do evil. Morpheus changed. He is no longer a gentle god."

"Oh." And we were still under his power. "Um, maybe we better wake up."

"We've tried, Miss Jones." Thorandryll folded his hands together. "And were unsuccessful."

It occurred to me that I may have dreamed everything. Morpheus could be any of the people around me. Maybe even all of them. "Let's try again."

The Queen's laugh was a silvery, musical sound. "I'm now aware of the matter. Awake."

I opened my eyes to a smooth surface and no feeling in the arm I lay on.

We had been moved. I groaned while rolling over onto my back, and heard enough to realize I wasn't alone.

Okay, I was alone in the little cell with its door of bars and smooth walls of dull black volcanic rock. Yet, I could hear Kate muttering, the rustle-flap of Percy's wings, and other sounds of people waking. My arm began to tingle and I grimaced.

"Cordi?" Logan and Dane called out at the same time, changing my grimace to a smile.

"I'm okay, is everyone here?" I rubbed my arm, wishing it would hurry up and return to normal circulation.

"Roll call," Kate said, and one by one, the members of our party gave their names. I sat up when no one mentioned the hounds or mare.

"Leglin." My hound buddy didn't appear. "Okay. I don't like this."

"We're in a dungeon. There's a lot not to like." Damian replied.

"None of the Unseelie are present," Thorandryll said. "The cell doors are spelled to prevent escape."

Ily yelped, and the prince sighed. "Don't touch the bars."

"It's all right. You don't have a mark," Damian told his familiar. The husky grumbled. "I've said time and time again, not to put your nose on things. " A slap of hand on rock followed.

"So we're trapped." Connor's statement. "Fantastic."

"The Queen is awake. She'll send people to search for us since she knows we're here." Kethyrdryll paused. "Whether that's before or after the Unseelie retake their realm..."

I huffed and climbed to my feet. My ass-kicking outfit was, of course, gone. The air felt chilly. "I'm not hanging out for rescue in my freaking night gown, people. Not really in the mood to freeze to death."

"What do you suggest, Miss Jones? We can't touch the bars and they are the only way out. There are spells to prevent magical egress." Thorandryll sounded as huffy as I felt. "As the young lion said, we are trapped."

"Un huh." I walked two steps, stopped shy of the bars. From my new vantage point, I could see two other cell doors across a narrow hall. "Hi."

Kate wiggled her fingers at me. Percy stood at her feet, his head turned. In the other cell, Logan smiled and lifted his hand. The bars looked like metal and radiated cold.

"Hm. Are there alarm spells? Like if someone escaped, would the Unseelie know?"

"Of course." Thorandryll's voice came from the left. I couldn't see him, but Kate must've been able to, because she pointed.

"Okay." Could I melt the bars? In theory, kinetic abilities were all about manipulating energy and matter. If I wanted ice, I made whatever moisture was present cold. Fire, I leaned on friction to cause air to super heat.

Metal was a little different. It didn't burn like air or wood or vampires. I'd have to try and make it melt. That would require a lot of concentration and focus to get right. "As long as I don't touch the bars, I'm good, right?"

"Or attempt spells," Kethyrdryll said.

"Bully for me. I don't know any." Deep breath, Cordi. It can't be that hard. "Okay."

"What are you planning to do?" Logan had moved closer to his cell door.

"I'm gonna give it a hot foot. Or try to."

Thorandryll snorted. "It won't work. Your abilities are a form of magic, Miss Jones."

"I don't cast spells," I pointed out. I didn't. I just...kind of directed my kinetic abilities' particular powers and manipulated them to do what I wanted.

With varying degrees of success, but oh well.

"I pray for you at times," the prince said. "I pray you'll survive your youthful arrogance."

"Gee, thanks ever so much. Don't think I don't know that's a fancy way of calling me an idiot, you jerk."

"He may be right." Kate rubbed her arms. She was wearing a lilac nightgown.

"I am right."

"And I am going to try this anyway, because I'm freaking cold," I said. "So shut up, Prince Snooty Pants."

"I'm merely attempting to save you pain," Thorandryll snapped. "Proceed if you wish. I await the opportunity to say 'I told you so' with an unseemly gleefulness."

"Stuff it." Okay, I was going to do this just to make him eat crow. "And be quiet, I have to concentrate."

Which part? I decided on the metal plate. The other side had a keyhole. I could see the keyholes on Kate and Logan's cell doors. "One metal hot foot coming up."

Air was easy to combust. You simply increased the friction of its molecules until they burst into flame. The one and only time I'd set anything with metal parts on fire had been when I'd first woken from my coma.

I needed to practice to fine tune my abilities but finding time on a regular basis wasn't exactly easy. Plus, I needed a safe place to practice with fire.

Didn't want to burn anything down. I usually didn't want to.

There had to be some air inside the lock. I concentrated on that, and a flicker of light rewarded my effort. Next step: heat the metal enough to melt. How many degrees was that? I had no clue, other than more than five hundred, since that was the high temperature for most ovens.

The best I could do was keep sending oxygen in and continue making the air molecules do a mad rhumba inside the lock. It was working, because I could smell the heated tang of metal.

I heard something give in the lock, and switched gears, hitting the door with a blast of telekinesis. It burst open and hit the edge of its stone frame on the hinge side. The dull clang-thump echoed as the cell door rebounded. I stopped it from closing with a TK block. "Hah."

Walking out, I turned left and put my hands on my hips while meeting Thorandryll's sour gaze. "Sorry dude, no 'I told you so' opportunity here."

"You may be out, but we're still trapped."

"Give me a minute, and your cloak. I'm freezing."

He actually rolled his ice blue eyes, but unpinned his cloak and dropped it. There was a slot at the bottom of his cell door, probably for food tray passage. Thorandryll used the toe of his boot to stuff his cloak through it.

I bent to pull the cloak through and gave it a shake before wrapping it around me. "Thank you."

My bare feet were turning into ice cubes, but the cloak was an improvement over running around in a nightgown and panties.

I studied his cell door before looking left and right. More bars blocked each end of the cell block. No handy keys, buttons, or switches to see. "Figures."

"Beg your pardon?"

"Nothing. Okay, stand back." When the elf complied, I concentrated on the lock of his cell. Maybe he'd figure out a way to help once he was free.

Hearing the crack of superheated metal, I moved aside and pulled his cell door open with TK. "See, I'm your get out of jail free card."

"My thanks." Thorandryll joined me in the corridor. I turned to cross to Kate's cell.

"Can you help me open these? I'm going to run out of juice if I have to do them all like this."

"I'll see what I can do." He moved to do Alleryn's cell door. I began to concentrate, but heard "tink tink" and turned to see what Thorandryll was doing.

"You carry lock picks?"

"Shh." He had his eyes half-closed. Shaking my head, I turned back and got busy. Once Kate was out, Percy took flight.

"Free, free. *La petite deesse.*"

I moved on while Kate scurried over to relieve Alleryn of his cloak as he left his cell. Her boyfriend produced another set of lock picks.

Logan stepped back, and I discovered it was hard to concentrate with him dressed just in pants. He was loads more distracting now, after the kissing and cuddling we'd done. My cheek had rested on his bare chest, and it had liked doing so.

Sproing-crack. I TKed his cell door open. "I bet you're cold."

"I'm okay," he assured me, his lips curving a touch. "How are you doing?"

"I'm considering setting my feet on fire."

"Give me a minute."

I nodded and went to the next cell. Damian waved, his other hand resting on Illusion's head. "Hello. Come to save the day?"

"Giving it my best shot." By the time I'd freed them, Logan appeared with a pair of thick socks. "Ooh."

"On loan from Kethyrdryll."

"Nice." I made short work of putting the socks on, hoping my feet would thaw out. The socks did provide insulation from the stone floor.

Before long, everyone was free. I'd ended up at one of the end doors, and sighed. "I'm tired."

My head was hurting too, and my stomach chose that moment to let me know it wanted food with a growl. "And I'm hungry."

A figure stepped into view on the other side of the bars. I shrieked and backed into Logan, lifting my hand to my chest. My heart was trying to leap out of it. "Holy crap! Don't do that."

The two elves on the other side of the bars paid zero attention to me. Logan and I stepped back as one of them began to unlock the door. They were both armed with swords and wearing dark gray armor.

"I want armor. Can I have cool armor?"

"If we make it home, I'll commission some for you. I know a guy," Logan said.

"Promise?"

"Promise."

"You continue to hold the title of Bestest Friend."

"Prince Thorandryll," one of the new elves called, as he entered the dungeon. I tried to stifle my giggles when he ducked Percy, who dropped a smelly bird bomb on his way out. It splattered on the elf's back armor. My sputtering noises earned me a look that killed my giggle urge.

"Hey, I didn't do it."

Percy shot back through the doorway, screeching and pooping as he went. Logan and I narrowly avoided being hit, plastering ourselves to the wall. Few others were as lucky, resulting in yells of outrage and arms swinging, trying to swat the parrot out of the air.

"Really, Percival."

"Miss Smith, control your familiar," Thorandryll ordered. Kate gave him a look that plainly told him where he could stick his order. Percy pooped on the prince's shoulder before landing on Kate's.

I buried my face against Logan's shoulder, trying to muffle my laughter. Trust Bird Brain to shake things up.

"I don't like your bird," Connor told Kate.

"Not very fond of him myself at the moment."

"Prince Thorandryll," Percy's first target said. "My Queen requires your attendance."

"Of course."

"Hey, any chance of some clothes?" I'd recovered from my hilarity. "I'm not dressed for meeting royalty."

The second new elf sneered at me. "And you are?"

"Lady Discordia Angel Jones, a queen of my clan, a protégé of Lord Whitehaven's, and the main reason you're awake with a hope in hell of taking back your realm."

I closed my mouth, quit staring at Logan, and nodded. "What he said, bub."

Kethyrdryll smiled. "She's also a rather powerful natural mage."

"I prefer psychic."

He bowed. "My apologies for forgetting your preference."

"Are you two officially dating yet?" Damian waved his finger between Logan and me. Kate smacked his arm. "What?"

"Not the time."

"It would be glorious if everyone who isn't me would stop speaking now." Everyone looked at Thorandryll. He smiled. "Thank you. Now, we are ready to meet with the Queen."

TWENTY-EIGHT

We were guided to the same ballroom we'd visited in the dream, which apparently doubled as Queen Maeve's throne room. Once again, we had to pass between lines of grim-faced, staring Unseelie. I didn't like it any better the second time around.

Though catching one or two of them wrinkling their noses at the odor of parrot poo kind of made my day.

The Unseelie Queen didn't looked impressed as she surveyed us from her throne. "You appear worse for the wear, my sons."

"There was an unfortunate incident," Kethyrdryll said.

"I would like some clothes before we go fight the bad guy. Please," I added when Maeve looked at me.

"You won't be accompanying us. This is an internal matter."

"He has human hostages we've been sent to retrieve." Kate slipped between Thorandryll and Kethyrdryll. I envied her ability to appear confident, dressed in a nightgown and cloak spattered with bird crap. "We have the right to claim our human kin."

"Here, you have only the rights I choose to grant you, little witch."

I freed one hand from my borrowed cloak and raised it. "Um, what if we're under the orders of a god?"

Maeve smiled. "And which god would that be, who orders you to trespass into my domain?"

I couldn't give her Sal's name, because I didn't know his real one, so I went with God Number Two. "The Horned God, Cernunnos."

"Really, Miss Jones," Thorandryll gritted out, shooting me an annoyed look.

"Don't you really me, bub. He told me to come here, to find what's missing. What's missing is humans. I'm here, and I'm going to find them."

"You're not one of us, nor an animal. Why would the Lord of the Hunt choose you as his emissary?" Maeve asked.

Good question. I stared back at her, before smiling as an answer presented itself. "He's the Lord of the Hunt. I'm a private investigator, which is a type of hunter, and I'm on a hunt."

Thorandryll sighed. "The Horned One did state that he found Miss Jones to be an intriguing child, when first they met."

"How did such a meeting come about?"

"She rode on a Hunt with us," Alleryn replied from somewhere behind us. "A dark elf survived."

Maeve's lips tightened. "I see."

"Miss Jones has proven herself useful in the past," the prince said. He hadn't lost his annoyed face though.

I grinned up at the Queen. "Not to brag, but I blew up a god at the end of that Hunt. Well, his Avatar."

Her lips parted, and she blinked. "We have a matter of grave importance to attend to. See to it that they're properly outfitted."

"Why don't we have armor?" I swept my hand from myself to Damian and Kate.

Logan double-checked the hang of the sword he'd been given. "Ever play an RPG?"

"Huh?"

"Role playing game. Dungeons and Dragons?" Damian shook his head at my blank look. "What do you do for fun?"

"Cook, read, watch movies." I pointed at Leglin. "He even got armor."

"Because he's a tank. Tanks physically fight. We," Damian waved his hand, including Kate and me in the sweep of his hand. "Are casters. We do damage from a distance."

"With a buffer zone of us to keep anyone from getting to you." Dane tightened the straps on Connor's chest plate.

"Oh." I eyed Logan's sword, which had a brilliant green jewel set in the pommel. "I want to start taking sword lessons."

"Every clan member can use one. I can teach you, or if you'd rather have a female instructor, I'd recommend Moira. She's hell on wheels with blades. Any type of blade." Logan surveyed us, and knelt to make adjustments to Leglin's armor. The chest piece of if didn't look quite right. "Who put this on him?"

"Well, I tried," Kate said, her hands landing on her hips. "It's not like I spend my days dressing doggies for war."

"I can tell," Logan said. "You put this on upside down."

She muttered something that sounded nasty and wandered off. I hid my smile by bending to pat Illy. He bared his teeth. Snatching my hand back, I asked, "What is your problem, dude?"

"He and Percy aren't happy we'll be facing a god."

Oh. I remembered how their familiars had acted during the Case of the Cursing Corpsicle, (who was Dalsarin). I looked at Illy. "You know, it's not my damn fault gods decide to turn evil and run around doing bad things to people."

The husky grumbled. I didn't understand what he said, only then realizing he didn't actually speak Dog. Or not the version of Dog I'd inadvertently learned. Was there more than one version? "Fine, be mad. See if I care, or ever cook you steak again."

Illy flattened his ears and skulked off. The call came to form up into lines. Kethyrdryll, dressed in silvery blue armor, joined us. "Hey, why aren't you up there with your mom and brother?"

"I've been assigned to your guard." He nodded at two more elves walking up to us. "As were they."

"Oh. Thanks." It sounded as though we wouldn't be near any actual fighting. Maybe the Queen didn't want to risk both her sons.

We began moving, the clanking of armor echoing as we marched down the hallway we'd gathered in. Nervousness fluttered in my stomach. I looked around at my companions, hoping we'd all go home in one piece.

"We'll transport to the Pit in groups," Kethyrdryll informed us. "There's not a gate or door to step through."

"Then how did that golem deliver the people to it?" Really, the Pit? Couldn't elves come up with a better name for their high-security prison?

He shook his head. "I don't know. There are layers of wards on the walls."

"Well, if I were your mom, I'd be scheduling a good, hard inspection after this." I thought about slipping the Queen Ronnie's card. Which reminded me that I needed to call Ronnie. My new place needed warding.

Elves were disappearing ahead of us. Magical transport, my favorite. Wait, I supposedly counted as a magic user. A natural mage. It did have a certain ring to it. Nah, after years of being called a psychic, I was comfortable with that label.

Our turn came, and we walked forward, the hallway disappearing and a square room replacing it. The walls were pale gray stone, and there was a wide archway at the opposite end. I checked over my shoulder. The wall behind us was solid.

Beyond the archway was a stadium-sized room or cavern, with dark stone walls. I wasn't sure how dark because the entire place was shrouded in heavy shadows. Nothing moved, and the only sounds I heard were the soft footfalls of elves as they formed a multilayered half-circle outside the archway. "This doesn't look like a hotbed of prison escapees."

Logan sniffed. "They're hiding. I can smell..."

The half-circle of elves had been slowly moving forward as more arrived. Something rose from the puddle of shadows across the middle of the floor. No one screamed. Instead, a rain of arrows flew, and whatever the thing was, it went down a pincushion. "The lighting sucks. What was that?"

"A giant, I think." Kate tilted her head. "Does anyone else hear wings?"

We all looked up, but the ceiling was completely blacked out. And that's when the goblins decided to charge. I let loose with my pyrokinesis, creating a wall of fire to block them.

"Cernunnos bless us," Kethyrdryll murmured as my fire lit the place up. There were cracks in every wall, and a lot of eyes reflecting flames. "They've been destroying the wards."

"Maeve," a voice roared at the far end, and a hulking, red beast strode out of a particularly large crack. "Face me, you elven bitch."

The Queen strode forward, her glittering armor adding a light show of blue and orange sparks as it reflected the fire. "Miss Jones."

"Yes, ma'am?"

She gestured at the fire with her sword. "If you'd be so kind?"

"Oh, sure." I put the fire out, aware of the elves in the front lifting their weapons. Good thing they did, because a wave of dark figures came forward.

"Goblins!" someone yelled and within seconds, everything was chaos. I lost sight of Kate as something dropped onto her, but saw Dane kick and slash at whatever it was. Illy was barking. I couldn't see Damian. The remaining elves poured from the archway, forcing us apart, and forward.

Connor cut down something with wings and a human face that flew at us with its clawed chicken feet outstretched. One of the two elves went down as four twisted, smoky figures leaped onto him.

I hit a looming figure with a blast of TK, knocking it away from Kethyrdryll, who was busy slicing away at a blobby creature with long arms. Logan snarled, fencing with a being made of shiny, silver light.

"I'm way out of," I sent a lance of fire toward what I thought might be a troll. "My depth."

Connor laughed. "Me too. Fun, huh?"

"Yeah, ahh." A concussion rocked the area, knocking us down. My stomach lurched. "What was that?"

"Ah, big and fiery. Going to say..."

Kethyrdryll finished Connor's sentence. "Fire elemental."

"Hey." I'd gotten to my feet. "Let me at it."

"Go for the heart," Logan called, already slashing away at nasties again.

"Heart. Got it." I focused on the tall, vaguely human-shaped figure. The elemental was shedding flames that became little firenados. "So, heart would be about...there."

I concentrated, channeling my cryokinesis, and the fire elemental stopped. A dark splotch slowly appeared on its chest. "Yeah, buddy. Chill with me for a while."

"Cordi!" Someone shoved me. I flailed sideways, managed to keep my balance, and turned in time to see an axe whistling through the air...and tearing through Connor's throat. Blood spurted as his headless body toppled forward. Blood hit me in the face, blinding me. My stomach heaved, rebelling against the taste of hot, salty copper that had splashed into my mouth.

"Cordi." Logan's voice was followed by a loud clang overhead as I ducked, frantically wiping my face. The first thing I saw after clearing blood from my eyes was Connor's head. His eyes and mouth were wide open, surprise etched deep by death. A massive cramp twisted my stomach, bending me double. I retched, and panicked as something came up, only to get stuck in my throat.

Logan grabbed my arm. I heaved again, whatever it was moving. It began to slide out of my gaping mouth: A long, thick ropy tube of white and green. I couldn't breathe, clawing one-handed at Logan. He dropped his sword, grabbed hold of the thing, and pulled. "Kethyrdryll!"

The elf's sword flashed, blocking a strike from a black sword that would've split Logan's skull. He yelled in Elvish, and we were quickly surrounded by Unseelie. Tears poured from my eyes. My lungs were burning. Logan hauled on the tube thing, doing his best to pull it out of me.

It was dissolving into a puddle at our feet. A puddle I was about to pass out into.

The last bit slipped free. Logan dropped it to catch me as I pitched forward. My throat was raw and my tongue felt burned. He dragged me away from the puddle, which had begun glowing. Elves scattered when the puddle exploded upward. Logan covered me, ducking his head. Everything paused for a few seconds.

Still busy sucking in air, I looked when Logan moved, to see Sal and Cernunnos standing there. They both looked at us then strode off toward Morpheus.

I didn't see much of what happened, too busy slapping away anything that didn't look like an elf with my TK. Logan recovered his sword, and Kethyrdryll came back to help us.

But I could see the blue lightning, as well as the globes of green and slashes of red. Look at me, kind of witnessing a battle between gods.

And then Morpheus screamed.

Everything just stopped, the abrupt silence causing my ears to pop.

TWENTY-NINE

The sound of Morpheus's scream ended the battle. Everyone seemed to want to witness the collapse of a god. He fell to his knees, his eyes wide, and held out one hand each to Sal and Cernunnos. "My brothers."

"You made the wrong the choices," my fairy godfather said. "This is the only way it could've ended."

"I've no stomach for taunting the defeated." Cernunnos put his hand on Sal's shoulder. "We finish this now."

"Of course." They walked toward Morpheus, who shook his head.

"No. Spare me."

"Too late." Sal shoved his hand into the fallen god's chest. Golden light burst from all three, growing brighter and brighter, until I had to close my watering eyes and turn my head. I could see the light even then.

When it finally faded, I expected them to be gone. Blinking tears from my eyes, I looked and they were still there. Morpheus lay still, his chest split wide open, charred and smoking. Sal held a small, glowing golden orb in his bloody hand. He turned, his wrinkled face set in grim lines, and spoke in a booming voice. "Witness the end of our brother, Morpheus. Behold the death of a god."

All who weren't already down dropped, even Queen Maeve. I was the only one who didn't bow my head, too curious to see what happened next.

Sal noticed. "Thanks for the ride, kiddo. We would've had a much harder time getting here without you."

"Yeah, you're welcome, and don't ever do it again." I saw Maeve's head turn, and ignored her wide eyes in favor of glaring at the two gods. "I feel like someone took me apart and put me back together wrong."

Sal laughed. "You'll be fine in a day or two."

"What is that?"

He looked at the glowing orb, and held it up. "This is the distillation of a godhood."

"Nifty. So he's really dead, no coming back?" I had enough dreaming issues. Didn't need a vengeful god of dreams showing up to further complicate them.

"Yes, he's truly dead." Sal handed the orb to Cernunnos. "Take it to be cleansed."

The Lord of the Hunt nodded before he disappeared.

"Maeve, stand before me."

The Unseelie Queen slowly rose to her feet. I saw her chest rise as she took a deep breath before walking across the smooth, black floor. She halted in front of Sal, taller by a good foot even with her head bowed.

"Your people are a powerful race, and you, their Queen, are the most powerful of them all. But you overstepped, Maeve, trapping and trying to hold a god. What were you thinking?"

"He tormented thousands."

"And he would've destroyed millions," Sal snapped. Lightning flashed around the cavern, and booms of thunder shook the ground. Maeve wasn't the only one cringing. "He was angry, not insane. Not until you buried him here. Because of your arrogance, he came close to unleashing all you were charged to collect and hold upon the world."

She slowly sank to her knees and offered up her sword. "I submit to your judgment, my lord."

"Oh, believe me, it would be immensely satisfying to separate your prideful head from your body." Sal sighed. "Yet your people are accustomed to your leadership, and your realm is now one with the others. They will need you to guide them."

"You are merciful, my lord."

"It's a terrible habit. We'll be watching you, Maeve. Don't screw up again."

"Yes, my lord."

Sal grunted and glanced at me. With a shake of his head, he left her kneeling and walked over to look at Connor's body. "What a mess. Were you fond of him?"

"He was my friend." Beyond that, returning his body to the Pride would probably end our alliance. Might even start a war, for all I knew. "I had a vision about him. He shouldn't have died here."

"I do owe you a favor for the ride." Sal bent down to pick Connor's head up by the hair. I gulped, my stomach juddering. He put it in place at the neck and paused. "Is this the favor you'd have of me?"

"Bringing him back? Yes, please."

"Now you're polite. Very well." Sal waved his hand, a flash of greenish white briefly hiding Connor's body from sight. The lion coughed up a wad of blood and gunk. Sal was gone.

Connor grimaced, dragging his hand across his mouth. "What happened?"

"Found them," Dane yelled from deep within the crack Morpheus had appeared from.

"Are they okay? Is anyone hurt?" I heard him asking, but didn't hear any responses.

Not before he said, "Everything's going to be okay. I'll get everyone untied."

Rico and Becky were the first to come stumbling out of the gloom, squinting against the light. I smiled. "This way. Boy, Rico, your mom is going to be so happy to see you."

"My mom?" He shook his head. "Who are you people? Where am I?"

Alleryn took charge of them. I guided the other captives to where he'd set up a triage area. Kate and Damian were assisting him. I'd been thrilled neither had been hurt.

Logan and Connor were off somewhere, helping the Unseelie to corral prisoners. I helped Dane with the last captive, and paused to look around. Morpheus's death had taken the wind out of the nasties' sails, but a few were resisting. The pockets of fighting were dwindling even as I watched.

Hearing a noise, I turned around and saw a slender, dark-haired woman creeping out of the crack. Crap, Dane had missed someone. "Everything's okay now. Are you hurt?"

She smiled, and threw out her hand. A strong blast of wind knocked me over, and I hit the ground hard. She kept throwing her hands up as she stalked past, and I could hear shouting. Rolling over, I saw that she was throwing people every which way as she went.

I struggled to my feet as she broke into a run. She reached Maeve first, and lifted the Unseelie Queen high into the air. Call me slow, but that was when I realized the woman was like me. She was a psychic.

Maeve screamed as her armor began crunching. The woman was using telekinesis to slowly crush the Queen. Arrows flew, but she waved her other hand. The arrows burst into flame, burning to ash before reaching her.

She was laughing.

Blood trickled from Maeve's nose and mouth.

I took a deep breath, and opened the room in my mental maze where I'd stored my newest ability: Electrokinesis.

The hum of electricity filled my mind. I pointed at the woman to direct it, and blue lightning shot out in a torrent. It struck the woman, lifting her to her toes and arching her back.

Maeve fell to the ground. The smell of cooking meat reached me, and the woman's dark hair caught fire. I was glad I couldn't see her face, especially when two loud pops sounded. She jerked, her skin blackening, and then fell.

I lowered my hand, and carefully closed off that mental room again.

"Her name was Rhaetha." Queen Maeve grimaced as her armor straps were cut. "She was the most powerful natural mage of her time."

"Why was she here?"

"You saw her. She was insane. A threat to all she encountered." Maeve allowed Alleryn to wipe blood from her face. "The stories I could tell of her."

"Don't." I didn't need to hear them. I'd seen enough in just those few minutes. But I did want to know one thing. "What made her go crazy?"

"Morpheus. It amused him to torment her with nightmares. She began to claim to see things even when awake." The Queen touched her ribs. Her fingers were trembling. "She grew unable to discern between what was, and wasn't, real. Due to that, she believed everyone was a threat, and murdered countless innocents."

"Oh."

Maeve waved everyone away. She studied me for a long, silent moment. "You saved my life, Miss Jones."

And had killed another psychic to do it. One she knew was a favorite target of Morpheus, and yet she'd thrown them into the same prison.

"I will not forget it."

I wanted to. I wanted to go home and forget all of this had ever happened.

"You're young, and I would warn you. Be careful whom you trust. People will want to use you, and they'll do whatever they must to bend you to their will."

Glancing at Rhaetha's corpse, I nodded. "Even gods."

"Yes, even gods."

As we walked out from under the stone arch into Thorandryll's sidhe, I grabbed Logan's arm. "I know."

"You know what?"

"I know what we should ask Thorandryll for."

"And what is it?"

"I have land, but it won't actually need much."

He nodded. "Okay. What needs some?"

"A pocket realm. A territory for the clan."

Logan blinked. "That's...a fantastic idea."

THIRTY

Solstice night was clear and cold. I had quite a lot to feel grateful for as I stood with Terra and Logan, between the crowd and the new, red stone arch set in the evergreens lining the front of my property. Everyone I cared about was safe. All the missing had been returned home.

And I hadn't seen Ginger since she'd led us through the maze challenge.

We'd decided to put the arch at the opposite end from my driveway, to preserve a semblance of privacy. A broad, Kelly green ribbon stretched across the arch, which was tall and wide enough to drive a small moving van through.

Tonight was the first time I'd seen Logan in four days. He'd been busy with Thorandryll's team of pocket realm experts, planning the clan's new home.

Tigers weren't the only ones present. The coven had been invited, and were attending with their familiars. Mr. Whitehaven and Tabitha had come, as had Kethyrdryll and Alleryn. Even my parents, Tonya, Betty, and my little brothers were there. And my three big dogs.

"I think Cordi should cut it." Terra tried to hand me the over-sized scissors.

"Nope, Logan should."

"It was your doing, and your idea," he said.

"Don't care. You did all the hard work to make it happen." No way working with seven snooty elves hadn't been hard.

"Good night, somebody cut the damn ribbon already," Kate called out. "I'm freezing."

"You're the Queen," Logan said.

"Both of you do it," I suggested, and after a few seconds, they agreed that was a good idea. The two halves of the ribbon fluttered to the ground amid cheering.

The three of us led the way in, down a short, paved road ending in a covered parking lot. From there, a wide, cobblestone path wound around trees. The path widened into a street after we passed the trees. At the far end of the street stood a large, two-story building. Nice houses of varying architectural designs lined both sides. Each had a mailbox out front, with a wooden name plate mounted on top.

"You assigned housing?"

Logan shrugged. "Less of a headache. If we let them choose, it'll be next year before we move in."

"What's the big building?"

"Meeting hall and offices. Behind it, there's a playground and our outdoor gathering area."

"This is awesome." Beyond the town on every side were more trees. I glanced up and realized the sky was familiar. "It's on Earth normal time?"

"Oh, yeah. That was far less complicated," he said. "And it's not as though we want to be separated. We just need a safe haven that's all ours. But, if it's ever necessary, we do have all we need to become completely self-sufficient here."

"Nice." I hoped it wasn't ever necessary, but was glad he'd planned for the possibility.

A couple of hours passed before everyone finished exploring and found their way to the gathering area, where food and tables waited. So did the massive pile of wood for the bonfire. Seeing it, I checked my pocket for the folded piece of paper inscribed with my wishes for the coming year.

I wondered if any of them would come true.

We ate, drank, laughed, and generally made merry for a couple of hours. Dane had won the drawing to light the bonfire, which he did with a loud whoop of joy, echoed by several others.

Flames shot upward, sending sparks high into the night sky. I watched the smoke rise, and saw the luminous circle of tiger spirits materialize above us.

Slow and stately, they marched around in their customary circle. I felt the lump of tears in my throat when I spotted the empty space among them. It belonged to the white queen who'd helped me find Logan in my dream. She was either trapped inside me, or gone for good. I had no idea which, but her willingness to sacrifice herself felt both pure and painful.

People began lining up to select pine cones or twigs to tie their Solstice wishes to, from baskets waiting to be emptied.

"You thought of everything."

Logan grinned. "Well, I tried to."

I selected a pinecone. So did he, and we walked to the bonfire together. I wondered what his wishes were, and if any of them involved me. I kind of hoped at least one might.

The festive evening came to a screeching halt for me when I tossed my wish-laden cone into the flames and Merriven walked out of the fire. His thirsty red gaze hit me like a punch, and a mocking smile stretched his lips wide.

"Cordi?" Logan slid his arm around my waist. "What is it?"

"Nothing."

He didn't believe me. "You're pale."

I was shaking too. "Okay, I'm feeling a little sick. Maybe my lunch is to blame. We tried a new place."

"Do you want..."

"I should go home," I said at the same time. "Wouldn't want to break up the party by tossing my cookies."

Logan insisted on walking me home. I agreed, not ready to be alone with my new delusion. The vampire lord looked as solid as Ginger had become the last few times I'd seen her. Way too real for comfort and a walk in the dark.

I'd thought maybe Morpheus had a hand in my Ginger delusion. That he'd been able to send out nightmares, and chosen the nearest psychic to torture with them. But he was dead, and here was Merriven.

I glanced at Logan while we climbed my front porch steps. I didn't want to end up hurting him, or anyone else. It wouldn't be fair to drag him along as I sank into utter madness.

"No, it wouldn't," Merriven agreed.

Son of a...he could talk. Ginger hadn't talked, except in dreams.

"I hate to leave you alone when you don't feel well," Logan said.

"I'm just going to take something and hit the hay. I'll be fine." Biggest lie of my life. "Besides, I actually don't enjoy having an audience when I puke. Throwing up god gunk aside."

He chuckled. "Okay. Do you want me to bring the dogs home?"

"Leglin will after they're done conning people out of food."

"All right." Logan began to lean forward, intending to kiss my forehead. I lifted my hand to his chest to stop him.

"I, uh, need to take a rain check on us dating."

"Oh." His brows drew slightly together, and he backed a few inches away. "May I ask why?"

Because I'm on a southbound train to Nutsville, with no stops in sight. Nah, couldn't tell him that. "I have some stuff I need to take care of. Personal stuff. I'm not sure it's a good idea to," my shoulders slumped, because I couldn't think of a way to end that sentence.

Logan looked into my eyes for a moment. "One question: Did I do anything to make you uncomfortable?"

"No, nothing like that. It's totally not anything to do with you. I just..." Gah, one of these days, I'd learn to say the right things. "Look, Merriven told me something when we were fighting, and it's been bothering the hell out of me. I need to get a handle on it."

"Is there anything I can do to help?"

I loved that he asked, but shook my head. "I don't think so, at least not right now."

Logan nodded. "But you'll let me know, right?"

"You bet." I didn't know whether to apologize or ask if he'd wait until I had my head on straight, if that were possible.

"All right. You know how to get in touch if you need me." Logan smiled. "I don't plan to go anywhere."

Relief put a smile on my face. "Great. Thank you."

He moved and planted a kiss on the corner of my lips. "I guess I'll talk to you later."

"Definitely." I stayed at the door to watch him leave, and waved when he did before he walked out of sight.

"This is the life you'll have without me," Merriven whispered in my ear. "Alone, forever."

Shivering, I called the dogs and went inside, refusing to look at him.

It's not like I knew where to begin getting a handle on this new development. Right now, all I could do was hope Merriven was wrong.

I didn't want to be alone forever.

About the Author

A sword-toting alien with a fetish for fur and four-legged creatures, she writes fiction and spends entirely too much time distracted by shiny things online, like Twitter.

She prefers Netflix because there aren't any commercials and she can ignore all the reality series. As a voracious reader, she enjoys both ebooks and physical books, though her ebook collection doesn't require regular dusting.

She writes scifi as G. L. Drummond, fantasy as Gayla Drummond, and other things as Louise Drummond.

If you're interested in news and future releases, you can find her on Facebook (http://www.facebook.com/G.L.Drummond), Twitter (@Scath), or visit her author web site at http://gldrummond.com.

The Discord Jones urban fantasy series has its own web site at http://discordjones.com.

Printed in Poland
by Amazon Fulfillment
Poland Sp. z o.o., Wrocław